THE
ELEPHANT'S
SAPPHIRE

THE
ELEPHANT'S
SAPPHIRE

S J T RILEY

Matador
Unit E2 Airfield Business Park,
Harrison Road, Market Harborough,
Leicestershire. LE16 7UL
Tel: 0116 2792299
Email: books@troubador.co.uk
Web: www.troubador.co.uk/matador
Twitter: @matadorbooks

ISBN 978 1803136 325

British Library Cataloguing in Publication Data.
A catalogue record for this book is available from the British Library.

Printed and bound in the UK by TJ Books Limited, Padstow, Cornwall
Typeset in 11pt Adobe Garamond Pro by Troubador Publishing Ltd, Leicester, UK

Matador is an imprint of Troubador Publishing Ltd

To my wonderful wife, Loly

OTHER BOOKS
ALSO IN THE LYNNFORD SERIES:

The Sea Breeze

Website
www.sjtriley.co.uk

ONE

A FATAL FALL

'Any fool can see it's a fake!'

The voice rasped like a metal file. Joseph Matthews recognised it and knew only too well its owner's brutality. A cold sweat slipped down his spine, and he slunk further back behind the pillar. It was all that was preventing the two men from seeing him – only a flight of stairs below. He held his breath instinctively for fear of disclosing his presence, and sharpened his ears.

The Queen's Fine Art Museum in Piccadilly was empty, and the altercation between the two men on the stairs of the cavernous foyer had broken out only seconds before. Bosworth, the dockhand from Alexandria Wharf in London's Docklands, had bounded up the stairs as if he had been about to unload a long-awaited ship on piece-rate. He had accosted Sir Christopher Fields, the museum's curator, on his way down the stairs, no doubt on his way out of the museum and home. There was no one else, as far as they

|

knew, left in the building except for the night guards, whose patrol had taken them beyond earshot. Still, the two men's crossed words were hissed in muffled tones, as if they were conspirators keen not to give themselves away.

'Your instructions are clear,' the heavy dockhand's voice rasped. 'We have a buyer.'

'Take it if you must,' the curator replied, already struggling under the other man's large hands.

'Walk away with a copy? They'd have me cut your throat.'

'Captain Morgan, is it now? This is London, not the high seas!'

The curator's quip ended with him choking for air, as the large man's hand grasped his throat in a single grip. 'Don't mess with me, Fields. You're no longer the king pin.'

'The original's been stolen! What can I do?'

'Get it back.'

'How?'

'Before anything else gets broken.'

Behind the pillar, Joseph Matthews winced, the curator's scream of pain piercing his ears. *The night guards must surely have heard that*, he thought.

'You've forty-eight hours, Fields. No more.'

Another cry of agony from the curator accompanied the dockhand's steps as he walked away, casually and seemingly unconcerned by the possible arrival of a night guard. Indeed, none came, and Bosworth made a mental note to pay off the two guards the next day. Only the curator's continuing moans broke the silence. Joseph Matthews summoned the courage to reveal himself, poking his head slowly round the pillar. The curator was alone, slumped over the stone balustrade, barely conscious, his arm hanging loosely by his side as if dislocated and broken.

Matthews hesitated, looking on, unsure of himself. He worked in the museum as one of the museum's warders. When he'd clocked in earlier in the day, little could he have imagined that he would witness such a scene. Even after the museum doors had closed to the public, and he had stayed on after the other warders had gone home, he'd had no premonition of what was to happen. He had simply strolled alone along the darkening galleries and corridors, as was his habit since his life had collapsed around him. Now, through some stroke of providence, he had before him, almost at his feet, the very man who had ruined it all – Sir Christopher Fields, the museum's curator. *How the once-mighty fall!* It was too much for him to take in. A flash of images rushed through his mind: lost moments of happiness, cruel memories of impotence and cowardice. His boy and girl lost to the curator's greed and immorality. He hesitated still. How many times had he wished for such a moment? To have the power of striking down with a single blow the cause of all his misery? To thrust a stake into his evil heart. He could never have done it before. Too weak and too cowardly. But now, revenge was within his grasp.

He walked slowly down the steps, careful not to alert his prey. And then, unable to take the strain a moment longer and fearing his resolution might dissolve, he rushed forward, bending down and gripping the curator by his legs in a single movement. The curator had only time to turn his head and, recognising Joseph, cry out in surprise, 'You!'

But Joseph, taken by his own energy, didn't flinch, hoisting the curator's legs above the balustrade and pushing with all his might. The weight fell from his grasp, the curator screamed in fear, and his body landed, crumpled, on the marble floor below, at the bottom of the immense museum stairwell. Joseph Matthews ran back up the stairs and hid, shaking and sobbing, unable to believe what he had done. *Tomorrow will be another day, come what may*, he consoled himself.

Matthews stayed in his hiding place all night. No one troubled him, unaware that such a place even existed. The night guards, the police, and everyone else must all have come and gone. He hadn't heard a thing. In the morning he crept out and, avoiding the main lobby, left the museum by a side entrance. He freshened up in the Lyons Tea House nearby, and afterwards, returned to the museum as if he were starting a day's work as usual, learning of the curator's death as if it were news to him and seeing everyone at sixes and sevens. The police took his statement, from which they learnt nothing. In the evening, he returned home and collapsed in his chair, staring for long hours into the cold fireplace, disturbed only by Janet, his daughter, slamming the front door, who, noticing him sitting in the dark, asked him why he was sulking.

'I'm not sulking, Janet,' he replied.

'Then what's wrong? And where were you last night? You didn't come home, did you, Dad?'

'It's over, Janet. It's over,' he repeated.

'What's over?'

'The filth, the misery, the humiliation; it's finally over.'

'What do you mean, Dad? You're scaring me.'

'The mighty Sir Christopher Fields is dead.'

Janet sighed heavily, as if looking back down a deep tunnel. 'Well then, good riddance!'

TWO

THE COLONEL'S PRIZE

Some months later, still in the same year – 1950, Lynnford, crime reporter for *The London Herald*, strode out of the newspaper's offices at Number 18 Fountain Street, City of London, letting the large entrance door close loudly behind him, blown to by a strong gust of wind. It was five-thirty and already dark. The late-afternoon air was cold and damp. December was only a week or so away, and Fountain Street was alive with people heading home at the end of the office day, most of them walking down towards Aldwych Underground Station, or upwards to Holborn or St. Paul's.

Lynnford turned into a cobbled side road, the damp stones glistening in the lamp light. Behind him, the passing crowds in Fountain Street pressed on, seemingly unaware of the small road's existence. The few shops in the road were now closed or about to close. Gates, the bookmakers, was closed, but next door the projecting sign of The Golden Fox was already attracting its regulars, including the two or three figures ahead of Lynnford, who all slipped inside. The Golden Fox public house was the favourite haunt of a mixture of newspaper people, particularly from *The London Herald*, and locals. Lynnford placed his hand on the cold metal latch and pushed open the door. Somebody was expecting him.

The chatter and bustle inside blew into his face as if carried outside by the escaping stream of warm, smoke-filled air. The public house was full.

'What's new, Lynnford?' A face, hidden behind a pair of thick-rimmed glasses, casually greeted Lynnford, breathing out a cloud of smoke above his head as he spoke.

'Thanks, Sanders. I'll speak to you later.'

Sanders worked on the foreign affairs desk at *The London Herald*. Lynnford steered his colleague to one side, giving himself room to pass by. Several other customers greeted Lynnford with a smile or a nod, letting him through with a friendly pat on the shoulder until he reached the bar, where Maureen, the landlady, was orchestrating the service with her usual, tireless effort. Lynnford squeezed himself in between a lone man and a couple of young women and caught her eye.

'The usual, Mr Lynnford?' The landlady asked, already bringing down a clear straight glass from the rack above her. The man next to Lynnford turned towards him.

'Ha! So it's you, Lynnford. Where have you been?'

It was Willy Tanner, Lynnford's counterpart in *The London Herald*'s rival newspaper, *The Daily Chronicle*. The journalist had removed his overcoat and jacket, and the shining forehead suggested that he had already had time for several drinks. Colourful braces held up his trousers around a frame that had long since lost its youthful sculpture. The cuffs of his creased white shirt were rolled back roughly, revealing two fattish forearms covered in thick blond hair.

'Trying to find a story?' he asked. 'You should change paper,' he continued in a mocking tone. 'They fall on my lap at *The Chronicle*. No need for me to go running round dark streets and back alleyways in the dead of night, looking through grubby dustbins for something to write.'

Lynnford smiled, refusing to take the bait and replying simply, 'You'll read about it tomorrow, Willy.'

'Mr Lynnford?'

Lynnford looked round. A man wearing a hat and a finely cut coat stood behind him, a folded umbrella hooked over his arm and a glass already in his hand. 'Mr Robert Lynnford?' the gentleman asked again, politely.

Lynnford nodded.

'We spoke on the telephone just now.'

'Yes, of course. Let's see if we can find a table.'

'Somewhere quiet, if possible.'

'Not much chance of that, I'm afraid.'

Lynnford led the man through the throng of customers to a table in a corner on the far side of the room, next to the telephone booths. 'This is the best we can do.'

'It's fine. As I told you on the telephone, my name is Philips, Edwin Philips.'

'Good evening, Mr Philips.'

The man removed his hat and coat, hanging them on the nearby stand, in which he had already placed his umbrella, and sat down. Sitting opposite each other, Lynnford studied the man, who less than five minutes or so ago had telephoned him, most likely from one of the telephone booths next to them, requesting a meeting with him, giving Mr Joseph Irvine, *The London Herald*'s proprietor, as a recommendation. A white-dotted burgundy handkerchief flowered out of his top pocket, matching the neat bow tie. His hands were finely manicured and his face polished. Even the lines on his forehead seemed to have been finely chiselled. A faint scent of perfume from his clothes floated across the table between them. *In his late fifties or early sixties, but very well preserved*, Lynnford observed to himself.

'Your good health.'

Edwin Philips lifted his glass. Lynnford returned the gesture, and took a long drink, the time to think. *Who might be this elegantly dressed man and what might he want of me?* he wondered.

'My name is Edwin Philips,' the man repeated. 'As I mentioned on the telephone, I am the curator of the Queen's Fine Art Museum.' He added, 'In Piccadilly.'

'I live in Knightsbridge, Mr Philips. Just up the road from the museum, so I know where it is.'

'Indeed. Yes, of course you do. In truth, I'm only its acting curator, pending a more formal appointment. Curator *ad interim*,' he added, as if the English needed explaining in Latin. 'And I have been for only a few weeks now.'

The man succeeded in combining pomposity and false modesty, irritating Lynnford.

'Here's my card.'

Lynnford glanced at the card and placed it on the table in front of him.

'I'd much prefer that you put it away. Prying eyes, you understand.'

'Of course.'

Mr Philips watched Lynnford pick up the card and place it in his wallet before resuming. 'Mr Lynnford, I believe that I have something that will interest you greatly, but what I have to say is absolutely and strictly confidential, and the less known about my conversation with you this evening, the better.'

Lynnford gave a dry smile. 'Perhaps, then, The Golden Fox isn't the best place to be.'

'It's safe enough.'

'It's full of journalists, Mr Philips.'

'Nobody knows me here. You didn't, Mr Lynnford.'

'No, I didn't. So, what is this story?'

'The first thing, Mr Lynnford, is that it's not a story.'

'Then it's not likely to interest me. And even less my paper. Not a good place to start, Mr Philips.'

'I'm sure it will interest you, and as for *The London Herald*, not only has Mr Irvine recommended you very highly, as I told you, but he's cleared your time in helping me, should you accept.'

'I see.' This time, Lynnford couldn't help a tone of irritation escaping him, but his companion chose not to notice it.

'Mr Lynnford, have you ever heard of the Elephant's Sapphire?'

Lynnford shook his head.

'The Elephant's Sapphire comes from Nepal. It's a perfect stone, the size of a large egg. Carved by ancient Nepalese craftsmen, it reflects a halo of dazzling blue light.'

'A priceless jewel, I imagine.'

'The Sapphire has immense value. It weighs four hundred and ten carats. It's not the largest in the world, but it's not far off.'

'And it has more than just monetary value, I assume.'

'Quite so, Mr Lynnford. It was fought over for generations, passing from one rival family to another. Eventually, it was acquired by a powerful statesman in the royal court, a nobleman, and worn by his favourite elephant as the centrepiece of a ceremonial headdress, placed in the middle of its giant forehead.'

'Quite a showpiece, then.'

'The nobleman would ride the elephant at the head of important processions, and the Sapphire would shine like a beacon in the sunlight. Magical qualities are even attributed to it. It is believed that it offers protection and good fortune in the hands of the good, and ill fortune in the hands of the bad and the unworthy. Imagine, Mr Lynnford, the splendour of the jewel.'

'And this sapphire is exhibited in the Queen's Fine Art Museum?'

The curator took a sip of whisky. 'Since 1882, but let me continue. In 1832, the wealthy nobleman's three-year-old boy was seized by a band of rebels and put up for ransom. The young boy was the elderly man's only surviving child and he doted on him, as you would expect. The rebels demanded no less than the nobleman's life for that of his son. A young British major, Major Urquardt, temporarily attached to the British representative in Kathmandu as a military advisor, and friendly with the nobleman, offered his help. He led a small group of the nobleman's trusted followers and rescued the boy. Overcome with joy and relief, the nobleman rewarded the major with a prize, the value of which far exceeded any wealth that the soldier could have imagined. The Elephant's Sapphire!'

'A nice tale. And that's the reason for its name, the Elephant's Sapphire?'

Edwin Philips shook his head and took another drink. 'No, that was much later. The Nepalese call it the Royal Sapphire. After his posting in Nepal, the major served in India, reaching the rank of lieutenant colonel. When he retired from service in the Army, he returned to England and commissioned a model cast-bronze sculpture of the king's elephant, some three and a half feet high, as a mounting for the Sapphire. He mounted the Sapphire on the model elephant, and it became known as the Elephant's Sapphire.'

The curator paused to take out a silver-plated cigarette holder and offered it to Lynnford, who waved his hand, declining the offer. 'No, thank you.'

'Mind if I do?'

Lynnford shook his head. The curator selected a cigarette, put away the box and took out a matching lighter, which he flicked open. A tall flame shot up. Bringing the flame close to the cigarette between his lips, he breathed in deeply and exhaled a white cloud of smoke as, with his free hand, he closed the lighter and returned it to his jacket pocket. Sitting back in his chair, somewhat more relaxed than before, Edwin Philips resumed his story.

'Lieutenant Colonel Urquardt died in 1882. In his will he gave the elephant and the Sapphire to the Queen's Fine

Art Museum on trust, where it was to be put on display for the benefit of the public.'

'That seems hard on his family,' Lynnford observed dryly.

'Perhaps so, but the colonel was a man with a strong sense of public duty and national pride.'

'A true Victorian.'

'Indeed.'

'A very interesting story, Mr Philips, but it's hardly news.'

'That's not the story, Mr Lynnford.'

'Oh!' Lynnford sat back, surprised. 'What is it, then?'

The curator leant forward, his voice falling into a whisper. 'Mr Lynnford, I'm taking a huge risk. What I'm going to tell you must absolutely go no further than yourself. I have been told that I can count on your discretion. I really must insist on it. Can I trust you?'

Lynnford nodded.

'Mr Lynnford, I have reason to believe that the Elephant's Sapphire has been stolen.'

'But surely you must know, Mr Philips. Either it has or it hasn't. Either it's there or it isn't.'

'It's not quite so simple. There is indeed a jewel on the elephant's forehead, but I believe it to be a replica, a fake.'

The curator cast a nervous look around the room.

'It must be a very good imitation for you not to be sure.'

'In fact, I am sure, Mr Lynnford. It's a fake.'

'And no one else has spotted it?'

'Not the public. And, fortunately, not yet the market. It's a very good replica, you see, exceptionally so. But it's only a matter of time.'

'When did you realise it's a copy?'

'Only a few days ago. I came upon it quite by chance.'

'So, you've no idea when the original was taken?'

The curator shook his head.

'So, it could have been last week as easily as last year or even longer, much longer?'

'Not so long ago. The exhibits are checked regularly. They were also checked when they were returned after the War.'

'That was five years ago.'

'As you say. Still, I think the theft must have been more recently, but I agree, there's no way of knowing precisely.'

'Obviously, your predecessor knew nothing.'

'There's no way of telling.'

'You could ask him.'

'Unfortunately, he's no longer alive.'

'I'm sorry to hear that. Who was your predecessor?'

'Sir Christopher Fields.'

'Sir Christopher? Ah, yes, I remember now. Didn't he commit suicide last summer? I apologise, I didn't make the connection.'

'There was no reason you should have. Yesterday's news, as they say, is soon forgotten.'

'Very tragic circumstances, if I remember correctly.'

'Yes, his body was found by the night guard at the bottom of the stairwell in the grand foyer of the museum. It seems he must have jumped from the top floor.'

'But how did that kill him? I could imagine him being left crippled.'

'He must have hit his head when he fell.'

'Didn't anyone see anything?'

'It was late in the evening. The museum was closed, and everyone had gone home.'

'And what were the reasons? Do we know?'

The curator shook his head.

'And I suppose that between his death and your appointment is the most likely time it was stolen. Is that what you think?'

'Yes. Obviously, everything at the time must have been a little disorganised, the staff shaken by the events. You understand?'

'Yes of course, but what is it that you want me to do?'

Edwin Philips did not hesitate in his reply. 'Find it.'

'The Elephant's Sapphire! Isn't that a job for the police?'

'Mr Lynnford, this is too delicate a matter. I can't afford to create the slightest suspicion that what is on display in the museum is anything other than the Sapphire and one hundred per cent genuine, and the presence of the police would surely do that. I need someone with discretion, who can work quickly. The police would simply spread out a large net, and within a day the whole world would know that the sapphire is a fake.'

'Can I think about it?'

'Not for too long. Come and see me at the museum first thing tomorrow morning with your decision, and you can see the elephant.'

Lynnford nodded.

'Then let's say nine-thirty.'

The curator got up and took his leave, collecting his coat, hat and umbrella from the stand. Lynnford watched him go. He looked at his watch. Six-fifteen. He had another appointment on the south side of the river, just past Tower Bridge, at seven-thirty.

THREE

ALEXANDRIA WHARF

Leaving The Golden Fox and catching a bus to Tower Bridge, Lynnford was soon crossing the Thames, an easterly wind blowing in a strong sea-smell from the far-off estuary. On the other side of the river, he was quickly thrown into another world. Quiet and foreboding, the lines of blackened-brick warehouses, standing slim and tall, were broken only by the turmoil of cobbled streets and alleyways that seemed to lead here, there and everywhere. Still, Lynnford walked with an assured pace, knowing his way. His appointment that evening was with Eddie Campbell in his shop.

Eddie Campbell owned a tobacconist shop. His business was suffering from large quantities of smuggled, duty-free tobacco arriving in London through the docks and flooding the local market. He also owned a couple of greyhounds that he raced at the track in Walthamstow in East London, and that was how he knew Stephan Maxwell, the sports writer at *The London Herald* with whom Lynnford shared an office in Fountain Street. Maxwell, who often covered the races at the Walthamstow Stadium, had told Lynnford about Eddie Campbell's difficulties, and Lynnford, quickly sniffing something far more important than a few cartons of tax-free cigarettes, had agreed to meet with Eddie to see if he could help him. His enquiries had led him to a quay in the docks on the south side of the river known as Alexandria Wharf, and to a particular ship, the *S.S. Martaban*, whose arrivals in Alexandria Wharf coincided closely with Eddie's loss of trade. But six weeks or so had gone by since the *Martaban* had last docked in London.

The tobacconist's shop stood at the corner of two terraced streets. Three other small shops across the road kept it company. All four shops were long since closed for the day. Lynnford knocked on the door to Eddie Campbell's darkened shop. Almost immediately, the light went on, shining brightly around the edges of the drawn blinds. Footsteps crossed the floor, stopping behind the door, a key fumbled in the lock and two bolts pulled back. The door opened and a man in his late forties stood on the threshold.

'Good evening, Eddie.'

Recognising Lynnford, the man said nothing. He simply stood back and allowed him in, closing the door behind them. The empty left sleeve of the cardigan he was wearing was pinned to his shoulder. He had lost his arm in an accident in the munitions factory in which he'd worked during the War. He lived above the shop.

'So, something new, Eddie? I got your message.'

'She's anchored out in the estuary, waiting to come in.' His voice was rough and tired.

'The *Martaban*?'

'Yes. Just off Canvey Island. I heard she will come upriver this evening, and dock in at Alexandria Wharf.'

'The same as usual?'

The tobacconist nodded. 'She's probably sailing now. The *Britannia* was occupying her place in the dock. That's why the *Martaban* had to wait. The *Britannia* only finished loading at noon today.'

'Any idea of what she's carrying?'

'Tobacco, of course, but there's definitely something else. She's registered as carrying African and Asian hard wood. But if it was just that, she wouldn't need to unload in the dark.'

'I don't see why they don't take off her special goods in the estuary. They might have done it already, don't you think? A couple of small boats, and they could have it on dry land in no time.'

'I don't think so.'

'Why not?'

Eddie shrugged his shoulders. 'Because it's safer for them in Alexandria Wharf. It's not so exposed. Once stored away in that labyrinth of warehouses that surround the wharf, the contraband can be discretely released through their network of agents. And anyway, I've heard that extra hands have been taken on at the wharf for tonight.'

'Tonight?'

'That's what I've heard.'

'When exactly?'

Eddie shrugged. 'Sometime either side of midnight. We should get there for eleven, just to make sure.'

'So you're coming along with me again?'

Lynnford recalled the previous occasion they'd spent watching the unloading of the *Martaban*, hidden behind a pile of barrels with the night's river mist all around them. It had been a damp and uncomfortable business that had gone unrewarded. Afterwards, he had returned alone to the ship several times before it had sailed, slipping surreptitiously aboard to check the ship's log and hold. But, apart from the untaxed tobacco, what the crew might have been smuggling remained a mystery.

Eddie nodded. 'But let's make it the last time. I've seen enough of their tobacco.'

'I know Eddie, but if we can only find out what else they are carrying... gold bars or South African diamonds, for example, that would be a real scoop.'

'You mean a good story for you. You make it sound like pirates' treasure. The tobacco, I'm sure about. The diamonds, I don't know. And how would you find them on a ship the size of the *Martaban*? The gold bars, possibly.'

'Patience, Eddie. We just need to be patient. They'll slip up soon enough.'

'But maybe not before they find out we're keeping tabs on them, if they haven't already,' Eddie replied dryly, adding, 'And then it won't just be my trade they'll be hitting.'

'It's only eight o'clock. Should I come back later or meet you there?'

'You might as well come upstairs. We can have a bite to eat whilst we're waiting.'

*

A hollow metal chime broke the silence, striking eleven o'clock. *The bell tower of Southwark Cathedral, further on up along the riverbank,* guessed Lynnford as he and Eddie approached Alexandria Wharf. Close to the river, the night air was damp and cold, and the cobbles underfoot were wet. Neither of them spoke.

Shortly, they arrived in front of an arched entrance, so dark within that what lay beyond could not be seen. They stepped inside and walked quickly yet cautiously forward. They were in a short tunnel driven under one of the warehouses that would lead them out onto Alexandria Wharf. Several short paces more and they were at its mouth, staring at the huge ship's hull that loomed up in front of them, dwarfing the dockside buildings. And, but for Eddie's restraining hand, Lynnford would have tumbled out onto the quay, where, a few paces away, twenty or so dockhands were engaged in ferrying out of the ship's hold crates of all shapes and sizes. Long lengths of timber already lined the quayside.

'The *Martaban*,' Lynnford whispered, half to himself.

Winched up by a crane that was mounted on the ship above one of the boat's holds, pallets piled high with wooden crates were being taken out of the hold, swung across the ship's side and then let down on the quayside, whereupon their ropes were untied and the crates whisked away on porters' trolleys into one or other of the warehouses surrounding the boat. Above another hold, a crane was extracting long lengths of timber.

A bearded giant of a man with cap and jacket was directing the unloading. Lynnford had seen him before on previous occasions, supervising the unloading of the *Martaban*. He had also seen him around Alexandria Wharf, almost bumping into him, some days after the *Martaban* had last sailed. So, he assumed the man was a dockhand, and not part of the ship's crew. As always, the man watched very closely the distribution of the crates, directing where each one should go. On his instruction, certain crates were marked with a bold cross and kept apart.

'Those are the ones we want!' Lynnford exclaimed under his breath.

The concrete surface glistened under the white light of the lamps fixed overhead. The heavy boots of the dockhands struck hard as they worked in silence. Another hour passed by before Lynnford could see signs of the unloading nearing its completion. Nobody during this time had made any move towards the place where Eddie and he were standing, or even looked their way. The crates marked with a cross had steadily grown in number, and now they were being ferried inside the warehouse. Tobacco or something else? There was no way of knowing without opening them up. Lynnford was hoping to find where they were being stored by following the dockhand inside the warehouse on his last trip.

The quayside was clearing, and most of the activity was now confined inside the warehouses. The supervisor had walked back up the gangway, the rope swinging under his grip, and disappeared into the side of the ship. On the wharf, a dockhand picked up the last of the marked crates and placed it on his trolley with two others. Lynnford, sensing this was his moment, got ready to step out of the protection of the archway and follow him.

Motioning to Eddie to wait where he was, Lynnford slipped out from under the archway, and was about to slide along the brick façade of the warehouse, shadowing the dockhand, when he felt a tug from behind and Eddie's quiet words, 'Quick, get back!'

Startled, Lynnford looked up, and immediately saw the reason for Eddie's alarm. A group of five or so men were walking hesitantly down the gangway under the supervision of the bearded dockhand, with others waiting behind him. He would only have to turn his head in Lynnford's direction to spot him. Without hesitating a moment longer, Lynnford stepped quickly back under the arch, his eyes now riveted on the men walking down the gangway.

Once on the quayside, the men stopped and waited whilst another group came out of the boat and joined them. And then another until they were about fifteen or so. The dockhand swaggered down the gangway and then, after briefly addressing the men, pointed in the direction of the archway into which Lynnford and Eddie had stepped a little further back so as not to be seen.

'They're coming this way. Damn it!' Lynnford expressed his frustration, as much at their having to vacate their hiding place as at the lost opportunity of seeing where the marked boxes had gone and of discovering what might be in them.

'Of course, it's the way out, or at least one of them,' Eddie explained, a little needlessly, before adding with some urgency, 'Come on! We can't stay here.'

And, turning back with Lynnford on his heels, he hurried through to the other side of the archway and out into the alleyway that had brought them there. Without stopping, they carried on until they reached the main street.

'Hold on!' Eddie had finally stopped, panting, his one hand holding his chest as he fought for air. 'It'll be the death of me!'

Lynnford stopped alongside him. 'Come on over here, behind the telephone box. We'll wait for them here and see where they go.'

Lynnford's curiosity had been awoken. He pulled Eddie away from the opening into the alley and behind the telephone box, where they waited for the group to catch them up. The minutes went by, but the alley remained empty.

'They must have found some other way out,' Lynnford concluded, frustrated. 'Who were they? The crew? Stowaways?'

'Paid passengers without visas, more likely. Probably worked their passage,' Eddie replied.

'Illegal immigrants, then. But they can only be a sideline, just like its official cargo.'

'It looks that way, but we're still no closer to finding your gold bars or your diamonds.'

'We should go back and find those marked crates.'

'Now? We'll never find them in the dark. Not in the maze of warehouses around the wharf. And whatever it is will be under lock and key by now, and under a careful watch as well, no doubt. You've missed your chance, Lynnford.'

'If only those men had come out five minutes later!'

'Well, even if it's only tobacco in those crates, I'm in for another hard knock. That's for sure.'

'What about calling the police?'

Eddie shook his head. 'They wouldn't find anything either. A police raid would just scare them into moving to another dock. Change ship, even, and then we'd be back to where we started.'

'Well, that suits me, Eddie. But I'll pay the *Martaban* another visit before she sails. Let me know if you hear when that will be.'

The two men shook hands and went their own ways home, unaware that some moments before someone had finally appeared at the entrance to the alleyway, standing discreetly to one side and remaining hidden in the dark shadows: the bearded charge hand who had been supervising the unloading of the *Martaban*. He had watched Lynnford and Eddie walk away, allowing no more than a light furrow of concern to wrinkle his forehead before turning round and walking back to Alexandria Wharf, pleased with the night's business.

FOUR
QUEEN'S FINE ART MUSEUM

Under its flat shade a bright electric lamp lit up the morning room. Outside, the grey dawn was drawing back the night sky, leaving the bare branches of the huge chestnut tree that rose up from the courtyard below to fill the window. Lynnford had opened the curtains before sitting down for breakfast, remarking, as on previous mornings, that the leaves and fallen fruit were still lying uncollected in large piles on the ground. His Knightsbridge flat, in Park Mansions, on the southern edge of Hyde Park, was on the third floor. He prepared his own breakfast each morning from whatever Mrs Wilson, the porter's sister-in-law, left him the night before. Mr Cobley, the porter, whose duties included tending the garden areas, didn't much care for gardening, bemoaning autumn and the mess left in its wake. Every year, he would put off collecting the leaves until he was sure there was nothing left to fall. *Still*, Lynnford had mused on drawing back the curtains that morning, *he's going to have to go out there fairly soon. It's nearly winter!*

He looked at his watch. Ten past eight. His appointment with Mr Philips was at nine-thirty so he still had time to read some more of the day's paper and change his ideas. Thoughts of the *Martaban* and Alexandria Wharf had been still swirling around in his mind when he had woken up that morning after a fitful night's sleep.

Mr Cobley brought up *The London Herald* newspaper for Lynnford each morning, leaving it on the floor outside the door to his apartment, something he didn't do for any of the other residents of Park Mansions. And, if questioned about it, he would reply curtly that it was a professional requirement of Mr Lynnford's employment to receive and read his employer's publication, by which he let it be understood that the privilege would not be extended to other residents. Lynnford had smiled when he heard this for the first time from one of his disgruntled neighbours. He guessed the porter was being sincere, and that he wouldn't bring him up any other newspaper should he ask, although he hadn't tested this idea.

At ten to nine Lynnford was downstairs. Mr Cobley was already at work, wiping clean the opaque glass squares of the two front doors, the left-hand door on which he was working being held ajar by a small iron weight. Having completed the upper part of the door, he was now kneeling on one leg as he tackled the lower squares.

'Good morning, Cobley.'

'Good day to you, Mr Lynnford. Fountain Street?'

'Not this morning. First off, the Queen's Fine Art Museum. What do you think of that?'

'Museums, sir? Oh, that's a strange business.'

'How's that?'

'Well, you know, looking into the past and all that. Best forgotten, if you ask me. Get on with the present and look to the future, that's my motto.'

'So, you'll be getting on with clearing up the leaves today, will you?' Lynnford quipped.

The porter made a face.

'Otherwise, you'll have them rotting into the New Year. Anyway, inspiration – that's what the Queen's Fine Art Museum is about.'

'And what's the editor of *The London Herald* got you going down there for?'

'Mr Kombinski? He doesn't know yet. At least, I don't think he does.'

The porter burst out with a laugh. 'Many as would like your job, Mr Lynnford. Being paid for doing just what you want.'

'You don't do so badly yourself, Cobley. Don't forget the leaves.'

Walking along the border of Hyde Park towards Piccadilly, Lynnford's thoughts spun around Edwin Philip's tale of the Elephant's Sapphire. Rich images of royal wealth, feuding families, parading elephants and forests full of the menace of tigers and bandits filled his mind. A comforting contrast to the cold dreariness of London! But how was he going to find a stolen sapphire? A needle in a haystack would not be harder. He was not an expert on South Asian art or history, nor for that matter did he know much about art in general. That was Victoria's speciality, his unannounced fiancée.

Lynnford's musings brought him quickly in front of the museum, a bust of Queen Victoria looking down upon him. As he stood on the steps craning backwards to read the crowning inscription that arched over the entrance, he almost lost his balance.

'I say, mind your step.'

A walking stick tapped him on the elbow, the accompanying voice patronising and confident. 'We don't want your leg in a plaster, do we, Mr Lynnford?'

Looking round, Lynnford met the gaze of Edwin Philips. The curator was smiling at him.

'Beauty lies in the eye of the beholder and not in its possession.' The curator read out loud the inscription. 'The Victorians were so uncompromising in their values. Don't you think, Mr Lynnford?'

'Indeed,' Lynnford replied, not knowing what else to say except to add the conventional greeting, 'Good morning, Mr Philips.'

The curator nodded. 'I'm glad to see you're punctual, Mr Lynnford. I like that. I'll take you in myself. We'll go and see the elephant straight away.'

The curator hurried through the museum, leading Lynnford through a series of galleries, and up and down several stairs, until he stopped under a painted archway that opened out into a large chamber. A subdued lighting pervaded the room. Gold-plated artefacts of all shapes and sizes lined the sides, richly patterned tapestries in reds and golds fell down from the ceiling, some so long as to almost brush against the floor. The curator broke the silence.

'The Nepalese Room, Mr Lynnford. What we want

to see is here. It would have been quicker to have come across the main hall, but I didn't want to attract too much attention, you understand?'

He took Lynnford along the length of the room, and then turned up an aisle that led off at right angles. Mannequins dressed in silks flanked their passage. At the end of the aisle, and just below his eye-level, two large eyes stared back at Lynnford, unblinking and unmoved, a blue jewel fixed between them, just above the trunk that curled up towards him. One of the elephant's thick, rounded feet was slightly raised and tipped forward as if to suggest movement, a slow processional march. Indeed, the animal appeared caught in a steady advance along the path in which Lynnford now stood, barring its way.

'So, this is the famous Elephant's Sapphire?'

Mr Philips nodded.

Or it would be if only it were the real one, Lynnford imagined the curator thinking to himself. He went up closer and placed his two hands on the glass display cabinet that encased the statue, looking down on the model elephant that filled its interior. The glass was cold to his touch.

'The elephant itself must be worth a fortune,' he observed.

'It's not solid, but yes, it's worth a lot of money in its own right. It's bronze, cast from a clay model.'

Lynnford held out his hand to measure the jewel, stretching out his thumb and forefinger. It was almost as big as a large egg nestling in the palm of his hand, a wide square-oval shape, held in place by a fine silver casket. Almost too large for the model elephant.

'Magnificent. Fascinating, almost. Are you sure? I mean it's hard to think that—'

The curator quickly cut him short, whispering quietly, 'Please, Mr Lynnford.' He raised a finger to his lips. 'Let's go to my office. We can talk there.'

Lynnford nodded, following the curator, and as he did so he caught sight of a middle-aged man dressed in a museum coat silently observing them from the shadows of the gallery.

'Mr Matthews, the gallery's warder,' the curator explained, paying no further attention to the man.

They retraced their steps to the immense hall at the entrance to the museum, whose open ceiling spanned the very top of the building, and from where the curator led Lynnford up the grand staircase, stopping in front of a heavy wooden door set under an oval arch on the uppermost floor.

'The museum offices,' he explained, pressing down the black metal door handle.

The door opened easily, and the curator stepped back to let Lynnford pass in front of him. The contrast with the vast exhibition rooms, and in particular the richly decorated Nepalese Room, was striking. The offices were small and confined, the ceiling low, and the walls bare. The floor was carpeted, with the underlay showing along the edges of the skirting board. A woman, her back to them, turned round on hearing them enter. She had just removed her coat and was hanging it on the stand behind her desk.

'Good morning, Mr Philips. The morning post is on your desk.'

'Thank you, Jennifer.'

The secretary smiled back at them and sat down. She lifted the cover off the typewriter, folding it away in the bottom drawer of her desk. The telephone rang abruptly just as she was closing the drawer. Straightening up, she stretched out her arm to pick up the receiver. The curator interrupted her.

'I'm tied up for the next twenty minutes. If it's for me, ask them to call back.'

'Certainly, Mr Philips.'

Leading Lynnford, the curator pressed on along the corridor. His office was at the end. Closing the door behind them, he waved Lynnford into an armchair placed in front of his desk, whilst he removed his coat and hung it on the back of the door.

'You can understand, Mr Lynnford, as I said yesterday evening…' The curator paused as he moved across the room, stepping behind his desk and glancing abstractedly at the letters that his secretary had arranged for him before looking up and continuing. 'I must be able to count on your complete discretion at all times in this matter.'

'Naturally.' Lynnford tempered his reply with a mild note of annoyance, adding, 'But you know that I work for a newspaper.'

'Yes, of course. As a journalist, you can make up any reason you like for being interested in the Sapphire.'

'But I do investigate crime stories.'

'Not everyone knows that. Sorry, I didn't mean to offend you.'

'No offence taken.'

Edwin Philips sat down behind his desk. 'Mr Lynnford,

what counts is your ability to work discreetly and achieve results, and on both counts, I'm satisfied. And I've heard that you know how to look after yourself. Knocked about in the War, I gather. Fighter pilot, wasn't it?'

'That and other things.'

'Action behind enemy lines. Intelligence work as well.'

'You seem to have done your research.'

'I'm a thorough man, Mr Lynnford. The art world is not kind to amateurs.'

'Then it will find out that your sapphire is a fake?'

'True, sooner or later, somebody will walk into the museum and tell me that it's not worth much more than the model elephant, if that. But, until then, a casual look in the semi-darkness is not going to reveal very much.'

'So, we have as long as it will take for news of the theft to filter out, possibly because someone's trying to find a buyer.'

'Not exactly.'

'Why's that?'

'Firstly, before we go on, Mr Lynnford, I need to know whether you are on board.'

'You realise, Mr Philips, that my editor is going to want me to give him a story?'

'Mr Irvine told me that it wouldn't be necessary.'

'He only owns the paper. The editor, Mr Kombinski, makes it sell, and for that he needs stories. Fortunately for me, I can afford not to work, but unfortunately for him, he can't afford to have me not working.'

'I would prefer to keep the museum out of the papers.'

'Let's see what I turn up first, Mr Philips. If we don't find the Sapphire, then it'll be too late to be worrying about protecting the reputation of the Queen's Fine Art Museum. If we find it, then that's another story. I'm sure we can come to some agreement.'

'You drive a hard bargain, but like your editor, I need you. So, as you say, let's see what happens. I don't see that I have any alternative.'

'And so, what is the urgency?'

'Well, as its curator, I can't permit the museum to engage in a public fraud, pretending the Elephant's Sapphire to be authentic when it is not.'

'No, of course not, but what is the real reason?'

Edwin Philips sat back in his chair, looking down, across his desk at Lynnford. 'Mr Lynnford, I don't know if you know anything about the political situation in Nepal at present, but it is particularly delicate. In fact, the country is in turmoil. Earlier this month the king was deposed, and he is in exile and there is fighting inside the country along the border with India.'

'Hasn't the king's grandson been enthroned?'

'Yes, he has. So, I see you are following what is happening.'

'I do read the newspapers, Mr Philips. As well as being a journalist.'

'Indeed. Of course you do. The grandson is only three years old and, so far, there has been no international recognition of the change of ruler. So, as you can imagine, the situation is still highly volatile.'

'And the relevance of the Elephant's Sapphire?'

'The Elephant's Sapphire is a highly prized political symbol and always has been since well before the creation of the modern-day state. Still, for the general peace, everyone's been happy for it to be kept out of harm's way, so to speak, on neutral ground.'

'Where it's been since 1882.'

'Exactly. With it in the Queen's Fine Art Museum, nobody has it. News that the Sapphire is on the black market would only fuel the instability in Nepal. It would be politically disastrous!'

'I see, but still, why the urgency? Why should the Nepalese ever find out? Nepal is not exactly across the Channel.'

'Because today is Thursday 23rd November, and on the second Saturday before Christmas the Sapphire needs to be back in Straw House Farm in Norfolk. Saturday 16th December, to be precise.'

'You've lost me, Mr Philips.'

'Straw House Farm is the family home of the Urquardts. You recall that it was Colonel Urquardt who won the Sapphire as a prize. His granddaughter, Mrs Stockton, lives at Straw House Farm. Strictly speaking, the museum only holds the Sapphire on trust, under the terms of which, every five years, the family is entitled to have it back to adorn a winter ball that it holds for the local well-to-do.'

'That must push up their insurance.'

'Above all, I doubt that the replica will withstand inspection under the bright lights of a party. Because of the War, the last time it went back to the family was, I believe, in 1936. Anyway, it is imperative I recover the real sapphire before the party, otherwise I'll have to inform the Board of Trustees – and Major Leonard Stockton, Mrs Stockton's husband, is on the Board.'

'That's only three weeks away!'

'Exactly.'

Lynnford reached into his pocket and took out a notebook. 'Do you mind if I take down some notes?'

'Of course not.'

'So, the chances are, as you said yesterday evening, that it was taken some time between the death of Sir Christopher last summer, which I checked happened on 15th August, a Tuesday, and your appointment, which was when exactly?'

'November 1st.'

'And when did you make the discovery?'

'A week or so ago. As I told you.'

'So long? What have you been doing?'

'Agonising with worry. What do you think? Believe me, Mr Lynnford, I am in a very delicate situation. And I had to confirm my suspicions.'

'You had it examined?'

'I have the necessary expertise, Mr Lynnford. I wasn't appointed as the museum's curator on a whim. But I wanted to be sure, and I had to be careful not to alert any of the staff to my suspicions.'

'Do you suspect anyone amongst the staff?'

The curator said nothing, his lips drawn together in a line.

'Do you have anyone in mind?'

'No.'

'You've not made any internal enquiries?'

The curator shook his head.

'And the replica, what is it made of?'

'Lead crystal glass, expertly worked by some master

36

craftsman, no doubt trained in France or Italy. The silver mounting is real enough.'

'And it's very impressive. That can't come cheap.'

'No, indeed.'

'And how exactly does someone make a replica of a jewel? It can't be easy.'

'No, indeed. The dimensions are given on the display, of course, but they would not have been much help.'

'So?'

'So, the most accurate way of reproducing the Sapphire would have been to make a wax copy of it. I imagine from an imprint of its shape or by studying it in detail, holding it, feeling its weight. Touching it. It's the work of a sculptor.'

'So, whoever it was would have needed access to the Sapphire, possibly taking it out of the museum for a while?'

'Yes, or to have visited the museum. But whichever way, it would have had to have been taken out of its display case.'

'And there's no record of that having happened, I suppose? Of someone borrowing the Sapphire or coming to the museum to study it?'

'No. And, really, I wouldn't expect to find such a record. Not if the purpose of making the replica was to steal the original.'

'No, indeed. So, how did they do it?'

'I believe that someone in the museum must have helped them. I cannot see any other way how it could have happened. Most likely by letting the person in when the museum was closed. But who, I've no idea, and I don't want to start questioning the museum staff. It would only make matters worse.'

'No, of course not. I understand. And so, how does a wax copy become an exact replica of a sapphire gemstone in glass?'

'Lead crystal glass,' the curator corrected him. 'The soft wax would have allowed a faithful reproduction of the jewel's facets. A moulding compound, mostly likely of plaster of Paris, would have been cast around the wax sculpture. Once the mould had hardened, the wax would have been melted out and the molten glass poured in, taking the shape of the copied Sapphire. Once the glass had cooled, the mould would have been simply broken away.'

'Clever!'

'Indeed, but it's been a popular technique for centuries. Since ancient times, some say.'

'And heating the glass and firing the mould, that would have required a furnace and heavy equipment?'

'No, not really. A small kiln and a workshop would have sufficed.'

'And what do you think has happened to the Sapphire? How easy would it have been to find a buyer?'

'No one would have taken the risk of stealing the Elephant's Sapphire without first having a firm order from someone.'

'Which means that it's no longer on the market, if it ever was. It's most likely already hidden away in someone's private collection. Unless it's already been cut up. What's your idea?'

'Obviously, I would prefer the first option. Really, I think it's the most likely. Cut up, the Sapphire would have much less value, although it would be much easier to sell.'

'Well, that's something.'

'Not really. My real worry is that it will be faceted.'

'I'm sorry?'

'You've seen the replica. You can see that it's not a sophisticated jewel. It has been cut in a very rudimentary way, with the techniques that were available at the time. Basically, it's nothing more than a rounded, head-like shape with a flat reverse. What they call a *cabochon*. Paradoxically, I suppose, that's what made it relatively easy to copy. It's the highly saturated colour and the almost flawless clarity that give the Elephant's Sapphire its edge.'

'And so?'

'And so, my fear is that someone has taken the Elephant's Sapphire with the intention of using modern cutting tools to transform it into a truly and literally brilliant jewel, at the cost of destroying its unique historical value.'

'And how much is the Elephant's Sapphire worth in its present state?'

'As much as anyone will pay to take it away from his or her rival. It is insured for one million.'

'Pounds sterling?'

The curator nodded.

'So, this wasn't a job for a back street fence. I guess there must be a small world of specialist art dealers willing to turn a blind eye. Any idea of who might handle such a deal? Or who might know someone who might?'

'Wheeler, Chambers & Son, art dealers. They're off St. Martin's Lane.'

Lynnford was taken aback at the alacrity and preciseness of the curator's reply.

'Sounds respectable enough. Why them?'

'They have a reputation. That is, not a good reputation – at least the son, Jeremy Wheeler, hasn't. I found their card amongst Sir Christopher's papers, something which I have to confess surprised me. Although, of course, there might be any number of reasons why it might have been there.'

The curator pulled open a drawer in his desk and selected a business card, which he placed on the edge of the desk in front of Lynnford.

'Thank you.'

Lynnford took the card. 'Do you think he might have discovered the theft? Sir Christopher, I mean.'

'But that would mean that the Sapphire was stolen before his death.'

'It's just an idea, Mr Philips. What do you think?'

'It's possible. In which case, that might have been a reason for him taking his own life. There doesn't appear to have been any other.'

'I hope it doesn't push you in the same way!'

'It's not something to joke about, Mr Lynnford.'

'No, of course not. I'm sorry. How do you suggest I take up this lead with the antiquarians in St. Martin's Lane?'

'Perhaps you could hint that you have the Sapphire for sale.'

'That would certainly set the cat amongst the pigeons!'

'Whoever has the Elephant's Sapphire could not help but be intrigued. You will raise the worry that they will always have: that possibly what they have is nothing more than a fake, despite whatever they have done or paid to acquire the real jewel. At the very least they would have to find out whether what you claim is true or not.'

'I'll try that. One last thing.'

'Yes?'

'It would help to have someone on the inside.'

'What do you mean?'

'I have a young lad who works at *The London Herald*. Could you recruit him temporarily? He could see and hear what's going on amongst your staff, things you wouldn't pick up. Maybe they're all above board, but just in case.'

The curator looked unsure.

'Of course, he wouldn't know anything about the Sapphire,' Lynnford added, hoping to reassure him.

'I don't like the idea, but I agree we mustn't be blind. If you can vouch for him, and tell him no more than absolutely necessary, then fine. Speak to Mrs Fellows, my secretary. Jennifer. She'll arrange everything.'

'Thank you.'

'Then, if that is all, perhaps we can conclude this meeting. I have a busy day ahead of me,' and so saying, the curator got to his feet. 'Of course, if you need anything else, Mr Lynnford, I am at your entire disposal. Although, in the circumstances, I would prefer to limit our contact to the absolute minimum. You understand, of course?'

Downstairs, in the grand foyer, Lynnford glanced back up the stairs, and wondered. It was a strange place for a suicide. Crippled, as he had suggested to Mr Philips, and a broken back, seemed to him the most likely outcome from such a fall. At least Sir Christopher had been lucky to have spared himself that.

FIVE
WHEELER, CHAMBERS & SON

Lynnford looked at the shop in front of him. Wheeler, Chambers & Son; the name was spread across the façade. The entrance door, inset between two window displays, one on either side, their glass corners rolling round into the recess, was made of oak and cut by a pane of frosted glass in the upper half, engraved with the words "antiquarians and dealers in fine art". Lynnford crossed the road and walked inside.

He imagined the interior to be large, but any idea of its true dimensions was lost by the profusion of objects placed almost on top of each other, in cabinets, on shelves, from the walls and ceiling, and on the floor. Even the objects on display had been called into service. Close to him, a human-size statue of Apollo propped up a gilt-edged mirror whose glass reflected the several gold rings dangling on chains from the extended fingers of one of the god's overhanging hands. A pedestal desk and a fine bow-legged table, each placed at an angle and facing the entrance on opposite sides, appeared to fulfil a dual role of reception and protective barrier for the remaining open floor space in front of them.

An open spiral staircase linked the shop floor to the upstairs and basement. Behind the pedestal desk, a white panelled door had been left ajar. A young man sitting at the desk raised his head on seeing Lynnford and was about to get to his feet to greet him when a woman, standing close to the window, turned round from the large copper plate that she was examining and interrupted him, 'That's all right, Thomas. I'll deal with the gentleman.'

She smiled at Lynnford. 'What can I do for you?'

Her hair was tied behind her head in a ponytail that was perhaps more youthful than her years. A cardigan covered her slight frame. She wore no jewellery, and her only decoration seemed to be the pair of tortoiseshell-rimmed glasses that she had removed after placing the copper plate to one side, leaving them to hang from a fine chain around her neck.

'Mrs Chambers,' she explained, adding, 'A bitter day, don't you find?'

'Indeed. December's not far off,' Lynnford replied, and taking in the contents of the shop with a sweep of his eyes, commented, 'A very impressive collection, Mrs Chambers. Is that Chambers as in Wheeler, Chambers & Son?'

The woman nodded.

'Mr Jeremy Wheeler was recommended to me. Would it be possible to see him?'

Mrs Chambers shook her head slightly and smiled. 'I'm afraid that he's away at present. Perhaps I can help?'

Lynnford looked around for something to say and his eyes alighted on the table. Several expensive white carnations in fresh water filled a cut-glass vase, and next to them was a silver figurine, an arm stretching out with a bow, and holding a lamp in its other hand.

'Zephyrus,' Mrs Chambers announced.

'Ah, yes. The Greek god of the west wind,' Lynnford added, keen to establish his credentials, and recalling his Classics at Oxford.

'It's a charming piece. Italian, about 1800. Silver. Delightful, don't you think?'

Addressing the young man behind the desk, she added, 'Thomas, fetch me the Archer. I'm sure the gentleman will like it.'

'Judith!'

The door behind Thomas opened with a burst, revealing a red-faced man towering over the seated assistant in front of him. He was well-groomed, in a blue-striped shirt, with white, silky hair that lined a balding crown.

'Can I just borrow Thomas a minute, Judith? Some stock-taking.'

'Really, Arthur, he's helping me with this customer, but I don't mind. I can manage without him.'

Mrs Chambers made a sign towards the assistant with an expression that combined permission and displeasure.

'It doesn't matter about the Archer,' Lynnford intervened.

'Really?' Mrs Chambers turned her attention back to him. 'Something else, perhaps? Tell me, are you buying for yourself, or perhaps a gift?'

Lynnford smiled, asking instead, 'And the copper plate you were examining a moment ago?'

'Oh yes. In fact, we've only just acquired it. A gentleman brought it in earlier this morning. Are you interested in it? I haven't really evaluated it. How much would you be willing to offer?'

'I'm not sure that I would want to offer anything without your opinion first.'

'Very sensible. A cautious man is rare indeed.'

'Perhaps not as rare as your collection.'

Lynnford and the antiquarian both laughed, politely. He could not see in her anything other than a simple historian lost in a world of trade. Certainly not a criminal. 'Tell me, Mrs Chambers, how can you be sure of the plate's authenticity? I mean, something like that, brought in off the street so to speak.'

'You mean whether it's a fake?'

'Well, yes,' Lynnford replied, a little taken aback by her unexpected directness.

'We are a respectable firm, I can assure you. But make no mistake, between the authentic and the fake there's a whole universe of copies, reproductions, inspirations from, and adaptations of. They all have a value. What we don't practise is deceit. Deceit is the death of a healthy business.'

'I'm afraid the copper plate is not really what I'm looking for.'

'What about this then?'

Mrs Chambers held up a cup and saucer. 'Russian, hard paste porcelain, enamelled and gilded with the imperial crown and eagle.'

'It's certainly exquisite.'

'But not your cup of tea!' Mrs Chambers gave another light laugh, replacing the cup and saucer. 'No, well then, there really is something that I'm sure would interest you.'

And she began to thread her way between the expensive *bric-à-brac*. After a minute or so she called out triumphantly, 'Here it is!'

Lynnford followed the antiquarian's outstretched arm and beheld a wooden sculpture, about a foot high and composed of two oriental figures sitting around a small, low table. Mrs Chambers brought it out and placed it on her table. The dark red wood revealed two finely sculpted men, capped and dressed in robes, sitting on the floor, one opposite the other, their concentration on the squared board between them.

'The Korean chess players. Solid mahogany, and I can guarantee sixteenth century. Admittedly it's a copy of something much older, but still full of character. Don't you think?'

On entering the shop Lynnford had had no intention of buying anything, but despite himself he couldn't help but be drawn to it. The two figures engaged his curiosity and imagination.

'Yes, I like it. Tell me, Mrs Chambers, I have a set of antique jewels to sell. Could you find a buyer?'

Mrs Chambers turned away from the pair of Korean chessmen.

'Not without seeing them. I thought you wanted to buy. Are you telling me that you want to sell instead?'

'I will need some money to afford the two chessmen.'

'What sort of jewels?' she asked sharply.

Lynnford made an expression as if to suggest that he didn't want to go into detail.

'Can I see them?'

Lynnford shook his head. 'I don't have them at the moment.'

'They wouldn't be stolen, would they?'

Again, Mrs Chamber's occasional directness was disarming.

'Of course not!' Lynnford replied quickly.

His tone was full of pretence, but Mrs Chambers was unperturbed. 'What sort of sum are we talking about?'

'Sufficient to make it difficult to find a good buyer. I understood you might be able to help, or rather, Mr Wheeler might.'

'You really won't need that much to acquire the chessmen, not for a gentleman of your quality, I can assure you.'

As Lynnford did not say anything, she leant over the table and opened the drawer, from where she picked out a business card.

'Jeremy Friedman,' she explained, handing the card to Lynnford. 'You'll find him down between Charing Cross Station and the Embankment. He might be able to help you.'

'Thank you. I'll go and see him right away. Don't worry, I won't say anything about you. But please keep the chess players aside for me. I'll be back.'

Mrs Chambers opened the door for him with a thin smile, adding, 'I can't promise anything for the chess players.'

*

In less than ten minutes and following the directions of a war veteran selling newspapers on the pavement outside Charing Cross Railway Station, Lynnford entered a covered passageway that descended several flights of steps to what appeared to be an impasse at the bottom. An iron handrail cut into the brick guided him down the broad steps. What must have been a recently erected glass canopy allowed the late-November daylight to illuminate the protected world below. A series of small shops filled the arcade, enjoying a privileged clientele, as Lynnford inferred from their select appearance. Outside the door to a silversmith, a brass plate indicated the premises of Jeremy Friedman Esquire on the first floor, above the shop. *Has money, but doesn't want to say how he earns it*, Lynnford commented to himself and, continuing in his thoughts, added, *If you're coming to see Mr Friedman, you must know what you're looking for.*

Lynnford pressed the bell and the door clicked open. At the top of the stairs, he was greeted by a slender man, dressed simply in a grey suit. Behind him, the door to his office was closed.

'Yes?'

The greeting, with its interrogation, was pronounced in a matter-of-fact tone, but with sufficient authority as to make it clear that Mr Friedman was not to have his time wasted or business interrupted with uninteresting trifles.

'Mr Friedman?' Lynnford replied, politely ignoring the question and putting his own.

The man nodded without moving, staring back at Lynnford, clearly expecting something more. Of average height, his head was narrow and ferret-like, with the features of his face centred on his nose.

'Mrs Chambers, off St. Martin's Lane, recommended you.'

Mr Friedman's face opened, almost as if Lynnford had turned a key in the man's mouth, just like an old clockwork doll. A smile broadened across his face, still without changing its guarded features but releasing an affable welcome, nonetheless.

'Of course, she advised me.'

With another nod, Mr Friedman bowed and, opening the door behind him, beckoned Lynnford to enter. The single room was sparsely furnished. A plain desk was placed next to the window. A black telephone handset on the desk informed Lynnford as to the likely means of communication between the shop off St. Martin's Lane and Mr Friedman.

'Buying or selling, Mr…? Forgive me. Mrs Chambers didn't give me your name.'

Lynnford made up a name. 'Taylor.'

'Ah, yes.'

Mr Friedman's tone indicated clearly that he both understood the name to be an alias and fully accepted to deal with Lynnford on that basis. 'I believe you are selling, are you not, Mr Taylor?'

'That's correct.' Lynnford took the seat offered to him in front of the desk. 'I had been hoping to speak to Jeremy Wheeler, but Mrs Chambers informed me that he's away.'

Surprisingly for Lynnford, the reply was straightforward.

'In fact, I'm one and the same. The Wheeler in Wheeler and Chambers is my mother. She and Mrs Chambers are twin sisters. For convenience, let's say, my preferred name is Friedman. Of course, you understand that, don't you, hmm, Mr Taylor? I'm the son in Wheeler, Chambers & Son, and, if you like, this office is a sort of backdoor for those people who, as yourself, like to be discreet.'

'And, if I wanted to buy?'

The change of direction did not appear to ruffle Mr Friedman. 'My aunt tells me that you already have your eye on something in the shop.'

'Two Korean chessmen, yes. But if I wanted something else, could you find it?'

'Mr Taylor, look around.' Mr Friedman opened out his hands in an expansive movement, offering Lynnford to inspect his surroundings. 'There's nothing here, as you can see. I find people, not objects. Buyers and sellers like yourself. What they have to sell or want to buy is their affair. I don't concern myself with that, only insofar as it helps me bring them together. What they have, it's their responsibility. So, tell me what you would like to sell, and perhaps I will have a buyer for you.'

'A jewel of considerable value, a unique jewel, but for the moment I cannot say much more.'

Mr Friedman laughed, and even his eyes seemed to sparkle. 'Well, that's all very well, but it's not going to get us very far. Can I see it?'

Lynnford smiled dryly and hunched his shoulders, saying nothing. Mr Friedman raised his eyebrows in what Lynnford could not help feeling was an assumed expression of surprise.

'Let's be frank, Mr Taylor, shall we? You have a jewel to sell, or rather would like to sell once you have it in your possession. Do I understand you correctly?'

And, as Lynnford remained silent, he continued, interpreting Lynnford's silence. 'How very interesting. A nice little puzzle. I wonder how you propose to obtain it, but perhaps that would be too indecent of me to ask?'

'As I understand you, that's my business.'

'Yes, of course. So, you want me to confirm that I can find a buyer in order to persuade you that it is worth your while acquiring this… this unique jewel. Is that it?' Mr Friedman nodded his head, as if in agreement with himself. 'And what is it you intend to acquire, Mr Taylor?'

'It's a sapphire the size of a large egg, of Nepalese origin.'

'It must be remarkable, to be of such a size. And I presume it has a name.'

'The Elephant's Sapphire.'

'How very nice.'

As they spoke, Lynnford heard the faint sounds of someone breathing and the slight scrape of a shoe. Was someone listening to them? But it wasn't clear where the person might be hiding. Mr Friedman remained impassive.

'And you can acquire this sapphire, Mr Taylor?'

Lynnford gave a look of assurance.

'And what price do you put on it?'

'Its value is outside the reach of a normal catalogue. An ordinary dealer would have difficulty in handling it.'

'That I can imagine, but it's not worth anything if one can't sell it.'

'Of course not, Mr Friedman. Could you find someone?'

'Possibly.'

'Who would this be?'

'Ah, Mr Taylor, please do not push the boundaries of indiscretion too far. I have told you that I might be able to find a buyer, and I will try, if you want, but it would be impolite for me to breach the person's trust by revealing their identity. Nor would it make much business sense for me. My work is not free – far from it.'

'Would this be a private collector, then?'

'Let's say, somebody who likes to enjoy their collection in private, among trusted friends, and who can afford to indulge a passion. There, Mr Taylor, I think that's enough said.'

Mr Friedman rose to his feet. 'Bring the Sapphire to me once you have it, and I will find your buyer.'

Once Lynnford had left Mr Friedman's office, a man appeared from behind a false screen, large and heavy in his movements. The screen was disguised by a *trompe-l'oeil* that reflected the sparseness of the room's decor.

'Well, Bosworth, that's a nice little coincidence, wouldn't you say?'

'He wants to sell the Sapphire?'

'You heard him, loud and clear like a foghorn, Bosworth. It seems this man, Taylor, knows where it is.'

'He only knows that it's been stolen, if that. He's fishing for information.'

'How's that?'

'Because his name's not Taylor.'

'I know that, Bosworth. I'm not stupid.'

'And, whatever he says he is, he's a newspaper hack. I've seen him around, sniffing around Alexandria Wharf.'

Jeremy Friedman's face turned grave. 'I see. So he's looking for a story. Is he dangerous?'

'He could be. It's time to put him out of action.'

'Couldn't he lead us to the Sapphire? We've no idea who stole it from Fields.'

'The newspaper man doesn't know where it is. If he did, he wouldn't have come here. He's told us all he knows.'

'That the jewel in the museum is a replica and the original Elephant's Sapphire has gone missing?'

'Exactly, and we don't need him to find it for us. Not with his snout already stuck into our business in Alexandria Wharf.'

'I understand. Still, I think you would be missing an opportunity, Bosworth,' Friedman continued. 'A bloodhound with the scent! Or as good as, that's what he seems to me. He could find the jewel for you and save you a lot of trouble. You're a little too hasty and violent, Bosworth.'

Jeremy Friedman immediately regretted his words and cowered within himself, expecting any moment to be thrown back against the wall. But Bosworth did not lash out, simply relishing his interlocutor's fear. 'We'll do what I say, Friedman. Remember that!'

SIX

BAKER'S TEA ROOMS

Leaving Jeremy Friedman's office, Lynnford almost collided with an elderly man as he hurried out of the arcade. Carrying a suitcase in each arm, the man was no doubt on his way to catch a train in the nearby Charing Cross Railway Station. It was almost two o'clock, and Lynnford was late for a lunch appointment in Baker's Tea Rooms in Kensington that he'd made with Victoria the day before. Would she still be waiting for him? he wondered. His thoughts raced ahead, hoping that she had the afternoon free, but, even if she did, he knew the November cold would be no match to her chilly fury at having been left waiting by him, once again.

'Watch out, young man!' the man with the suitcase called out.

'Sorry,' Lynnford apologised, his hand already up and flagging down the black cab he had just spotted coming along the Strand.

For the last two years or so, Victoria had been Lynnford's undeclared fiancée, although he'd known her for much longer. Indeed, ever since she'd picked him up in an Auxiliary Territorial Service recovery truck after crashing his plane in a Suffolk field on return from a mission in the early years of the War. Her French husband had died in a road accident shortly after the War, whilst she had been studying in Paris, at the Sorbonne. She continued to refer to herself as Mrs Beaumont.

'Baker's Tea Rooms, Kensington,' he called out.

The cab driver nodded, sliding shut the communicating window, and, shifting back in his seat, he joined the traffic swimming around Nelson's Column in Trafalgar Square.

Outside Baker's Tea Rooms, standing on the pavement as his taxi drove away, Lynnford could see Victoria sitting at a small table, squeezed in behind the entrance and window, looking out onto the street. She had spotted him getting out of the cab, and was now beckoning to him energetically, but silently, through the glass.

'You're late, Robert,' she admonished him once he was inside, pointing to the remains of her lunch on the plate in front of her. She was now smoking a cigarette. 'Where have you been?'

'Some of us have to work, Victoria.'

'And you're not one of them.'

Lynnford's tardiness had sharpened Victoria's sarcasm. 'Why Paul Kombinski took you on at *The London Herald* I will never know. There are so many journalists who need the work.'

'Because you asked the proprietor, Joseph Irvine, and he asked Kombinski; and anyway, I like what I do.'

'Ah! So now we have the real reason why you're always late,' she sniffed, with what she hoped was a contemptuous air. 'What have you been up to?'

'Well, to be honest, Victoria, you could help me out on this.'

Lynnford pushed away the empty plate and handed Victoria an ashtray from the table behind him.

'Tell me.'

'The curator of the Queen's Fine Art Museum in—'

'I know where it is, Robert!'

'The curator has asked me to find a stolen jewel. I met him last night in The Golden Fox.'

Victoria let the fine scent of her cigarette blow across Lynnford's shoulder. 'And what's the problem with that?'

'Don't you think that he would be better going to the police?'

Victoria shrugged her shoulders, shaking her head. 'Not really. I imagine he wants as few people as possible to know about it.'

'Exactly.'

'I'm surprised you're even telling me about it, Robert.'

'Victoria! Anyway, I haven't told you which one.'

'If you want me to help then you need to trust me.'

Lynnford, feeling he was walking across a minefield, said nothing, and Victoria continued, 'He's probably got a fake on his hands and hopes that you can recover the original before its loss is apprehended by the art world.'

'But, Victoria, how did you know?'

'It's obvious, Robert. Why else would he have searched you out personally yesterday evening in The Golden Fox and not got his secretary to arrange an appointment at the museum?'

'Perhaps he should have come and seen you, Victoria.'

'He'd have been wasting his time. So, what's his pickle?'

'His pickle, as you so elegantly call it, is that the jewel could have been taken really at any time, but most likely during the last three months. It could be anywhere by now, and in any state.'

'Has he got any idea who might have taken it?'

'Mr Philips?'

'Is that his name?'

'Yes. No, not really. He suggested I start with a firm of antiquarians whom he considers to be a little below board. I went round there this morning. They seemed straightforward enough. But to tell you the truth, I don't really have the experience to judge. That's what I hope you can help me with: art expertise. That's your field, isn't it?'

'And who are they?'

'Wheeler, Chambers & Son. Just off St. Martin's Lane.'

Victoria shook her head, dismissively. 'I've not heard of them.'

'Anyway, they have a back office for their clients who are seeking discretion, run by the son. Mr Philips suggested that I pretend to have the jewel for sale. I've just come from there.'

'Tell me more about this jewel.'

Victoria folded her arms and sat back in her chair, looking at Lynnford, an inquisitive look on her face. Lynnford recounted the tale that he had been told by the curator. When he had finished, Victoria's eyes flashed and she released her arms, 'That's a nice story.' She leant forward and, picking up her cigarette, gently tipped loose the long line of ash.

'Yes, but where's the jewel now? That's the question.'

'Well, for what it's worth, if you want my opinion…' Victoria paused, with a smile on her lips.

'Yes, Victoria? Come on.'

'Well, I doubt that it's been cut up. Of course, it's a possibility, but I would think that if somebody has gone to the trouble of making such a good copy as to fool everyone, then it's because they want to enjoy the authentic jewel in private, or at least their client does. If they were going to cut it up there'd be no need to have put such an effort into making a good copy. Don't you think?'

'Yes, that sounds plausible. You should be a journalist.'

'Well, for that, Robert, I have better things to do. Did he say it was a glass copy?'

'Lead crystal glass.'

'Then it must have been done using the French or Italian technique.'

'Yes, he said that.'

'Only something like that could have achieved the quality that this replica appears to have. Whoever made the copy is most likely to have been a master craftsman.'

'Yes, Mr Philips is of the same view. You haven't got any ideas on possible collectors with money to burn?'

'Certainly not! But it might be useful for you to visit an auction to see what happens, who's there, and who's bidding for what, that sort of thing.'

'It sounds a good idea.'

'Guildford's of Kensington is just round the corner. They hold an auction every Thursday afternoon.'

'You're a regular?'

'Robert!' Victoria responded with scorn. 'I don't just spend my time on charities and visits. How do you think I furnish my apartment? Where do you think the Queen Anne dining table and chairs came from? And the watercolour of the Lake District?'

'What watercolour?'

'You're hopeless, Robert. Come along, it's Thursday, isn't it?'

*

Outside the auction hall, Victoria had another idea.

'Listen, Robert, what you need to do is find the person who made the copy.'

Lynnford stopped. 'That's not a bad idea. Let's think about it for a moment.'

Victoria shrugged her shoulders dismissively. 'You can do all the thinking you like, but I must be off. Don't forget the auction.'

'Victoria! Aren't we going in together?'

'Not this afternoon, Robert. I really must be going. I have an appointment at four o'clock. You were late for lunch, remember.'

So saying, she hailed down a taxi and disappeared inside. Before the taxi drove off, she wound down the window and leant out. 'Can you pop round this evening?'

'Of course, we'll have dinner at Oscar's.'

'Lovely!'

The taxi pulled away, Victoria's arm stretched out, giving a little wave, leaving Lynnford to enter the auction hall by himself.

*

Two hours later, and after having sat through the auction at Guildford's Auction House for just over an hour, Lynnford entered the offices of *The East London Gazette* with an idea for finding the person who had copied the Elephant's Sapphire.

'Afternoon, Lynnford. What wind brings you out here?'

Lynnford had stepped into a small office with a counter stretched between two partition walls, painted in white up to just two feet below the ceiling, where a glass panel ran round the three internal walls. Empty, straw-seated chairs lined the room on his side of the counter. The reception to *The East London Gazette* had nothing spectacular about it, and the absence of an imposing figure like *The London Herald's* head clerk leaning over the counter seemed to underline the newspaper's lowly local status. Still, whilst other local newspapers had come and gone, *The East London Gazette* had been printing since 1908.

The man who had welcomed him was Walter Duff. Unlike Lynnford, Walter Duff had always worked on newspapers, apart from during the few years of the War, when the Royal Air Force had brought him and Lynnford together. It was Walter Duff who had first introduced Lynnford to the world of newspapers, telling him what he did for a living in civilian life. He was not just someone who wrote stories, but a reporter who carried out his own investigations, and it was this memory that Victoria had unconsciously touched on when she had had the idea of asking Joseph Irvine to offer Lynnford a job on his newspaper. Back from the War, Walter now worked on everything at *The East London Gazette* and, although he was not its proprietor, he seemed to be everything else. An energetic, slim-built man of medium height with strands of glistening black hair swept backwards behind his ears. Lynnford glanced at the collection of selected front pages pinned up on the wall behind Walter, celebrating his scoops and headline stories.

'Still grinding away at the mill, Walter?'

Several lines arched across Walter's forehead as he opened his hands, exclaiming, 'What else?'

Lynnford tore out a piece of paper from his notebook and handed it to him.

'What's this?'

'Just an advert, Walter. I'd like you to run it in the classifieds.'

'Knowing you, Lynnford, nothing's just an advert. What are you up to?'

A hint of suspicion hung in Walter Duff's eyes after the flash of surprise. 'Why the personal visit? It must be a very hot story. Any clues?'

'It's much too early to tell you. Is there still time to get it into this week's edition? It comes out tomorrow, Friday, doesn't it?'

Walter nodded and took the paper, reading out loud the text, 'Sapphires and diamonds. Fine quality lead crystal replicas sought for overseas customers. Reply in confidence to the editor or telephone Knightsbridge 3434.' He looked up at Lynnford. 'I didn't know you were into antiques, Lynnford.'

'A possible lead. Nothing more than a shot in the dark. Can you run it for the next few weeks?'

'Sure. Under what?'

'Antiques.'

Walter laughed. 'That's not a big section in the East End. Better try "miscellaneous" or even "services wanted".'

'Fine, I'll leave it up to you. It's a long shot, as I said. I can't count on a reply. Although, if whoever I'm looking for does exist, then I'm sure he or she is an avid reader of local papers. I'll have it run in several others as well.'

'Then you'll need to get cracking if you want to make their deadlines. Most of them come out on Friday like me.'

Lynnford looked at his watch. 'Well, that doesn't leave much time. It's five already. Anyway, I've made your paper.'

'Leave it with me, Lynnford.'

Walter took the pencil stump from behind his ear and scribbled a few lines of instructions at the foot of the piece of notepaper, pressing hard against the counter as he wrote.

'Thanks, Walter. Let me know straight away if you get a reply. You've got my number?'

'Somewhere. Isn't this it?' he asked, pointing to the Knightsbridge number that Lynnford had inserted in the advert. 'More likely than not, whoever it is will call you directly.'

'Yes, of course. Tell you what, Walter, can I use your telephone? I'll ring round, it'll be quicker.'

'Sure, Lynnford. No problem. Use the one in the office next door.'

Within twenty minutes, Lynnford had made all his calls, reading out the same advert that he had prepared following Victoria's suggestion. His own local paper, *The Chelsea and Knightsbridge Times*, had been the last on his list. It only remained to be seen if the person who'd copied the Elephant's Sapphire would take the bait. *Thank you, Victoria!*

*

Was it the lull before the storm? Joseph Matthews could not decide, and the uncertainty was making him irritable. The Nepalese Room was quiet, and the warder sat on his stool staring blankly at the exhibits around him, as he had been taught to do by the others, lost in his own thoughts. It was almost five o'clock and the museum would shortly be closing for the day.

Nothing had happened to disturb his routine in the three months since he had pushed Sir Christopher Fields to his death that balmy night in August. The coroner and the police had concluded a suicide and Bosworth, the dockhand, and his gang had not been back to trouble Matthews. Indeed, he hadn't seen any of them in the museum since the death of the curator. He should learn to enjoy his freedom, he knew, but still he was uneasy. He wondered if they had recovered the stolen Elephant's Sapphire that Fields and Bosworth had been arguing about. They certainly had the means, but he hadn't heard anything. And he wasn't going to tell them that he knew who'd stolen it. Why should he? Hadn't Fields stolen it from the museum in the first place? The thief had most likely sold it already and made his fortune.

Voices and footsteps suddenly rushed into the Nepalese Room. Joseph looked up to see three boys talking excitedly, their younger sister behind them, pulling on the hands of her mother. Instead of the sadness over his own broken family that the scene might have evoked for him, Joseph was surprised at the warmth, albeit slight, that he felt in witnessing the children's innocence and attachment to each other. He should have called out for silence, he knew, but they were alone in the gallery and so he let them run up and down until their mother came up to him, all apologies. And then, almost in no time at all, they were gone; the children laughing as they chased each other out into the corridor, tickled by their mother's light scolding.

And as their voices trailed away, another voice spoke up, but this time filling Joseph with dread.

'Hello, Joseph.'

A large man stepped in front of him, casting a shadow as if he held a curtain, drawing a close to the warder's brief calm. Bosworth! What did he want? Nothing good, Joseph was sure, but the man didn't give the warder any time to think.

'I've got a job for you.'

He speaks as if nothing has changed since the death of Sir Christopher Fields, thought Joseph. *Maybe nothing has.*

'Come outside,' Bosworth ordered, adding, 'We can't speak here.'

Joseph let Bosworth leave the gallery and then, with a

sigh of resignation, got to his feet, following the dockhand out of the museum and onto Piccadilly. He found him in a side street. Bosworth went straight to the point. 'Has anyone been sniffing around the Elephant's Sapphire?'

'The replica, you mean?'

'Don't be clever, Matthews.'

'What do you expect? It's an exhibit.'

Bosworth snarled, without saying anything.

'No,' Joseph replied, quickly.

'No one? Not the new curator?'

'No.'

'What about this man?'

Bosworth gave a description of Lynnford.

'Yes. He was here with Mr Philips, the new curator.'

'The curator showed him the Elephant's Sapphire?'

'Yes, this morning.'

Joseph closed his eyes momentarily, anticipating the blow. None came, and he opened his eyes to Bosworth's smirking face. 'Shit-scared as always, Matthews?'

Joseph said nothing, nervous fear consuming his shame.

Bosworth continued, 'I have a job for you.'

Joseph recoiled within himself. So, he wasn't free of them after all. Just of Sir Christopher Fields. 'What is it?'

'A little day out for you, tomorrow.'

'I have to be at the museum.'

'Call in sick.'

Joseph shrugged his shoulders. What could he do otherwise?

'You're to take the lorry to Portsmouth.'

'What needs picking up?'

'Nothing. The man you saw with the curator this morning will be driving back from Portsmouth tomorrow afternoon.'

Joseph knew better than to ask Bosworth how he could possibly know such a thing. He just did, somehow. Bosworth continued, 'Make sure he has a road accident. Drive him off the road. All the better if it's fatal. Whatever it takes. But make sure he doesn't come back to London.'

'You want him dead?'

'I don't want to see him again.'

'How am I supposed to find him? It's a long road and—'

'Shut up!'

Joseph let his mouth drop.

'He drives a blue four-door Morgan, and he'll be visiting this shop.'

Bosworth scribbled down an address and handed it to the warder, adding, 'Get there early in the day so that you see him arrive. Then you can follow him back onto the Portsmouth Road, or lie there in wait. It's up to you. Just make sure you don't miss him.'

Joseph turned to go, his head down.

'Haven't you forgotten something, Joseph?'

'What?'

'These!' Bosworth handed Joseph a set of keys. 'For the lorry. You'll find it at the wharf in its usual place.'

SEVEN
JACK CHANGES JOB

'That's better.'

Lynnford turned back with a smile from the window looking down onto Fountain Street. It was Friday morning. The fresh damp breeze from the open window whisked through the stale, smoke-filled air that had greeted him on pushing open the door to the office a few moments before. Moving across the room to Maxwell's desk, he picked up the ashtray next to the typewriter that had been overlooked by the cleaner, and tipped its contents into the green metal wastepaper bin, letting up a cloud of ash that made him cough.

'Well, Jack, what do you say?' Lynnford addressed the young lad who had followed him into the office, and who was now standing in the middle of the room. An over-starched white shirt filled out around a buttoned waistcoat that touched the waistband of a faded pair of black trousers.

An inquisitive and young face, topped by an untidy mop of light brown hair, made him look like a boy in a working man's clothes. Jack Worth was employed as a clerk-cum-messenger boy for *The London Herald* and had been since leaving school just over a year ago. Much to the annoyance of George, the head clerk, under whose authority Jack was placed, he was always more than ready to help Lynnford out on one of his stories whenever he was asked. Lynnford had met him on the stairs that morning and had wasted no time in mentioning his idea of having Jack work for him at the Queen's Fine Art Museum.

Jack scratched nervously at the back of his head before replying, excitement overcoming his uncertainty. 'An undercover agent! Gosh! You want me to work as an undercover agent at the Queen's Fine Art Museum?'

'Now, Jack, don't get carried away,' Lynnford tried tempering his excitement but could not help laughing. 'They're looking for some extra help to cope with the school visits and that sort of thing at this time of the year, and I know you'd fit the bill. A young man, discreet, and quick-witted.'

'But what exactly do you want me to do?'

'Mix in as one of the museum warders and keep your eyes and ears open. Get their trust. Listen out for anything that might seem dodgy, not quite correct. I'm particularly interested in a warder called Joseph Matthews, and anything about the former curator, Sir Christopher Fields, whose body was found at the bottom of the great stairwell last August.'

'A murder!'

'No, a suicide. At least that was the coroner's verdict,

so I've been told, but see what the staff say about it. Try to find out about what they do in their spare time. Where do they go after work? Do they have cash problems? Who are their friends? See what they do with their time in the museum. You never know what little sidelines they might be running.'

'That's a lot to find out!'

'That's right, Jack, so no sleeping on the job! I need someone whom I can trust one hundred per cent.'

Jack's face blushed crimson despite himself, and he glanced down uncomfortably at his shoes.

'And to be clear, Jack, you'll be working as if you were a journalist, not a secret agent.'

Jack nodded and Lynnford continued, 'So, if you hear anything interesting try and get it corroborated.'

'Yes, sir.'

'Good. I'll need a report from you every day, of course,' continued Lynnford. 'There's a Lyons Tea House close by to the museum, at the bottom of Regent's Street.'

'I'll find it.'

'Good. Unless I tell you otherwise, I'll meet you there at five-thirty, every day. Remember, you mustn't tell anyone that you work for *The London Herald*.'

Jack had got over his embarrassment, and his eyes shone again with excitement.

'That's it, Jack. So, you've agreed?'

'When do I start?'

'This morning, I hope.'

'Gosh!'

Jack could not retain his surprise; little could he have

expected this turn up for the books as he ate his breakfast only an hour or so earlier.

'Of course, I'll have to clear it with George, which isn't going to be easy. Leave it to me. Not a word to anyone, least of all to him. Don't let him hear anything until I've spoken to him, otherwise he'll be as stubborn as an old rhinoceros.'

Jack was still laughing at the image when the door opened. Maxwell strode in, a broad smile on his face. 'What's this? Secrets? This is a newspaper, not the War Office. A good morning to the both of you. What are you up to, young Jack?'

As he spoke, Maxwell removed his jacket and squeezed round his desk, sitting down with a sharp exclamation. 'Brr!' he shuddered. 'Close that window, will you, Lynnford? We might as well sit outside with that gale blowing through our hair.'

Lynnford laughed as he addressed Jack. 'Be ready in the next hour or so. I'll let you know once I've got it set up. Until then, not a word, and don't get lost.'

'What's up then?' Maxwell asked, shaking out a cigarette as Jack left their office.

Lynnford didn't reply, only tapping his nose with his finger, before turning round to bring the window down. Maxwell crumpled up the empty cigarette packet, throwing it in the bin beside him. The noisy clatter of the telephone broke up their conversation. Lynnford picked up the handset. '*London Herald*, crime desk.'

'Mr Lynnford, this is Philips.'

'Yes, what can I do for you?' Lynnford replied, deliberately not addressing the curator by name.

'You might try an antiquarian in Portsmouth, Montageau's. I heard last night he has some Nepalese *bric-à-brac* on sale, which might be of interest to you.'

'I see. Who told you this?'

'I'd prefer not to say, but I believe the information is reliable.'

'Fine. I'll drive down today.'

'Thank you, Mr Lynnford.' The curator cut the call.

'Interesting?' Maxwell asked.

'Maybe. At the very least, a drive down to the coast once I've sorted Jack out.'

'Sounds like George isn't going to be too happy.'

'When is he ever?' Lynnford remarked dryly, leaving the office and going downstairs.

*

'Paid absence for a week!'

The blood in the cheeks of the head clerk's face had turned a deep purple. Lynnford's proposal that George release Jack for several days' alternative employment outside *The London Herald* had shaken him to the core. 'Never, Mr Lynnford, never. This is not a charity. I don't need to remind you of that.'

Ever since his forced retirement from the King's Hussars, George had had difficulty in adjusting to civilian life. He understood only too well, however, the need for a business to make a profit. Although Lynnford guessed that it was more likely the rude breach of convention and lack of respect for authority that had provoked the clerk's violent reaction.

'And what would Mr Kombinski have to say if ever he heard of it?' George evoked the possibility of a complaint to the editor, and Lynnford was only too aware that his proposal would not please him.

'I thought that perhaps this could stay between the two of us, George. If ever he should find out, I shall of course take full responsibility. In the meantime, perhaps I could do something for you in return?'

'A bribe!' George was even more scandalised.

Lynnford back-pedalled rapidly. 'No, no. I didn't mean that, but perhaps Jack could put in some extra hours.'

'Mr Lynnford.' The clerk gave a deep sigh, his cheek muscles relaxing slightly, and the normal colour of his face beginning to return. 'Mr Lynnford, it's only out of my respect for your war record that I don't throw you out. Jack Worth is a very junior clerk, basically a messenger boy. He's not a journalist, and certainly not a secret agent, for that matter.'

'I know that George, but Jack is different. He likes the chance to get out and prove what he can do.'

'Don't I know! It happens far too often with you, Mr Lynnford.'

'What if it's very important this time?'

The clerk paused before replying. 'Mr Lynnford, you're bending the rules too far, but I dare say I can overlook young Jack's absence. Mind he's back by the end of next week! That's my final word, and on your head be it if Mr Kombinski finds out.'

A knock on the glass panel behind him drew his attention. There was someone standing in the lobby.

'Anyway, Mr Lynnford, I've got my own work to do, even if nobody else has.'

The clerk got to his feet and, turning his back on Lynnford, pulled open the reception window to speak to the delivery man who had just arrived.

A few minutes was all that it took Lynnford to arrange with Mrs Fellows, the curator's secretary, the employment of Jack as a temporary warder standing in for an absent employee at the museum, and to dispatch him on his way to the museum with a simple set of instructions.

*

Half an hour or so later, on his way downstairs to the lobby and his motor car parked outside, he crossed Sanders, *The London Herald*'s foreign affairs correspondent.

'Morning, Lynnford. Flying out already?' Sanders' eyes smiled up at him behind his glasses.

'If only!' Lynnford replied. 'Listen, Sanders, have you got a minute?'

'Of course. How can I help?'

'Nepal. What can you tell me about what's going on there, apart from the deposition of the king?'

Sanders leaned back against the banister, with one foot on the next step up. 'Bit of a tinderbox, I'm afraid, and rather worrying with the Chinese having just marched into Tibet.'

'And the fighting?'

'The Nepalese army seems to have regained control of the area. The reports on Monday were that the anti-government Nepal Congress forces had moved back over the border into India.'

'So the situation has stabilised?'

'For the moment, but I'm not sure it's going to last.'

'Why is that?'

'We just heard yesterday that India has decided not to recognise the new king. And so, most likely, nobody will. Not Britain, nor the States.'

'So, two contenders for the crown! The old and the new. That's a recipe for disaster if there ever was one.'

'As you say. We'll see what happens, but my assessment is that it's going to be a bumpy ride down to the end of the year. The old king is believed to be more than sympathetic to the anti-government forces and the opposition to the government is still very active. You know that it's reported that it was Nepal Congress party members, in league with disaffected army officers, who were behind the plot last September to assassinate the country's Prime Minister? And he's the man who pulls all the strings, for the moment at least. So, I don't think the rebels are going to give up that easily. I would say that the fire is smouldering, not out. What's your interest?'

'Fine art, that's all. Nothing to do with politics,' replied Lynnford, cautiously.

Sanders couldn't resist a smile. 'And where's the crime in that?'

'I just wanted some background, that's all. Thank you, Sanders, that was very helpful.'

'Any time, Lynnford.'

*

The late afternoon winter sun was lying low in the sky behind him, shining in the rear-view mirror, almost dazzling him when he looked. The sky was now beautifully clear, the rainclouds earlier in the day having blown away, and Lynnford, driving with one hand on the leather-bound wheel of his Morgan motor car and the other hanging loosely over the open window, let the miles of macadam pass carelessly by. The open road was something to enjoy, and an opportunity to forget the disappointment of Portsmouth, now some distance behind him. Montageau's had been a red herring with nothing more to show Lynnford amongst the *bric-à-brac* than a troop of seven teak elephants, each sporting two paste rubies, the tallest no more than a foot high. Mr Montageau, the proprietor, had been of no real help, having to all appearances voluntarily marinated his insides in gin for the last decade or so; a habit that he had topped up several times during Lynnford's brief visit.

The road was almost his own. The little traffic there was on the road was heading mostly in the opposite direction, towards Portsmouth and Southampton on the coast. Lynnford drove steadily with little interest in speeding. He had to be back in London in time to meet Jack at five-thirty, that was all, and he had plenty of time for that. Coming out of a bend, a long straight stretch of road opened out before him, almost tempting him to press down the accelerator pedal, but he maintained his speed, fixing his attention instead on the oncoming lorry that he'd spotted in the distance, allowing his mind to play through the mathematical gymnastics of calculating the exact point on the road where the two vehicles would meet, and drawing there an imaginary line.

As they approached each other, the straight road appeared to be pulling the driver of the lorry along ever faster, and so Lynnford was kept busy in adjusting the imaginary line that he'd drawn, a line that was getting ever closer, very quickly. Suddenly, the lorry was upon him, much larger than he'd thought. He shook his head as the memories of his wartime aerial combats came flooding back, only to realise that it was a combat. The lorry had crossed in front of him and would have crushed the sports car under its speeding weight had not Lynnford's sixth sense made him spin the steering wheel round in time, taking the Morgan onto the other side of the road, and out of the lorry's deadly path by a hair's breadth.

Blaring horns awoke him to the presence of at least two cars heading directly towards him, but still some distance away, giving him just time enough to steer back onto the correct side of the road. By the time he could look safely in the rear-view mirror, the lorry had corrected its path and was back on the left-hand side of the road, continuing its journey as if nothing had happened. *Maybe the driver dozed off momentarily*, Lynnford reasoned, but he retained the distinct impression of having seen a man high up in the lorry's cabin, gripping the steering wheel with eyes of steel focused on Lynnford in his Morgan. Why and who he was were the questions left spinning in Lynnford's mind as he pressed down the accelerator, with the wish now to get back to London as soon as he could.

EIGHT
JACK'S FIRST DAY

'So, tell me about your day.'

It was five-thirty, and Lynnford and Jack were seated around a white-clothed table in the Lyons Tea House in Piccadilly Circus, not far from the museum. Lynnford had left his Morgan in Park Mansions and caught a bus, arriving just ahead of Jack.

'Aren't I supposed to be able to go home now?'

'Don't be so cheeky. You're lucky I don't send you back to *The London Herald*. George wants you to put in some extra hours to make up for this.'

'He should try it. Museum warder and secret agent all in one!'

The waitress approached their table.

'Then you'll be hungry. Would you like a cup of tea and something to eat?'

Jack's eyes opened at the invitation.

'Two sausage rolls would be fine, and maybe…' He hesitated, waiting for Lynnford to indicate his approval, 'a buttered teacake.'

Lynnford laughed. 'Fine. That should be enough to get you home all right. Your mother's bound to have your tea on the table. Now, tell me what happened.'

Jack bristled with importance.

'Well, the gaffer called me into his office as soon as I arrived.'

'Mr Philips?' Lynnford questioned, surprised.

'No. Mr Hill, the head warder.'

'Tell me about him.'

'A bit full of himself. Takes himself for a bit of an art expert.'

'Well, he does work at the Queen's Fine Art Museum, Jack. How long has he been there?'

Jack shrugged his shoulders. 'I don't know exactly, but judging from his office, cramped full of junk and bits and pieces, more like a private study, he looks pretty well established. Pretends he went to college, but really it was no more than a private boarding school in Brighton for duffers.'

'But he probably knows more than you. What did he ask about you?'

'Nothing. I don't think he expected anything from me. Said he was glad to have someone to fill in at such short notice. I told him that I'd been working in a packing firm that had folded up.'

Lynnford burst out laughing, stopping suddenly. 'Don't do that again. You're lucky he didn't throw you out on your ear. Not everyone appreciates a sense of humour.'

'He takes life too seriously to spot his leg being pulled.'

'Still.'

Jack got on with his report. 'It was about eleven o'clock when I arrived, so I missed the tea break. Straight away, he sent me to look after the gods, as he put it.'

'What's that?'

'A gallery full of broken bits of stone statues. Antiques. Anyway, I didn't have to know anything about them, Mr Hills said. *Just stay there and make sure nothing happens to them*, he told me. No fear of that! They couldn't be any worse off if somebody played rugby with them. No one came in the whole morning except a couple of students, from the nearby art school, I think. But they made no fuss, just sat and drew copies. I was bored off my feet.'

'Try and use your time better, Jack. George wouldn't be pleased to learn that you'd spent the morning nodding off on a chair. Hardly the profile of a budding journalist!'

'I didn't fall asleep!' Jack replied, indignantly. 'Just no one came. They closed the doors at one o'clock for lunch.'

'What did you do then?'

'Mr Hill came down and took me along to the canteen. Really, it's nothing special. No more than a cabin set up in the courtyard at the back. It's reserved for the museum staff.'

'What are they like, the other warders?'

'They're all right; a bit different from the lads at *The Herald*. Quiet. They don't talk much.'

'Didn't they ask who you were?'

'Mr Hill told them I was the temporary lad, but nobody seemed to take much notice of him. I'm not sure they heard what he said. He's not like George.'

'Yes, George is unique. Well, we hope he is!'

'Eileen serves up the food. Like Mum's friend, Mrs Tunn. Do you remember her? She works as a dinner lady at Marsh Street School.'

Lynnford knew Mrs Tunn better than Jack realised. Working as a conductor on London's buses during the War had fuelled Mrs Tunn's gregarious character, giving her – arguably – through the many acquaintances, casual contacts and friends of a friend that she had made during her time on the buses, an unrivalled knowledge of the city's underbelly, of its shady dealings from bootlegging to moonlighting and back to burglary. Shortly after Jack had started at *The London Herald*, his mother, realising Mrs Tunn's potential, had introduced Lynnford to her, and very quickly, unbeknown to Jack, she had become one of Lynnford's best sources, always ready to give him a tip-off at the drop of a hat.

'I think she comes in especially at lunchtime,' Jack continued, referring to Eileen. 'She's funny, cracking jokes with the warders. She gave me a free lunch, like it was my first day, and she told some of the warders to look after me, otherwise I don't think they would have said a word.'

'Joseph Matthews? Did you get a chance to speak to him?'

'No.' Jack shook his head. 'He was off sick today.'

'That's odd. I'm sure I saw him yesterday and he seemed well enough then. What's wrong with him?'

'I don't know. Mr Hill just said he was off work, sick.'

'Does he have any particular friends amongst the museum warders?'

'Nobody seemed very concerned about him, although they say he's chums with Mr Hill. It seems the old curator also took an interest in him, but not the new one.'

'Really? Why did they say that?'

'I don't know. Why are you so interested in him?'

'He's someone I want you to keep an eye on, Jack. I told you.'

'Well, it seems that he and Mr Hill are always plotting, that's what Bill said. He's the one who chatted to me most. We even played cards during the lunch break.'

'What about the others?'

The waitress interrupted them, placing a hot plate on the table in front of Jack.

'At last!' Jack picked up one of the warm pastries in his fingers. 'There's Harry.'

'Harry?'

'Well, he calls himself Harry, but it's not his real name. He must be Polish or something like that. He sat in front of me but didn't say much. As I said, Bill was the only one who really talked. Out of all of them, only Mr Hill pretends to know anything. The others just put in their hours. I reckon they turn off at nine o'clock as soon as they start work, doze until lunch, and then take a nap until it's time to go home.'

Damp flakes of pastry stuck to Jack's fingers as he picked up the second sausage roll.

'Anything else?'

'Not really.'

'What about Mr Philips, the curator, the new one?'

'Nobody really mentioned him.'

'And Sir Christopher, the one before?'

'The one who topped himself?'

Lynnford nodded.

'Again, nothing. Except his interest in Matthews. I didn't want to come across as too nosey on my first day.'

'Of course not. You did right, but tomorrow start asking some questions. And to Mr Philip's assistant, Mrs Jennifer Fellows.'

'That'll be hard. She has her tea taken up to her by Mary. That's Eileen's help. She also cleans.'

'Think of something.'

'Oh, there's also Mr Collins, he does odd jobs. He wanted me to help him move some heavy furniture. He was happy enough to talk. He was telling me about how much they have stored away. Almost twice as much as what they have on display. He said that the previous curator had a habit of putting more and more into storage.'

'Interesting. Anything else?'

Jack hesitated before replying. 'Nothing really, except you did tell me to keep my ears open.'

'That's what you're there for, Jack. Well?'

'It's nothing really, but he started chatting about his retirement. I suppose he doesn't have long left now.'

'Who? Mr Collins?'

Jack nodded. 'He went on about what he would do when he retired and that he'd need to make some more money, somehow. He said that there was money to be made in importing copies of antiques. Sculptures, frescoes, ceramics. That sort of thing.'

'Really? Go on.'

'He said that art colleges here in London were always

willing to buy copies so that their students could study them without having to go abroad. It seemed an odd thing to me, but he was sure of it. He said it saved them a lot of money. According to him, there's a market for such things in places like Italy, France and Holland. It's a real business, apparently. He would buy them cheap, he said, bring them back, and make a profit. He had it all worked out. I don't know, it still seems far-fetched to me. I can't see art schools having money to burn. Maybe it was just an idea of his to go travelling and give himself something to do.'

'Maybe. People always dream of what they will do when they stop working.'

'He even said that if I'd some spare cash, and wanted to make an investment, I could do no worse than hop over to Paris – as if I could do such a thing in a million years.'

'Why? Why should you go to Paris?'

'He'd heard there was, right now, a second-rate artist passing off copies of the museum's exhibits, which he thought I could sell off back here for a nice profit.'

'Legitimate copies?'

'I suppose so.'

'Did he mention any in particular?'

'Sapphires. Very popular, he said. Like the big blue one in the gallery that Mr Matthews sits in. You know, the Nepalese Room.'

The Elephant's Sapphire! It must be, Lynnford exclaimed to himself, the information making his mind bristle with excitement. Already, Jack's presence in the museum was paying dividends. Still, he played his poker face. 'Very interesting, Jack. Did he say where exactly in Paris?'

'An island, he said. In the middle of Paris. Is there such a thing?'

Île St-Louis, Lynnford guessed. In front of him, Jack licked the running butter from his fingers, munching through the toasted teacake, unaware of the importance of what he had just revealed.

NINE

CHANDRA BHAT

Friday evening. Outside was black. The giant chestnut tree was almost lost in the darkness. Sporadic lights shone out strangely like fallen stars from behind the curtained apartments that looked onto the internal courtyard of Park Mansions. Above, the low evening sky, which seemed almost to touch the roof of the building, was strangely blue, the clouds full again of imminent rain. Lynnford drew the curtains of his drawing room, letting the heavy cloth fall from his hands, and turned his back on the window.

A floor lamp with a large silk shade standing next to the fireplace cast the rest of the room in a warm half-light. The bars of the electric fire in the hearth glowed brightly, and the rug in front of the fire seemed a bed of warmth. But Lynnford had no time to rest. He was busy packing, collecting his papers and putting together some clothes for a short stay in Paris. Jack's tip-off about the sapphires in Paris was too good to miss. The boat train for Dover was leaving at midnight, and he already had the tickets for himself and Victoria. The telephone rang abruptly.

'Knightsbridge 3434,' he replied.

'Mr Lynnford?'

'Yes?'

'Mr Lynnford, this is Mr Philips.'

'Oh yes, of course,' he answered, recognising now the curator's voice. 'Good evening.'

'Mr Lynnford, I was just wondering whether anything turned up in Portsmouth? You went there today, didn't you? I didn't hear from you.'

'A red herring, Mr Philips. I'm sorry.'

'Oh, I see.' Disappointment tinged the curator's voice. 'I'm sorry too. Anything else?'

'I'm off to Paris tonight.'

'A lead?'

'Possibly. Rumours of someone selling a copy of the Sapphire, but it could well be the real thing. I need to check it out.'

'Of course. Well, good luck.'

'Oh, by the way, Mr Philips!'

'Yes?'

'My lad, Jack Worth, started today.'

'Good.'

'Tomorrow, could you give him a message from me? Tell him that the daily meetings are off until I get back. I assume the museum's open all day on Saturdays.'

'Yes it is, and yes, I'll do that.'

Edwin Philips rang off. No sooner had Lynnford replaced the receiver than the telephone rang again.

'Mr Lynnford?'

'Yes?'

This time he didn't recognise the voice.

'Mr Lynnford, I understand you have something to sell that might interest me. Would you have time this evening to receive me?'

The gentleman's voice and vocabulary were refined, holding back before the pronunciation of each word, as if to avoid intrusion, and at the same time to imply the seriousness of his intentions. *Somebody who has had to prove himself in a hostile environment whilst considering all the time such efforts beneath his dignity*, mused Lynnford.

The man continued, 'Are you alone?'

Lynnford ignored the question, instead asking bluntly, 'You are?'

'My name is Bhat, Mr Chandra Bhat. Mr Lynnford, my time, like your privacy, is precious. May I come up straight away?'

'Of course.'

Lynnford felt he had little choice. 'When should I expect you?'

'In a couple of minutes.'

With a click the line went dead, and almost immediately, it seemed, the doorbell rang. *He must have been in the telephone box just outside Park Mansions*, thought Lynnford as he went to open the door to the apartment. A man in his late thirties and wrapped in a fine camel-coloured Kashmir overcoat stood on the landing, a charming smile on his face.

'Mr Bhat?' Lynnford volunteered, already giving way to his visitor.

'Thank you, Mr Lynnford.'

The stranger accepted the invitation and stepped inside. 'It is most generous of you to receive me in your home and at such short notice.'

The man's politeness was polished. He remained where he was, standing in the middle of the room without removing his overcoat, waiting for Lynnford to close the door, surrendering himself, as it were, to the rules of his host's hospitality. Lynnford chose not to oblige him until he had some clearer idea of the purpose of his visit. 'You said you were interested in something I might have for sale?'

'Yes, indeed. Perhaps if we might sit down, we would be more comfortable.'

The visitor smiled agreeably again, his tone both patient and confident. Lynnford relented, and in response to his gesture, Mr Bhat untied his belt and removed his coat, revealing a thin frame clothed in a finely cut suit. The starched collar of his white shirt rode high up his neck, and the gold cufflinks and ring on his finger matched the richness of his straight jet-black hair, cut short and swept neatly back above his ears. He offered his coat to Lynnford.

'Would you like something to drink?'

'Thank you, but not this evening.' Mr Bhat declined the invitation with a voice that conveyed a deep apology. He sat down, lightly adjusting the shirt cuffs around his wrists. He repeated his earlier query, this time with further precision. 'I understand that you have a fine jewel for sale. Am I right?'

Lynnford still chose not to reply. He guessed Mr Bhat

must have seen the advertisement in one of the local papers that had come out that day, but what his visitor went on to say suggested otherwise.

'You are wondering how I'm party to this privileged information? Let us say that I'm aware that the precious sapphire of Nepal, the very jewel in its crown, has been stolen, and that for several months now, the Queen's Fine Art Museum has been exhibiting nothing more than a replica, which is of course a great insult to our country. Yet I am a realist, and I can accept this state of affairs, for the time being. The liberation of the real Sapphire increases our chances of recovering it. You understand, Mr Lynnford?'

'Your country, Mr Bhat?'

'Yes, Mr Lynnford. I'm Nepalese.'

'You represent your government, then?'

'I represent my country, Mr Lynnford.'

'They're not the same?'

His visitor smiled, without conceding defeat, and placed the tips of his fingers together. The enamel of the manicured nails gleamed in the room's shaded light.

'The Sapphire, Mr Lynnford, represents a great symbol for my country. Its disappearance from our land over a hundred years ago was a sad mistake. A misplaced and foolish act of gratitude.'

'It was a reward for the rescue of a young boy, was it not?'

'So, I see that you are familiar with its history. You would not have it were you not. The boy was nothing more than the son of a tyrant who abused his privileges.' Mr Bhat maintained his smile and cool authority.

'I see. Why wait so long? Surely the longer you wait, the more expensive it will become.'

'Not necessarily.'

After a moment's silence Mr Bhat continued. 'I've been waiting for it to surface as soon as we learnt that the exhibit in the museum was no longer the authentic jewel.'

'How was that?'

So much, then, for the curator's desire to keep the loss of the Sapphire secret, Lynnford mused, but he realised that his visitor was able to provide him with a lot of useful information, and he was keen that he should talk as much as possible. He wondered how widespread the knowledge of the Sapphire's theft might be.

'It stares you in the face!' Mr Bhat replied to Lynnford's question, surprise flashing instinctively in his eyes, only to quickly disappear behind a smile that restored his composure.

No ordinary dealer, Lynnford remarked to himself. *He's too emotionally attached to his jewel, and shocked that anyone might not appreciate the difference between it and the copy.*

'Nonetheless, it's a very good copy, can't you agree?' he remarked. A look of disdain tinged the edges of Mr Bhat's smile, and Lynnford continued, 'I doubt very much that you came across the substitution by accident. Am I right?'

'No, indeed not. I arrived in London some weeks ago, as soon as I heard through friends that the Sapphire was on the market.'

Edwin Philips' worst nightmare, thought Lynnford. His visitor's remark appeared to confirm that art dealers, or at least some, were already aware that the exhibit in the museum was no longer authentic.

Mr Bhat continued, 'Please excuse me, Mr Lynnford. I have already intruded sufficiently on your generous hospitality. Your time is valuable; so is mine. Allow me to come to the point. What is your price?' And, not allowing Lynnford time to reply, he continued, 'Mr Lynnford, I know you don't have the Sapphire physically in your possession.'

Lynnford could not prevent a look of surprise.

'The contrary would surprise me. Yet I understand that you intend to acquire it, and that you will. Is that correct?'

Lynnford acquiesced with a nod of his head, wondering now how his visitor had learnt about him.

'So, if I might repeat myself, what is your price?'

Mr Bhat clothed his insistence in velvet. Lynnford replied quickly, 'I haven't a price. Once I have it, I shall let you know.'

His reply did not seem to surprise Mr Bhat, who inclined his head in agreement. Leaning forward, he offered his business card. 'Please do not hesitate to contact me as soon as you are ready, Mr Lynnford. I'm sure we will come to terms.' His teeth flashed in an open smile. 'And now I think that I must take my leave.'

Closing the door behind his visitor, Lynnford turned the card over in his hand. Mr Bhat's name was not on it, only the name and telephone number of a firm: Everest Art, dealers in Asian antiques and curios. The address was an apartment in Bayswater. Perhaps he had walked across the park, but somehow Lynnford doubted it.

Well, that's a turn up for the books, Lynnford exclaimed to himself, returning quickly to his packing. Mr Bhat may have seen the advertisement in one of the local London newspapers, but it seemed unlikely. And he most certainly wasn't the person who had copied the Sapphire. That was clear. So how had he found him? Through Mr Friedman? Somehow Lynnford doubted that the art dealer had arranged the visit. He was sure that Mr Friedman would not allow his clients to meet each other independently of him. He had, after all, his commission to look after. Yet Mr Friedman was the only person with whom he had spoken and given a description of the Elephant's Sapphire. If there had been someone eavesdropping in Mr Friedman's office, as he half-suspected from the sounds he'd heard whilst he had been there, then maybe it had been Mr Bhat, but he wasn't sure that there had been anyone else in Mr Friedman's office. There had been nowhere to hide, after all. And with Jeremy Friedman, in his office, Lynnford had assumed the name of Taylor, so how had Mr Bhat learnt his real name, and found out where he lived? Lynnford shrugged his shoulders. He had a train to catch, and very shortly.

TEN

ÎLE ST-LOUIS, PARIS

The streets around Victoria Railway Station were already deserted. Lynnford walked quickly through the open entrance. His footsteps echoed loudly around the vast interior, most of which was closed and without light. A stale smell filled his nostrils, the end of a spent and tired day. Even the pigeons had gone to sleep, high up and hidden among the metal girders of the station's roof. Litter and cigarette butts dotted the dirty, grey surface of the huge vestibule. Lynnford headed towards platform one, the only part of the station that was still lit, and alongside which was drawn the midnight boat train to Dover, ready to depart. Here, the remaining life of the station was congested, attracted like fluttering moths around a night lamplight. He spotted Victoria, standing with her suitcase at her feet, waiting for him.

'Come along, Robert! It's twelve already, and the train leaves in six minutes.'

As he hurried forward, he sensed running steps catching him up. He glanced sideways, and recognised Stephan Maxwell. 'Max! What are you doing here?'

'Catching the boat train, with you and Victoria. Come on! We'll make it yet.'

'At last, Robert!' exclaimed Victoria. 'Have you got the tickets?'

'Yes. Coach eight.'

'Are you with us, Max?' asked Lynnford, surprised to see *The London Herald*'s sports writer climb aboard the same carriage as them.

'Coach four. But I'll join you if you don't mind. There must be plenty of room.'

Maxwell swung his holdall up onto the luggage rack above the empty seat in front of Lynnford. 'There!' And the three of them settled down as the train began to pull out of the station.

'So, Max, is this just a happy coincidence?' Lynnford asked with a smile.

'Victoria called me. She guessed you wouldn't have time to think of telling me.'

'And what for?'

'I've won some money on the races and couldn't resist the temptation of a weekend in Paris. And there's the *Prix de l'Arc de Triomphe* at the *Hippodrome de Longchamp*.'

'But you've missed it. It was last month.'

'I know, but there's horse racing every Sunday, and I thought it would be a good opportunity to look the place over. Preparation for next year, that sort of thing.'

Lynnford burst out laughing. 'It's just an excuse for a

night out in Paris! Still, it's good to have you along, Max. Here, you can help me finish the crossword.'

Maxwell took the newspaper from Lynnford.

'Is that *The Times*, Robert? There's a piece you should see.'

'What's that, Victoria?'

'May I have the newspaper, Stephan?'

Maxwell handed Victoria the paper, and she opened it.

'It's here on page three, at the bottom. It's about the Jaipur Diamond. Apparently, it was auctioned by Christie's for a record sum of twelve thousand pounds after having been illegally exported out of Calcutta. A local firm of jewellers has been convicted and fined for having breached the Antiquities Export Control Act.'

'So, this is what it's about!' Maxwell opened his eyes wide.

'Victoria, Max doesn't know anything about it,' warned Lynnford. 'Listen, Max, we're trying to find a jewel, and we've got a tip-off that it might be in Paris. And that's all you need to know.'

'Lips sealed. But Paris is a big city to find a small gem.'

'*Place Vendôme* is the place for expensive jewels, Robert,' Victoria observed, 'but I don't think you'll find it there. The *Île St-Louis*, the island in the middle of the River Seine, as Jack was told, seems more likely. Less showy, more discreet, but still central. Yes, I'd place my bet on the *Île St-Louis*.'

'Well, then the *Île St-Louis* it is,' declared Lynnford. 'And although the story Jack was given was of replica jewels being for sale, my bet is that it's the real one. At least, that's what we're going to Paris to find out.'

*

Paris was grey. A white sky outside the *Gare du Nord* railway station cocooned the city's buildings in a single sheet of stationary cloud. Lynnford, Victoria and Maxwell, a little numb from their broken night's sleep on the boat crossing the Channel and the long hours on the train from Calais, cast their eyes about the scene before them, hoping to find a hotel without having to look too far.

The *Hôtel de la Gare* stood directly opposite them, a tall narrow building squeezed into a row of blackened buildings, the dull uniformity of whose façades was decorated at street-level by a collection of cafes, restaurants and shops. They crossed the street, letting the traffic hoot around them.

The entrance to the hotel was open, the door jammed against the lobby wall by a wooden wedge. The doorframe had a tired, shabby appearance. The long, narrow hallway was poorly lit.

'Well, I'll leave you here,' Victoria announced, taking Lynnford and Maxwell by surprise.

'Where're you going?'

'You don't think I'm going to spend a night in a flea pit like this, do you?'

'So, where're you going to stay?'

'I'll go round to my in-laws, instead. They'll be more than happy for me to stay with them. I told them I was coming, so they'll be expecting me, and they have an apartment in the 6th *arrondissement*. We can meet for lunch on the *Île St-Louis*. The cafe *La fleur de Lys*. You can't miss it. It looks onto the bridge, the *Pont St Louis*.'

96

Lynnford shrugged his shoulders and followed Maxwell into the hotel. There was no point arguing with Victoria.

His room was bare and dispiriting. Victoria was right! The carpet was threadbare, and the mattress on the low bed sagged in the middle. A cracked basin propped against the wall was supplemented by an old water-jug placed on the table between the bed and the rickety wardrobe. A few minutes were all it took to hang his clothes in the wardrobe, and he was back down at the bottom of the stairs handing his key to the receptionist. Maxwell appeared shortly afterwards. He made a face:

'Bit of a dive, *n'est-ce pas*? Eh, Lynnford?'

'I couldn't agree more.'

'Still, it's handy for the station.'

'You'll find the *Hippodrome* in the *Bois de Boulogne*, Max. The Metro will take you there.'

'Don't worry, Lynnford, I'll find my way there. In the meantime, I've got some plans for a bit of sightseeing. That's if you don't need an extra hand?'

'No, that's fine, Max. Victoria will interpret for me, if necessary. We'll meet up later.'

For the rest of the morning, Lynnford trailed alone across the little island in the middle of the River Seine, from boutique to boutique, explaining that he was an English collector of rare sapphires but gaining little more in reply to his queries than haughty disdain. In the afternoon, after lunch with Victoria and her help, the doors of the antiquarians and art dealers opened a little more easily.

They explained that they were hoping to acquire a very fine and large sapphire that they understood someone on the island was trying to sell, and they asked whether such a person had been into their shop and whether they had seen the Sapphire. Yes was the reply, there was someone, an Englishman, trying to sell such a jewel, and from the descriptions they were given, Lynnford had no doubt that it was indeed the Elephant's Sapphire. And a real sapphire, not a replica, because none of the art dealers they spoke to had questioned the stone's genuineness, even if they might not have recognised its historic value. Still, none of them had, however, been willing to meet the seller's price – *or*, thought Lynnford, *they had been too uncertain about its provenance to take the risk of buying it.*

What intrigued both Lynnford and Victoria was why the Sapphire was being sold only now, in late November, unless the theft was more recent than Mr Philips, the curator of the Queen's Fine Art Museum, supposed. If it had gone to a collector, as Victoria thought, why was it back on the market again so soon?

More frustratingly, no one was able or willing to give a useful description of the man or suggest where he might be staying. He hadn't left a business card, so no credentials, but, yes, according to one dealer, he'd come in only yesterday, or the day before, and he was most certainly still on the island. They'd surely come across him, they were assured with condescension.

'Let's try one last shop before calling it a day,' Victoria suggested. 'This one.'

Lynnford looked up at the name plate fixed to the wall. *Jean-Michel Dubrueil, Antiquaire, membre de la Compagnie Nationale des experts.* 'Very impressive!' commented

Lynnford. 'Antiquarian and member of the national society of experts.'

On the other side of a glass-panelled door, a man was reaching up to pull down the blind, an elderly man wearing a tweed jacket over a white shirt and tie. Tufts of white hair covered his head. Seeing them, he raised his wrist and, pointing to his watch, showed them the face of the dial, shaking his head.

'Just two minutes,' Victoria pleaded in French. 'Just two minutes, *s'il vous plaît*.'

The man opened the door. 'I am closing.'

'Yes, I know. We're sorry. We won't take up much of your time. We are gemologists and jewellers from London,' Victoria invented. 'We believe there's an Englishman on the island with a large sapphire for sale, which we would like to acquire. Have you seen him?'

Reluctantly, the man opened the door further. 'Come in.'

The shop was in darkness except for the area near the entrance. Although elderly, the antiquarian was spritely, his back held perfectly straight.

'What sort of sapphire exactly is this man selling?' he asked, carefully.

Lynnford described the jewel and Monsieur Dubrueil nodded. 'He was here earlier today. I had been considering his offer but, finally, I decided that the price was far too high.'

'You don't have his address, by any chance?'

'No, but he has been seen a lot on the island and I'm sure he eats locally. Try the restaurant or one of the bars at the top of the road.'

'Can you describe him, monsieur? It would help us greatly.'

'Yes, of course. You cannot miss him. Very English. He was wearing a checked green tweed suit with a waistcoat. An English country gentleman, no doubt. Younger than me, but older than you.' The antiquarian smiled, adding, 'He carries a stick, a walking stick.' He then motioned to the entrance. 'Now, if you will excuse me, it's time for me to close.'

*

Sunday morning. The bottle-green tables outside the cafe *La fleur de Lys* were still mostly empty. Lynnford had picked a table next to the open entrance that gave him a good view of the bridge, the *Pont St-Louis*, that brought people onto the island from the larger island next to it, the *Île de la Cité*, as well as a splendid view down the full length of the *rue St-Louis en l'Île*. There was almost too much to watch over. A large net with which to catch his fish! He could only hope that the mystery vendor would come again onto the island and try his luck. He and Victoria had spent long hours the evening before sitting in the very same cafe, playing with the breadcrumbs on the tablecloth, hoping, somehow, they would spot him.

The giant bells of the cathedral *Notre Dame* had just announced the Sunday morning mass. Victoria had gone to church with her in-laws. Maxwell had gone to the races in the *Hippodrome de Longchamp*. The strong smell of coffee made Lynnford look up to see the waiter standing beside him with his pot of coffee and croissant on a tray.

He had got out of bed early that morning, his bare hotel room encouraging him to waste little time in getting ready. The cold water from the enamel jug had made him shiver, and without warm water, the stubble round his face had cut badly as he stood shaking in front of the frameless mirror fixed haphazardly to the wall above the basin.

A west wind blowing along the river had broken up the blanket of cloud of the previous day, moving it eastwards. Streamers of disorganised white lines now fanned out across the sky, and sharp gusts of November wind whipped around from behind the corners of the buildings.

Lynnford flicked idly through the well-thumbed menu, the contents and prices of which he now knew by heart. The tables outside the cafe were filling up. People were staying longer; some looking out across the bridge and river, their thoughts known only to themselves, a cigarette in hand; while others, behind the open pages of a newspaper, an empty cup of coffee on the table in front of them, were engrossed in events further afield.

'Any luck?'

Lynnford looked up and recognised the antiquarian from the previous day, Jean-Michel Dubrueil. 'May I join you, monsieur?' he asked, taking hold of the back of the seat with his hand.

'Of course.'

The antiquarian unbuttoned his overcoat and sat down, beckoning the waiter, who came immediately and took his order.

'A morning stroll?' Lynnford enquired.

'Hardly. Breakfast before work. I'll open the shop for

a few hours. Sunday morning is a good time for business. Nobody buys anything, but they look around. They're more relaxed than during the week. Invariably they come back during the week and buy. Or perhaps a week or so later. We must be patient, you know, like yourself.'

The antiquarian smiled before lifting the small coffee cup to his lips, sipping slowly. He replaced the cup carefully and continued, 'May I ask what your field of interest is?'

'Antique sapphires.'

'Yes, of course. You said so yesterday. Like the piece you are hoping to buy here on the island?'

'Yes, we heard it was on the market. It seems it could be just what we're looking for.'

'And so, you must still be looking for the person who wants to sell it?'

Again, Lynnford nodded.

'Well, then you may well be in luck.'

Lynnford gave a start.

'I believe that's him,' explained the antiquarian.

'Where?' exclaimed Lynnford.

Monsieur Dubrueil turned his head. 'Over there, look, he is just about to cross the bridge *St-Louis*.'

Lynnford followed the antiquarian's gaze. Striding firmly towards the bridge, he saw a man of stout and middle-aged appearance, wearing a raincoat, and swinging a walking stick, uncaring for those around him. *He must have just walked past*, thought Lynnford, annoyed that the antiquarian had distracted him.

'No doubt he's been visiting one of my colleagues in *rue St-Louis en l'Île*,' the antiquarian suggested. 'Still, I must be going. It's been a pleasure talking to you again. Have a good day. And good luck with your search!'

They shook hands. Lynnford, his eyes on the receding figure, fumbled in his pocket for some money to pay for his breakfast, and, leaving the coins on the table, he dodged past the tables and was about to cross the road when the waiter called him back. 'Monsieur!'

He turned round, annoyed.

'The second coffee,' the waiter explained, holding the tray in his hand with an apologetic look on his face.

And he's walked off without paying to boot! exclaimed Lynnford to himself, looking desperately back over his shoulder and along the bridge as he searched in his pocket for some more French francs. He returned quickly to the waiter, dropped the extra coins with a rattle on his tray, and rushed back out of the cafe, his coat flapping about him.

'*Attention!*' A woman cried out as he brushed past, catching her hair with his coat. Lynnford took no notice, his eyes fixed on the man now progressing rapidly along the bank on the other side of the river. If he didn't hurry, he was going to lose him all together. A pedestrian in front forced him out onto the road. A car horn blared behind him. Back on the pavement, he was almost at the end of the bridge. The man with the walking stick was still in sight, glancing back over his shoulder before crossing the road. Another person in front of Lynnford slowed him down, and another car, the horn pressed hard, kept him on the pavement. Once off the bridge, the crowd dispersed, allowing Lynnford to free himself, but the man with the walking stick had vanished.

A taxi drove past on the opposite side of the road, almost

scraping the pavement, and pulled up outside a hotel several yards further along. The back door swung open, letting out a suited gentleman and a woman in a fur coat; and, as if it were a revolving door, the man with the walking stick suddenly appeared from out of the hotel entrance. He hailed the taxi driver and took the place of the couple in the back of the cab.

Lynnford watched, unable to do a thing, as the taxi pulled away and melted into the busy Parisian traffic. For the second time that morning, the mystery vendor of what he assumed to be the Elephant's Sapphire had eluded him. He entered the hotel. The wide lobby was richly carpeted, and behind the polished counter a hotel clerk in a maroon livery greeted him.

'*Bonjour, monsieur,*' the clerk smiled.

'Good morning,' Lynnford replied in English. 'I have a meeting with one of your guests,' he made up. He noticed a room key left on the counter that he guessed had just been left by the man with the walking stick, and added, 'Can you call room twenty-one, please?'

'*Je suis désolé.* I am sorry, Mr Bell has just left this very minute.'

Lynnford's face expressed disappointment, encouraging the clerk to be helpful.

'He's taken a taxi to the *Gare du Nord*. Monsieur Bell is returning to England. You might just catch him before his train leaves.'

'Maybe, if I get there in time. Did he leave a forwarding address?'

Lynnford pushed a folded French franc note across the counter.

'*Non,*' the clerk replied, slipping the note into the palm of his hand. 'But this is his home address.'

Lynnford read the registration card that the hotel clerk had moved towards him with the tip of his finger: "The Old Vicarage, Lambsholm, Surrey".

'Many thanks.'

'*Je vous en prie, monsieur. Merci.*'

The clerk replaced the card in the box below the counter and handed the room key to the cleaner, who appeared from the depths of the corridor as Lynnford hurried out of the hotel entrance, hailing a taxi in his turn. '*Gare du Nord, s'il vous plaît.*'

He knew there was a boat train for Calais leaving early in the afternoon. Perhaps he would be just in time to catch it, if the taxi driver was quick enough. Maxwell could always pick up his things at the hotel and make his own way back to London on a later train. Victoria had already told him that she would be staying on for a further day.

ELEVEN

THE BOAT TRAIN

'Too late, sir. It's leaving.' The station guard shook his head, indicating the moving carriages, their wheels rattling against the rails, a noisy racket filling the station; and adding with a supercilious air, 'The Calais train leaves at two.'

The large coin-shaped clock hanging above the platform entrance confirmed the hour. Two minutes past two.

'What time's the next train?' Lynnford asked, not without unintended impatience.

'For Calais? At five o'clock. But, of course, you will miss the boat, if that's what you want.'

The station guard took out a timetable and, with his broad flat finger, ran across the lines of times and places. 'The next boat train leaves at eight o'clock tonight. You'll arrive in London at five o'clock in the morning.'

'And there's no other way of getting the earlier boat?'

'*Non, monsieur,*' and the guard left Lynnford to rejoin a colleague at the end of the platform, stuffing the timetable back into the outside pocket of his jacket as he walked away.

What a slippery fish, and so close! Three times already. Lynnford couldn't hide his frustration. *What now?* he asked himself, his mind racing ahead whilst he paced around in circles on the empty platform. He didn't want to lose track of the man with the Sapphire, not after having been so close. Of course, the hotel clerk had given him the man's address in England, but that was hardly much use with him being stuck in Paris. *The London Herald!* Maybe he could get one of his colleagues to meet the Dover train in London. Sanders, possibly, if he was at work.

Back in his hotel and squeezed inside the telephone booth with the receptionist from the day before staring lazily at him from her counter, Lynnford waited for the operator to put him through to the switchboard in Fountain Street. Eventually, a familiar voice replied and, recognising Lynnford, surprisingly suggested that he could speak to Jack Worth, who she knew was at that moment in Lynnford's office. The line went quiet momentarily as he was transferred.

'Mr Lynnford's telephone,' a young voice replied cautiously.

The line crackled with interference.

'Jack, it's Lynnford. What are you doing?'

'Nothing, Mr Lynnford, I just dropped in after church.' He sounded embarrassed.

'Listen, Jack, I haven't got much time. Can you go down to Victoria Station and meet someone coming off the Dover train at ten this evening?'

'Yes, of course, Mr Lynnford. Won't you and Mr Maxwell be on it?'

'No, Stephan Maxwell and I will be back tomorrow, at five in the morning. I want you to look out for a Mr Bell. You don't need to meet him. Just check he arrives and find out where he goes.'

'You want me to follow him?' Jack's excitement almost buzzed along the line.

'Yes. You shouldn't have any trouble picking him out. He's stoutish, quick on his feet, mid to late forties. Most likely he'll be dressed in tweeds, a three-piece suit. Green check, possibly. Wears a trilby. Dark brown hair, from what I could see. And he'll be carrying a walking stick, and wielding it like a retired officer. That's if he can find a porter for his bags.'

'He'll be so lucky.'

'What's that?'

'Nothing. I'll be there.'

'Good, I'm counting on you, Jack.'

Lynnford replaced the receiver and as he did so, he spotted Maxwell step into the hotel entrance, filling the corridor with his frame. 'Any luck?' he asked.

'Not a single French franc, but I've a piece for tomorrow's edition and that's got to be worth something. What about you?'

Lynnford shook his head ruefully. 'I just missed him! He slipped through my fingers like a Thames eel. But do you know what? I've just spoken to Jack Worth. He was sitting in our office, and on a Sunday!'

Maxwell laughed. 'No need to make that face. He's only practising his typing.'

'Typing! What for?'

'Well, we type, don't we?'

'Only because we have to.'

'Exactly!'

'I see, but there are better ways for him to spend his Sundays.'

'Like trailing jewel thieves?'

'I'll tell you about it soon enough, Max, don't worry. For now, the man with the jewel we came to Paris for has taken the boat train back to London and I've just asked Jack to be there when it arrives.'

'And what about us?'

'We'll take the next one. It leaves at eight o'clock this evening.'

*

High up on the uppermost deck, Lynnford and Maxwell, leaning over the ferry's rail, looked down at the approaching quayside. At one o'clock in the morning, the damp cold air broke down what remained of their slumber. Above them, moonlit clouds deepened the darkness aboard the boat.

'It's a chilly night, Lynnford. Let's hope that Jack picked up your man all right.'

Lynnford nodded, adding, 'And that the boy's safe and sound.'

The boat shuddered against the quayside.

'Come on, Max, it's time to go.'

Half an hour or so later, having passed slowly through the passport and custom controls, they found themselves an empty compartment on the waiting train to London. Settling into their seats, they fell quickly back into a deep sleep as if the cold disembarkation from the ferry had been nothing more than an unpleasant dream.

Soon, however, it seemed to Lynnford, his mind was racing round in a whirl. Along the narrow Parisian roads of the *Île St-Louis* he hurried, the drab hotel opposite the *Gare du Nord* railway station colliding with the bridge and the cafe, Monsieur Dubrueil becoming one with the man with the walking stick, leaning out from a balcony and laughing at him. He awoke with a start. His neck aching, he opened his eyes. Maxwell was snoring quietly, but there was someone else in the compartment, a man standing with his back to Lynnford. He was searching for something in the case that he'd placed on the opposite seat, its top resting open against the back of the seat. Looking up at the luggage rack, Lynnford noticed that his suitcase was no longer there.

The stranger must have sensed Lynnford looking at him, or the slight movement of his head had disturbed him. In a flash, he lifted the case in both hands and, turning round with its contents falling onto the carriage floor, threw it at Lynnford, who fell back on his seat with surprise whilst the man pulled open the compartment door and vanished into the corridor.

'Max! Wake up!'

Lynnford got to his feet. Stepping on the clothes strewn across the floor, he ran into the corridor and caught sight of the man disappearing into the next carriage. He hurried after him, checking his balance with every other stride as the train, speeding along the rails through the night, rattled from side to side. The interconnecting carriage door behind him slammed shut, leaving him on the shiny connecting plates between the two carriages, slipping around the pivot and making his footing uncertain. The noise was abrupt and raw, the rails hurtling under his feet. He pushed open the door of the next carriage, letting it close behind him with the same violence as the one before. The corridor was empty. Where had he gone? Lynnford crossed over into the next carriage. The door banged loudly behind him, and Maxwell appeared, breathless.

'What's happened?'

Lynnford explained in a few words.

'Has he gone into one of these?' Maxwell indicated the closed compartments, their blinds down.

'He could have, but we'd never be able to pick him out in the dark. We'd be wasting our time. And we'd have a lot of angry passengers on our backs. You stay here. I'll see if he's got to the end of the train.'

Several carriages further on, Lynnford reached the end of the train without finding the man. He turned back and returned to Maxwell.

'No luck?'

Lynnford shook his head.

'What was he looking for?'

'No idea,' Lynnford replied, adding, 'there was nothing of value in the case. My passport and wallet are in my coat pocket.'

'Still, he wouldn't have known that.'

'No.'

'What about the jewel you went to Paris for?'

'It's possible, but if he'd been following us, he'd have known I hadn't got it.'

'Still. Did you catch sight of him? Would you recognise him again?'

'No. It was dark, and he always had his back to me.'

The train began to slow down. 'We must be approaching a station. It can't be London yet, can it? Where are we?'

Maxwell looked at his watch. 'Four o'clock. We can't be far off. I'll go and see if I can find some hot tea.'

Through the blackened windows, Lynnford could scarcely pick out anything. Pressing his forehead against the cold glass, he tried to see more clearly. Too late! The reflection in the window appeared and disappeared almost as soon as he felt the arm thrust around his neck and a blow to his head. Still conscious but heavily dazed, he felt himself being toppled backwards, dragged into the compartment behind him and dropped on the floor. The door clicked shut; the sound of heavy footsteps faded along the corridor. Recovering quickly, Lynnford got to his feet and pulled at the door, but it didn't budge. The lock had jammed! Frustrated, he pulled hard until it finally gave, and he burst out into the corridor just as the train began to pick up speed again, knocking him off balance.

'Mind out there!' admonished a gruff voice behind him.

Lynnford felt two hands grab him awkwardly under the arms, hauling him to his feet. Raising his head, Lynnford met the stern gaze of the train conductor.

'Not so fast, sir. We've another hour before London.'

The conductor squeezed past Lynnford. Seconds later, Lynnford heard him shout out again, this time a note of alarm in his voice. 'What the devil!'

The rest was lost in the roar of the train as it passed through a tunnel, the carriages clattering one after the other. The low light in the corridor diffused a yellow glow. Lynnford found the conductor at the end of the corridor, pressed against the wall of the last compartment, holding onto the handrail, a wall of blackened bricks racing past, startlingly close, the open carriage door banging wildly.

'Wait till we come out of the tunnel,' the conductor warned.

Lynnford nodded, and whilst he waited, holding onto the rail next to the corridor, his thoughts raced back to the man who he had been following through the train and who he now guessed must have jumped out through the open door. Had he, indeed, been after the Sapphire, as Maxwell had suggested? The conductor tugged at his sleeve, indicating the black open space filling with the distant shapes of houses and other buildings. They had come out of the tunnel. Lynnford leant out and pulled back the door, the stream of air running along the length of the train slamming it shut. Suddenly the carriage seemed quiet, and the two men relaxed.

'What happened?' Maxwell had reappeared, without any tea.

'Some fool without a ticket must have jumped off,' the conductor replied, straightening his jacket and putting the dangling watch chain back into the pocket of his waistcoat. Maxwell glanced at Lynnford, with the same thought as to who it had been in his mind. 'We always slow down there,' continued the conductor. 'And there's always someone who's taken his chance of a free ride up to London, or almost, and jumps out. Regular passengers, if you like.'

Lynnford and Maxwell returned to their compartment and began picking up Lynnford's clothes from the floor and packing them back into his case. Frustratingly, the man's image in the reflection was too confused in Lynnford's mind for him to recall it clearly. It could have been anybody.

'What a night!' he remarked.

*

On the platform at Victoria Station, a familiar figure was waiting for them.

'Jack! You're up early,' commented Maxwell, surprised.

Jack Worth put his hand to his mouth, resisting a yawn. 'Not really. I never went to bed.'

'Jack! What must your mother be thinking?' exclaimed Lynnford.

'It's all right, Mr Lynnford. She knows I'm safe. I telephoned her a couple of times during the night.'

'And that's another thing she won't thank me for! Still, that was a good idea of your mother's, to have a telephone put in when you started at *The Herald*.'

'We could do with some tea,' Maxwell interrupted. 'There was nothing on the train.'

Jack shook his head, his face filling with another large yawn that he tried to resist. 'No chance of that. Nothing's open yet.'

'Pity. So, what're you doing here so early?'

Jack gave a look of embarrassment, full of disappointment, and Lynnford started. 'You missed the man with the walking stick?'

'Oh no, he arrived all right.'

'So, what happened?'

'I lost him. Or rather he lost me.'

'Oh, Jack!'

'Well, perhaps I was a bit obvious. But still, I don't see how he could have spotted me.'

'What happened, then?'

'Well, I spotted him easily enough, coming off the train. He took a taxi to the Royal Park Lane Hotel, where I suppose he checked in.'

'What do you mean, "suppose"?'

'Let him tell his story, Lynnford.'

'You should have checked with reception,' continued Lynnford.

'I did!' protested Jack. 'Later.'

'Don't mind him, Jack. Lack of sleep and a knock over the head on the train have made him grumpy.'

Jack continued, 'Shortly afterwards, he came out of the hotel and that was when I lost him. Not straight away. He spent some time at a night club, the Oyster Club off Piccadilly. It was when he walked out around midnight that I lost him in Mayfair. I assumed that he was heading back to the Royal Park Lane Hotel, so I went straight there and waited by the railings of Hyde Park opposite the hotel entrance. But he never turned up.'

'Jack, there are two entrances to the hotel! The forecourt is in Park Street, on the other side of the building. You were standing outside the Park Lane entrance.'

Jack was silent for a moment, both pride and embarrassment confusingly welling up within him.

'Jack! What happened?'

At last, he spoke up. 'My cousin was watching over the Park Lane entrance.' And before Lynnford's surprise could manifest itself in words, Jack continued, 'Mum wasn't going to let me stay out all night by myself, was she? So, when I called her last night to tell her I was still in Mayfair and that I could be out all night she told me to go and get my cousin Norman when he finished work.'

'Your cousin Norman?'

'Yes, he's a year older. He works in a hotel in Piccadilly in the kitchen as a trainee chef.'

'So, you went to pick up your cousin and that's when you lost our man.'

'No!' protested Jack. 'We were both outside the Oyster Club when he came out. I went ahead to wait for him outside the hotel in Park Lane and Norman followed him.'

'And Norman lost him, is that it?'

'The man must have guessed he was being followed,' Jack admitted, shame infusing his words. 'We stood outside the hotel for a while, Norman in Park Street and me in Park Lane. After a while, I went into the lobby and asked after him, but they had never heard of Mr Bell.'

'Did you describe him?'

'Yes, but the night porter didn't know anything about him. He'd only just started his shift.'

'And so he hadn't gone back to the hotel, otherwise the porter would have recognised him,' Lynnford concluded. 'And you'd left your cousin to follow him. That was your job, Jack, not his.'

'We waited a little longer outside the hotel. By four-thirty he still hadn't turned up, so I thought I'd come down and meet you off the train.'

'Where's your cousin?'

'He's gone home.'

'Sounds like a story of too many cooks spoiling the broth,' commented Max, trying to make light of what had happened.

But Lynnford had already decided to temper his reaction. 'You did well, Jack, in the circumstances. It could have happened to anyone, but be careful about delegating next time. You didn't tell your cousin anything, did you?'

Jack shook his head.

'Good man. Don't mind me being short. You'd better go home now and get some sleep. You need to be at the Queen's Fine Art Museum for nine sharp. Here's some money for a cab.'

And then, as Jack was about to walk off, Lynnford added, 'By the way, did you find out anything about the museum warder in the Nepalese Room, Joseph Matthews?'

'Not about him, I'm sorry. His children, though, are real villains, if Bill can be believed.'

'How's that?'

'The son was killed in Belgium, shot by the police. He was trying to smuggle paintings out of the country when they caught up with him. They had been stolen from a collector in Brussels. As for the daughter, she's an opium addict, so Bill told me, and she also paints copies of old masters, which are either passed off as the original or used to cover up the theft of the original.'

'Not such a pretty picture, then! Well, thanks Jack,

you've done well. Oh, and by the way, Jack…'

'Yes, sir?'

'As you've been up all night, I think it better that we skip this afternoon's meeting in the Lyons Tea House, don't you agree? You need to catch up on your sleep.'

'What'll you do about your man?' Maxwell asked once Jack had left them.

'I've got an address, although I don't hold much out for it. If the name's false, so is the address, most likely.'

'That's what I was thinking. But I don't mind spending the morning checking it out for you. You never know.'

'Really, Max? Can you spare the time?'

'It's a village down in Surrey, isn't it?'

'That's right. Lambsholm. Here's the address.'

Lynnford took out his wallet and handed Maxwell the piece of notepaper on which he had written the address. 'You should be able to get a train in an hour or so. I'll take your bag round to Fountain Street.'

'Righty-ho.' Maxwell slapped Lynnford on the back and was about to leave when he remembered something. He took out a folded sheet of paper from his coat pocket. 'Here's some more copy for the sports page. I didn't have time to call it through so it'll have to be for tomorrow's edition, if Kombinski will accept it. Could you get it typed up? I'll check it over when I get back.'

TWELVE

VICTORIA CALLS FROM DOVER

The ringing telephone broke through the routine newsroom clatter and commotion. Maxwell had already returned from Lambsholm with confirmation that neither Mr Bell, nor anyone fitting his description, lived at The Old Vicarage or was known in the village, and Lynnford had reported to Edwin Philips on the events in Paris and on his belief that the Elephant's Sapphire was safe and sound and now back in London, or at least somewhere in the country. He lifted the receiver. '*London Herald*, crime desk,' he answered.

'Robert! I had to call you.' It was Victoria.

'Good afternoon, Victoria. What's up? Where are you?'

'Dover. Listen! I've just come off the boat. I'm waiting for the train. I haven't got long, but it's the Elephant's Sapphire, I can't get it out of my mind.'

'Go on.'

'I got your message that you and Max had gone back

to London. What happened to the man with the Sapphire? Did he give you the slip?'

'Yes. He's back in London, or England at least.'

'Get next month's *Home & Woman*. It's already out.'

'Why?'

'On page ten. Have you got that? There's a photograph you absolutely must see.'

'What, right now?'

'Yes! It's the Sapphire! Well, I guess it is from the description you gave me.'

'It can't possibly be, Victoria. We've just seen it, or almost, in Paris.'

'I tell you it is. Don't be tiresome, Robert. If it's not, then it's another replica.'

'Well, that's no good.'

'Yes, it is! It's as likely as not as to have been made by the same person who made the copy in the museum, and maybe it'll lead us to him. Whichever way, we win.'

'When do you think that photograph was taken?'

'A few weeks ago at most. Maybe last month. Listen, Robert, I'm running out of coins. Bring round the Morgan to my flat this evening. We'll drive up to Dundee straight away. As soon as I've had time to change and freshen up. My train gets in at five.'

'Dundee?'

'Yes, Robert, Dundee in Scotland.'

'But that's almost four hundred miles.'

'And so? You know you like a long drive. And we haven't been anywhere together in the Morgan for ages.'

'You want to drive through the night?'

'It'll be fun, Robert. I must go. I'll speak to the people in the photo as soon as I get home and arrange for us to visit them tomorrow. Their address is Edgar Terrace. Bye, Robert. I'll see you this evening.' And the line went dead.

Down in *The London Herald's* library, Lynnford quickly found December's edition of *Home & Woman*. Thumbing through the pages of the magazine, he found the photograph that had so excited Victoria. Two proud owners, Mr and Mrs Duncan, were exhibiting their drawing room, and beside them, decorating the top of a walnut sideboard, was the Elephant's Sapphire. Well, at least something that resembled it very closely. The man in the photograph, however, wasn't the man he'd seen in Paris. So, had it been stolen from the couple in Dundee? Possibly, but how then had the Elephant's Sapphire made its way from the museum in London to their home in Scotland? It had to be another replica.

Back in his office, Lynnford telephoned Edwin Philips and explained about the photograph and his plan to travel up to Dundee. 'Another goose chase, don't you think, Lynnford? You said this morning that you believed the jewel to be back here in London.'

'London, or somewhere else in the country, Mr Philips. We can't overlook a possible lead, though. If it's a replica, finding the person who made it could eventually lead us to the thief.'

'Very well, Mr Lynnford. I'm in your hands, but don't waste too much time up there.'

He looked up at the clock on the wall: Four-forty. Joseph Matthews, the museum warder, would be home soon. Sitting every day in the Nepalese Room with the Elephant's Sapphire in his view, Joseph Matthews had to know something about its theft or of the replica that had been made to take its place. That's why he had singled him out to Jack Worth. It was a conversation that he had been waiting all day to have, thinking it best to catch the warder at home, in private, rather than at his workplace in the museum. He still had time, if he hurried, to visit the warder and get back home in time to make his rendezvous with Victoria around half-seven in the evening. Lynnford grabbed his hat and coat, left the offices of *The London Herald* in Fountain Street, and crossed London Bridge, heading towards Borough Market. He had been given the museum warder's address earlier in the day by the curator's assistant: a modest council house near the market.

THIRTEEN

THE WARDER'S DAUGHTER

'Who are you?'

A woman in her early twenties stood in the narrow hallway to Joseph Matthews' house, holding open the door. She was tall and thin, with smooth chestnut hair and unusually pale features. She was wearing a coat, carelessly buttoned as if she had just thrown it on and was about to go out.

'Is Mr Matthews home?'

'Dad? He's not back yet. What do you want with him?'

'Are you his daughter?'

'What of it?'

'Just to know who I'm talking to.'

'And you still haven't told me who you are. Fine manners!'

Lynnford replied with the same name he had assumed

when he had visited Jeremy Friedman, 'Taylor, but your father doesn't know me. We have a mutual friend.'

'I was about to go out.'

'I can come back.'

The woman hesitated, then seemed to make up her mind. 'No, he shouldn't be long. Come in.'

She stepped aside and let him in, still watching him with a mixture of suspicion and curiosity. She closed the door and hung her coat on the end of the banister.

'Go straight ahead, into the kitchen. It's warmer there.'

Then, suddenly, she pushed past him, rushing into the kitchen in front of him and, reaching up to a shelf above the cooker, brought down a biscuit tin. Holding onto the base, she stretched her long fingers around the lid, pulling it open and letting it fall noisily onto the cooker. Her hand dived inside the tin, only to throw it away immediately in disgust, letting it bang on the floor, her hand empty. Sweeping back her hair, she turned her attention back to Lynnford, who had bent down to pick up the tin, her bloodshot eyes being the only colour in her face.

'You can leave it.'

Although surprised by the sudden outburst, Lynnford ignored her and quietly placed the tin on the kitchen table. He recalled what Jack had told him about the daughter's opium habit. The table was covered in breadcrumbs, and the dirty plates in the sink gave witness to a hasty meal earlier in the day.

'Are you from the museum?'

'No, I'm not,' Lynnford replied.

'Where are you from then?'

As she spoke, she fidgeted around the kitchen, unable to stand still, and not waiting for Lynnford to reply, she asked suddenly, 'Can you spare ten shillings?'

Lynnford smiled.

'Dad hasn't left me anything.'

'When will he be back?'

'I said soon, didn't I? He finishes at five-thirty. Have you got a job for him? Is that it?'

At last, she stopped fidgeting and sat down at the small kitchen table, sweeping away the breadcrumbs with her arm and looking up at him. 'I'll have a cup of tea if you're making one. The tea's in the cupboard.'

Despite her coarseness, she spoke well. Willing to oblige, Lynnford looked around for the cups.

'They're in the sink. You'll need to wash them.'

As he walked over to the sink, the young woman made a surprising offer. 'I'll sketch you.'

'I beg your pardon?'

'I'll sketch you.' She smiled as if to entice him.

'What for?'

'Ten shillings.'

'Do you paint?'

'Of course, but I'm not going to paint, I'm going to draw you. It's different.'

Lynnford didn't reply directly, simply smiling and busying himself in making the tea, taking his time, hoping by his quiet presence to ease himself into her confidence.

'So, you're an artist, a painter and someone who sketches. Is that right?' He dried and placed two blue cups and saucers on the table. 'You don't look like a painter.'

'The young woman as an artist!' She laughed, adding, 'And how should painters look, in your opinion, Mr Taylor?'

She laughed again, but this time her voice was hoarse and croaking. A violent cough shook her body, and, pushing away her chair, she got to her feet and leant over the sink, spluttering. The spasm ceased and she remained a while leaning against the side of the sink, saying nothing, breathing quietly. After a few moments she regained her chair.

'Sorry,' she mumbled.

Lynnford cleaned up the sink, then poured the tea and sat down. He pushed the sugar bowl towards her. 'Take it easy.'

'Thank you.'

She helped herself, stirring in the sugar with a distracted air.

'In fact, I feel like I'm as old as Hell,' she said at last. 'But I can paint. I went to art school with my brother. You wouldn't think it, looking at this place, would you?'

Almost purring like a cat, she looked at him slyly and tried again. 'You want me to draw you then?'

Lynnford laughed. 'If you like, but it's got to be good.'

She made a face as if to show she was offended by the insult.

'Ten shillings?'

'Ten shillings,' he agreed.

A smile crossed her face and she got up.

'There's some paper and a board upstairs. I'll get it. Wait here. Don't go anywhere.'

Lynnford followed her movements scuffling about in the room above what he assumed was the sitting room next door. The footsteps came back along the landing and down the stairs.

'Here we are.'

She was holding a large board. She sat down in front of him. Pushing her chair back, she slipped a band around her hair, and with her feet tucked on the rung below the seat, rested the board on her lap and against the edge of the table. A large sheet of thick white paper had already been clipped to the board. She seemed to have transformed herself from sloth to artist in the flash of an eyelid.

'How long are you going to take?'

'Shush!' she snapped.

She began to trace firm broad lines with her pencil, her eyes twinkling as she drew, glancing alternatively between Lynnford and the board, concentration orientating the movements of her hand. Lynnford, resigning himself, stretched out his feet.

'Don't move. You know that's not allowed. Ten shillings whether you move or not, remember.'

She paused for a moment, reflecting, before continuing. This time, with her mounting confidence, the movements of her pencil became ever quicker, scratching across the surface of the paper. As she drew, Lynnford let his thoughts drift back over the recent events since Mr Philips had recounted the extraordinary tale of the Elephant's Sapphire; coming back to the same question: what did Joseph Matthews have to do, if anything, with its disappearance? Could he tell him who had made the replica? That would be something, at least, but how was he going to get into his confidence? Lynnford still didn't know how. He would have to think of something before the warder turned up from work.

'There, it's finished now.'

'Can I see?'

'Ten shillings, first.'

Smiling, Lynnford took out a ten-shilling note and handed it over to her. She picked it out of his fingers and handed the board to him in exchange.

'Is this how you see me?' he joked, turning the board round.

'It's a first-class likeness.'

Indeed, the sketch was well executed.

'You haven't signed it.'

'An anonymous artist,' she replied, unclipping the paper and rolling it up. 'There you go. The price was for an unsigned portrait. Twenty shillings for the signed work.' She picked up her cup of tea, as if the matter was settled. 'Ugh! It's cold.'

'I'll pour you another cup.'

'Don't bother.'

Her voice cooled, not with hostility but more with disinterest. A slow glazing of her eyes presaged her withdrawal, turning in on herself as if retreating from the outer walls of her body and leaving her external senses abandoned. In a few seconds she was no longer the same person, as if a change of scene had brought in an understudy. Although conscious of Lynnford's presence, she had lost her vivacity. She sat in front of him, her hands resting on her lap, her head moving as her eyes roved around the confines of the kitchen, seemingly taking in her environment until a despondent air took over, her head slumping under its weight.

'Miss Matthews!' Lynnford tried to shake her out of her reverie. 'Miss Matthews,' he repeated.

He leant forward and lifted her chin gently with his hand. 'What is it? You must snap out of it.'

But all he could see were the distant eyes of someone lost to opium. To his surprise, he felt a warm, light weight press around his leg, and, looking down, gazed into the green eyes of a golden ginger-haired cat, its head turned up towards him, its clear glassy eyes and pink nostrils appealing for attention. It purred loudly, a long gravelly sound. The call penetrated the senses of the museum warder's daughter, whose head jerked up as if pulled by a cord.

'Gingerbread,' she called out affectionately. 'What are you doing? Where have you been all this time? Where's Daddy? Tell me.'

And as she spoke the cat moved away from Lynnford's leg, slipping under the table and brushing up against the warder's daughter, purring with hunger.

'So what's the matter, then, Gingerbread?'

She lifted the animal up onto her lap; her fingers lost in the white fur round its belly, the friendly contact sparking life into her once again.

Lynnford watched as the museum warder's daughter busied herself with the cat. She took a bottle of milk and filled a chipped saucer that was lying on the floor, and then sat back down in her chair, watching the cat, its pink tongue licking up the cold liquid.

'Don't give her too much milk, you'll spoil her.'

The man's flat voice made them turn.

'Dad!'

'You!' the warder cried out with alarm, recognising Lynnford's face.

Joseph Matthews stood in the doorway to the kitchen, staring straight at Lynnford. He hadn't heard him come in. *He must have let in the cat*, he thought. Sensing danger, the cat deserted the saucer of milk and, dashing through the museum warder's legs, ran out of the kitchen and back into the hall.

'Dad, what's wrong?'

A worried look crossed the daughter's face. 'What do you want?' she asked, turning to Lynnford. 'What do you want?'

Then, stunned, she saw her father turn and run.

'Dad!' she shouted after him.

Her voice was lost in the clatter of chairs and the stampede of the two men down the short hall, but the museum warder did not have time to even reach the front door before Lynnford stood there, barring his way.

'I recognise you now, Matthews. You were in that lorry on the Portsmouth Road last Friday.'

His words provoked another shriek from the daughter, and a plate smashed against the wall, just missing Lynnford's head.

'It's all right, Janet.'

'It's not all right,' she stormed, standing menacingly in the kitchen doorway. 'Who is he? One of them?'

'What do you want?' Joseph Matthews repeated his daughter's earlier question.

'Well, for a start, I'd like to know why you tried to drive me off the road.'

'Dad, what's he doing here? What's he talking about? Don't listen to him.'

'What choice do we have?'

'Plenty of choice.'

Janet Matthews pushed past her father. 'I'm not staying here,' she snapped, angry with scorn and disappointment. 'I thought you said it was over,' she hurled at him as she picked up her coat from the end of the banister and pushed her way out of the house.

The museum warder closed the front door with a soft push, sadness infusing his movements. 'It was an accident. I lost concentration.'

'You knew perfectly well what you were doing, Mr Matthews. But why?'

'I told you. It was an accident.'

'What exactly were you doing there?'

'I was making a delivery. I was driving to Portsmouth.'

'For the museum?'

'No, a private matter.'

'So, you have a second job?'

'That's my business.'

'Perhaps Mr Philips, the curator, will see it quite differently.'

'If you tell him.'

Could it have been an accident after all? Lynnford asked himself. Matthews had lost control of the lorry; that's why his face was so set, trying to regain control. But he wasn't too convinced. Matthews had to know something about the theft of the Sapphire and this incident on the Portsmouth Road simply reinforced Lynnford's suspicions. After all, the warder could even have switched and stolen the Sapphire himself. Surely he had had plenty of opportunity, and from what Jack had told him, his son had been mixed up in stealing works of art. But how could the warder have procured the replica? That would have cost him a lot of money. He would need to shake him if he was going to get anything out of him.

'I would like to know something about one of the museum exhibits in the Nepalese Room – the Elephant's Sapphire,' Lynnford continued.

'What about it?'

Lynnford sensed relief in the warder's reply, almost as if he had feared some other question, but Lynnford wasn't going to allow him any peace of mind. 'You don't seem too surprised at my question, Mr Matthews.'

The warder looked confused and Lynnford clarified his remark. 'Don't you think it odd that I should be asking you about the Sapphire? Why is that, Mr Matthews?'

Joseph Matthews didn't know what to say. He felt trapped. He could not shake free of the image of Bosworth, as large as life, telling him to drive this man off the road because of his interest in the Elephant's Sapphire. Of course, he knew that the Elephant's Sapphire had been replaced by a replica, and he even knew who had stolen it, but that information was too precious to give away and he wasn't going to tell anyone, least of all this stranger.

'I know about your son, Mr Matthews,' Lynnford continued.

'What of him?' The warder felt again as if he were being thrown off balance.

'I gather he was caught by the Belgian police in possession of stolen paintings, and, unfortunately, shot dead whilst trying to escape.' Lynnford sensed Matthews' anger swelling up, displacing his confusion. 'I guess that couldn't have been easy for you.'

Silence.

Lynnford continued, almost remorselessly. 'And your daughter, Janet. I understand she makes accomplished copies of old masterpieces – Rembrandts, Titians, Turners and the like – when she's not high on drugs.'

With a silent scream of pain, Matthews lunged at Lynnford, but without any strength or direction. Lynnford took hold of his hands and pushed him back down onto one of the chairs.

'So, Mr Matthews, we understand each other now. All I want to know is the name of someone who could make me a replica of the Elephant's Sapphire in the Nepalese Room. Good enough to be passed off for the genuine one. Can you help me with that?'

'What for?'

'I have a wealthy client who wants me to swap one for the other.'

Again, Lynnford could feel the warder deflate with an almost imperceptible sense of relief.

'You're going to steal the Elephant's Sapphire? That's a laugh!' the warder replied, spluttering a nervous chuckle.

'Think about it, Mr Matthews. I wouldn't want to make life unpleasant for you. Call me on this number. My name's Taylor.'

Lynnford wrote out his Park Mansions telephone number, reminding himself that he should have the name on the letter box changed. And Cobley, the porter, would need some explanation. He handed Matthews the number, adding, 'There'll be a nice commission for you.'

Joseph Matthews closed the door once Lynnford had left, with the rolled-up portrait of himself in his hand, and returned to the kitchen. So, after all, he had nothing to worry about from this man. Too easily he had started worrying for no reason at all, seeing danger in the smallest things. He'd spent too long fretting, a lifetime almost. It had become a habit. This man, Taylor, was only interested in the Sapphire, and much good that would do him! He wanted to make a replica of a copy! And Joseph almost felt like laughing. He didn't know who had copied the Sapphire, but he could easily find someone for him. He picked up the biscuit tin from the table and put it back in the cupboard. Another habit. Clearing up after his daughter.

What now? Joseph turned towards the front door. Someone was banging loudly on it. Another visitor! He shuffled along the hall and opened the door. *Him again*, he exclaimed desperately to himself.

'Janet's not here,' he announced, and immediately he was sickened by his cowardice, fear making him hide behind his own daughter, pretending she was the reason for the man's visit, and not him.

'It's you I want to speak to, Matthews,' his visitor replied with veiled smoothness. 'Why is he still alive?'

'Who?'

'The newspaper man. He left a few minutes ago. You were supposed to drive him off the Portsmouth Road.'

'It wasn't so easy. Is he a reporter?'

'You're a useless old man, Matthews. Good for nothing. Like your children. So, what did he want?'

'Nothing.'

The giant dockhand lifted his fist menacingly.

'He wants to make a copy,' replied Matthews, hastily.

'Of what? As if I couldn't guess!'

'The Elephant's Sapphire in the museum. He doesn't know it's a fake.'

'That's what he told you, is it? Well, I don't like him. Frighten him off, Matthews.'

'How?'

'Think of something. And make a better job of it than last time. I don't want to have to come and see you again.'

FOURTEEN
A DRIVE NORTH OF THE BORDER

On returning to Park Mansions from the museum warder's home in Borough, Lynnford brought out his Morgan motor car and went to collect Victoria from her apartment in Chelsea. They shared the driving through the night, stopping just south of the Scottish Borders in the early hours of Tuesday morning for a couple of hours sleep in the car before completing their journey, arriving in the Scottish city of Dundee shortly after midday. Victoria parked the car in Edgar Terrace and they got out, relieved to be able to stretch their limbs before walking leisurely along to the Duncans' townhouse.

*

The Duncans' drawing room in Edgar Terrace was smaller than Lynnford had imagined from the photograph, and likewise, the house itself was much less elegant. A not-so-newly attired maid had shown them into a parlour, asking them to wait whilst she informed Mr and Mrs Duncan, who were at luncheon, of their presence and the purpose of their visit. A few minutes later, she had returned and introduced them into the drawing room.

The Sapphire, or rather its copy, throned the sideboard, taking pride of place on an elaborate silver mounting. To Lynnford's eye it was a match to the exhibit Mr Philips had shown him in the Nepalese Room in the museum. Ten minutes or so later, Mr Duncan entered the room and flicked on a light switch. The crystal chandelier hanging from the ceiling in the centre of the room exploded into a brilliant ball of light, and the jewel on the sideboard glinted in the resulting blend of natural and artificial light, adding to Lynnford's confusion as to its authenticity.

'A beautiful jewel, wouldn't you agree?' Mr Duncan's soft, melodious accent was deep and rich.

Looking up, Lynnford and Victoria beheld the man they had seen in the photograph, standing this time in the open entrance to the room, his finger still poised on the light switch. He let his arm drop and entered the room, his thick, round hand outstretched, introducing himself. 'Gordon Duncan, how do you do? Very pleased to meet you both.'

'Thank you for letting us see the jewel, Mr Duncan,' Victoria responded, both she and Lynnford having got to their feet. 'And at such short notice! We do apologise.'

Their host smiled, waving towards the sofa. 'Not a bit of it. You are both very welcome. Please sit down. My wife, Kathleen, will join us in a minute.'

As if on cue, the smart woman from the photograph entered the room, the fingers of one hand unconsciously playing with the string of pearls around her neck. Her pale, oval face was framed by a bob of straight, dark, glossy hair.

'Please excuse me,' she apologised. 'I was detained,' Mrs Duncan explained, more to her husband than to their guests.

'So, why are you interested in our blue jewel? Not as valuable as its size would suggest, but still.' Mr Duncan sat down in an armchair with an air of casual superiority, adding, 'You don't mind if I smoke?'

'Really, Gordon!'

But he took no notice of his wife's objection, pulling out a cigar from his pocket, opening the end with a snip of his penknife. 'I'm pleased to tell you whatever I know. I have Council business this afternoon, so I don't have to go back to the office. I'm on the Council, and I have just been elected chair of the fire brigade subcommittee, you know. It has a meeting at the Town Hall at four o'clock, so we have plenty of time.'

'I was wondering, Councillor, to cut to the chase, would you be willing to sell the jewel?'

Mr Duncan didn't hesitate. 'And if I were, Mr Lynnford, what would you be willing to offer?'

His wife looked at her husband with surprise, Lynnford sensing a feeling of relief as if, as he suspected, the jewel had been an expensive folly on her husband's part.

'I imagine you paid a handsome price.'

'Several times over.'

'Undoubtedly. Would you object if I had it valued first?'

'Of course not. Your valuer will have to come here, though. I'm not parting with it, you understand?'

'Yes, of course I understand. Perhaps you can recommend someone? I don't know the city. If you agree, I can come back this evening with the valuer.'

'Excellent! Joseph Keys & Hamilton and McGregor's are both first-rate jewellers. Either one of them should do. You'll find them in Church Street. Evening suits me as I'm not sure when exactly my meeting this afternoon in the Town Hall will finish.'

Lynnford and Victoria took their leave of the Duncans.

'That's a clever ruse. Getting a valuation to find out the jewel's real value,' Victoria commented once they were back in the car.

'At least it suggests Gordon Duncan doesn't think it's an ordinary piece of glass.'

'Why are you stopping?'

Lynnford had pulled up outside a row of shops. 'Because I don't think we can trust the jewellers here for an honest valuation of this particular piece. More likely than not, they'll be in the pocket of Councillor Duncan. That's why he recommended them. So, I'm going to see if Mr Philips at the Queen's Fine Art Museum can recommend someone. There's a telephone box just in front of the shop over there.' Lynnford indicated a newsagent's shop. 'Have you got some loose change?'

*

'Well?' Victoria asked, as Lynnford got back into the car.

'He's given me the name of a jeweller in Edinburgh who we can count on. We're going to go and pick him up this afternoon. The curator will speak to him and arrange everything with him whilst we're driving there.'

It was nearly seven o'clock in the evening by the time Lynnford and Victoria returned outside the Duncans' house in Edgar Terrace, this time accompanied by Mr McPhearson, a loquacious gentleman in his late sixties who had entertained them during the journey back to Dundee with long tales of his adventures in India as an antiquarian in the museum of New Delhi. The curator of the Queen's Fine Art Museum having agreed to cover the full cost of his time, he was only too happy to make the visit, even though Lynnford had explained little more than that he wished him to carry out a valuation of a precious stone.

Mr Duncan opened the door himself, beckoning them in. 'You are clearly a serious man, Mr Lynnford, somebody ready to do things properly and without wasting any time. No nonsense, I admire that. Do come in.'

'Thank you.'

Lynnford introduced Mr McPhearson, and they all entered the house.

'I see you didn't take up either of my recommendations?'

The councillor looked at Lynnford and Victoria as if requiring an explanation. Lynnford replied, 'No, Mr McPhearson was recommended by a friend.'

'Well, Mr McPhearson, let's not waste your time. This is what you've come to see. Let's see what you make of it.'

Mr Duncan indicated, with an open hand, the blue jewel shimmering in the light of the chandelier and the coal fire that had been lit. Mr Duncan took a step backwards to allow Mr McPhearson to approach the sideboard, taking a long pull on his cigar, slowly releasing the smoke as he looked on with satisfaction. Lynnford noticed the jeweller give an almost imperceptible start. Mr McPhearson approached the sideboard, staring for some time at the mounted jewel before moving the mounting very slowly through a full circle, pausing nearly every second. Reaching into his pocket he took out a jeweller's eyeglass and a small pocket notebook; and folding back the cover of the notebook, he began to scribble notes over several pages before placing it on the counter of the sideboard; then, screwing the eyeglass against his right eye, he picked up the square oval-shaped jewel, and, balancing its weight in his hands, subjected the whole surface to an intense examination, quiet and absorbed in his work. The others were silent, mesmerised by the jeweller's careful attention. Only the pendulum clock in the hall and the crackling fire disturbed the silence.

After a few minutes or so, Mr McPhearson replaced the jewel carefully on its silver mounting, and took up his notebook again. Only after completing another two pages of notes did he finally look up, almost as if he had forgotten the presence of the others.

'Ah yes,' he said, removing the magnifying glass and bringing down the glasses that he had pushed up onto his balding forehead. 'So, what is it you would like to know?'

'Why, how much it's worth! What do you think?' Mr Duncan replied, stumping his cigar out in an ashtray that he'd taken from the chimney piece.

'Is this confidential?' Mr McPhearson addressed

himself to Lynnford. Lynnford shook his head. 'I think, as Councillor Duncan says, we just want to know the value that you would place on the piece,' he replied, adding with a little emphasis, 'Nothing else.'

'Well then,' Mr McPhearson coughed and scanned through his notes. 'Hmm, let's see.' And he shook his head slightly from side to side, as if balancing the weight of the jewel on a pair of mental scales. 'Not to put too fine a point on it, approximately one hundred pounds, not much more.'

'A hundred pounds!' Mr Duncan's voice exploded. 'Daylight robbery! You're a thief, man, not a jeweller.'

Mr McPhearson smiled politely but declined to reply.

'I paid one thousand pounds to a dealer in York. You can't buy a sapphire for a hundred pounds.'

'Regrettably, sir, it's not a sapphire. What makes you think it is? A thousand pounds wouldn't buy you a sapphire this size.'

'What is it, then?' Mr Duncan almost spluttered with indignation.

'A piece of glass.'

'Damn you, you scoundrel!'

'That is my valuation, sir. That's what I have been asked to give. It's not my intention to deprive you of the item.'

'But even a piece of glass would cost more,' the councillor objected, clearly beside himself.

Mrs Duncan looked on nervously.

'Well, Mr Duncan, it's clearly not what it seems,' resumed Lynnford. 'I can understand that you would not wish to sell the jewel at a loss.'

'I certainly would not!' the councillor fumed, looking furiously at his three guests.

'Then I can only apologise for wasting your time,' Lynnford replied. 'Perhaps, however, as a matter of interest, Mr Duncan, you might give me the name of the shop in York you bought it from. It might have something similar. You never know.'

'They certainly won't sell it to you for a hundred pounds, if that's what you think. But you can have the address for what good it will do you.'

*

Back in Lynnford's Morgan, and driving back towards Edinburgh along the dark roads, Mr McPhearson addressed Lynnford, 'Mr Lynnford…'

'Yes?'

'I hope you don't mind me saying, but you seem pleased enough for not having purchased the item.'

'Tell me, Mr McPhearson, what was it that gave you such a start when you first saw it?' As he did not reply, Lynnford continued, 'It must have been something important enough for you not to have mentioned it. What was it?'

Still the Edinburgh jeweller said nothing, staring out of the side window in the back of the car. Lynnford waited patiently, concentrating on the road ahead. At last, Mr McPhearson spoke.

'The decorative item is certainly an expensive piece of lead crystal glass. Excellently crafted, but manmade, nevertheless. However, on first seeing it, it reminded me of something else, something much more valuable.'

'The Elephant's Sapphire in the Queen's Fine Art Museum in London?'

'Yes, if you like. I'm beginning to suspect why my old friend, Mr Philips, sent me up there this evening. He wanted to know whether that was the Elephant's Sapphire. That's it, isn't it? But that can only mean one thing…'

'Yes, that's right, Mr McPhearson,' Lynnford interrupted him, not wishing him to express his thoughts. 'It's a very good copy. That's right, isn't it?' Lynnford glanced up at the rear-view mirror to see his passenger's face. 'Have you any idea who could have made such a copy?'

'Not really. A skilled artisan with years of experience, most likely French or Italian. Ours is a small world. But that you surely know already. I couldn't point you to anyone in particular. The replica has been made, most likely, from a compound of melted silica, soda, lime and potassium. And with lead oxide, of course. The intense blue, to make it resemble a sapphire, has been obtained from the skilful addition of cobalt, and a large amount of it to judge by the depth of the colour. What we've just seen is worth much more than a hundred pounds, but that was the figure Mr Philips told me to give.'

'Yes, that was what I told the curator to tell you, just so that I didn't get landed with it.'

'Well, you succeeded! The councillor wasn't too pleased with me.'

'No, he certainly wasn't. And you certainly put on a grand show, Mr McPhearson!'

And the three of them laughed.

They arrived in Edinburgh around eleven o'clock in

the evening and drove the jeweller straight home. Lynnford accompanied him to the front door, where he settled his fee.

'I trust that we can rely on your discretion, Mr McPhearson.'

The jeweller nodded, and Lynnford wished him a good night.

'Well, he's not cheap,' Lynnford remarked on returning to the car.

'So, York next?' Victoria asked, her hands on the wheel.

'Yes, and quickly. Mr Philips is in a real flap. He's just learnt that the Prime Minister of Nepal is expected in London for urgent talks sometime next week. The Maharaja himself. Obviously, it's about the situation in Nepal, but he will certainly also want to see the Elephant's Sapphire. The real one!'

FIFTEEN
YORK TO IPSWICH

'Where are we?'

Victoria squinted in the sunlight. Her eyes were sticky with sleep, and she was cold. She knocked her stockinged toes as she stretched her legs under the dashboard.

'Just outside York,' Lynnford replied, his eyes on the road ahead, smiling.

'What!'

Her tiredness fell away as she sat bolt upright. 'What do you mean? You said we'd stop after an hour or so after I gave you the wheel.'

'You fell asleep.'

Lynnford yawned, his mouth open wide. 'And I did stop, for a couple of hours or so.'

'Where?'

'Off the road, in a lay-by.'

'Robert! I thought you meant a hotel.'

'I didn't want to wake you, and it seemed easier.'

'But now you're tired and you look a mess. Heaven knows what I must look like. Dreadful, I imagine.'

'We'll stop for some breakfast.'

'Do whatever you like, but I'm tidying myself up before I do anything else, so find me a rest room.'

Shortly, they entered the outskirts of York and very quickly were in the centre of the city.

'Here, the Castle Hotel!' Victoria called out. 'This will do fine.'

*

The bells of York Cathedral rang out the hour as Lynnford entered Bell Yard, a stone's throw, it turned out, from the Castle Hotel, and where the hotel's receptionist had told him he would find Jenson's Antiques and Curios, the dealer who had sold Mr Duncan the replica sapphire. Ten very loud bells.

Bell Yard was so close to the cathedral that, standing within the courtyard, the stony masonry of the cathedral was lost from sight, except for its spire, piercing the grey winter's sky. Bell Yard, once devoted to ecclesiastical workshops, was now filled with smart boutiques. Jenson's faced the entrance, and Lynnford imagined Gordon Duncan sneaking off the main street towards it. Inside, there was a musty smell and an almost deafening silence in the aftermath of the bell ringing. Lynnford put his hand to his forehead, the last strike still resounding in his ears.

Someone was speaking to him, faintly. 'Can you hear

me?' A woman dressed in a plaid skirt was smiling at him pleasantly. 'Don't worry, you get used to it after a while.'

'They're not quiet, are they? They sound like they're ringing in the shop,' Lynnford commented dryly.

'People certainly don't dawdle, and try to come and go between the hours. And avoid the mornings! Anyway, how can I help you?'

'You sold a decorative crystal piece to a friend of mine who lives in Dundee a month or so ago, and I'd like to find something similar. My friend absolutely refused to part with it at any price.'

'What was it? Let's see if I can remember.'

'It was blue and oval-shaped, about the size of a large egg.'

The woman's face lit up, her eyes opening. 'Oh, yes, it was an excellent choice and very reasonably priced. I'm sorry, sir, I don't have anything else like it.'

'Maybe the person who sold it to you?'

'He's in Doncaster. He often picks up interesting items from local auctions. Most of it *bric-à-brac*, but occasionally he has something of value. As a matter of fact, I do believe that he had only acquired it that very day! I didn't have it in the shop more than a day myself before the Scottish gentleman came in. Is he the friend to whom you are referring?'

'Yes, he is. He thought he was buying a sapphire.'

'Did he indeed? I wonder why. I can assure you that I would not part with a sapphire for the price he paid. Not a sapphire that size.'

'You didn't tell him it was a sapphire?'

'Certainly not! But he wouldn't be the first to believe

they've unearthed a treasure unbeknown to the person who's selling it.'

'It seems to be changing hands very quickly.'

'Yes, it does happen occasionally. Other things just collect dust.'

'You wouldn't know where your supplier in Doncaster acquired it from, by any chance?'

'He did tell me, but I can't remember now. You can, of course, ask him yourself if you happen to be going down that way.'

'I might just do that. I'm driving back to London today. May I have his address?'

*

Victoria was ruminating over a cup of coffee in the hotel lobby when Lynnford returned to the Castle Hotel.

'Well?'

Cheerfulness bloomed out of Victoria like a flower, her hair once more in place.

'Doncaster, next stop,' Lynnford replied.

'At least it's a little closer back to London. What did the antique dealer have to say?'

'Nothing much really. She said she didn't pass the jewel off as a sapphire and she gave me the address of the shop owner in Doncaster who sold her the replica.'

'Any idea that she was passing on a replica?'

'Not in the least. I doubt she's ever heard of the Elephant's Sapphire, nor Duncan for that matter. Step by step, we'll get to the source, I'm sure.'

'Even if it's only an old leather boot.'

'Victoria! Honestly.'

'Well, that's the risk of anyone who goes fishing in a dirty river. Either they pull out a wriggling trout or just a sodden piece of footwear.'

And she burst out laughing at Lynnford's consternation. 'Come on, Robert! I'm pulling your leg. I'll do the driving, and you take a rest. Doncaster's not even fifty miles. We'll be there for lunch.'

The day passed quickly for Lynnford. Too tired to sit in the front beside Victoria, she stopped the car shortly after leaving Doncaster and pushed him into the back, throwing a blanket over him. From Doncaster to Lincoln and then to Ipswich, they swam back upstream, along the chain of transactions that had led to the rapid northwards movement of the replica sapphire to Dundee. In Ipswich, following the last set of indications given to them, they found themselves standing outside a second-hand furniture shop. The shop front was shabby with dirty white paint flaking off the woodwork. The loose-fitting door was locked. Inside, the light had still not been turned on, but they could make out the shape of someone moving about. Lynnford banged heavily on the glass panel inset in the door.

'Careful, Robert, it'll break,' Victoria cautioned. She pressed her face against the glass. 'Someone's coming,' she added, stepping aside.

The door was opened abruptly by a large man whose shoulders sloped down to his waist, almost. He was wrapped in an open cardigan that fell over loosely fitting trousers, his bespectacled and shaggy-haired head leaning forward. Lynnford could not help thinking of a bear roused from a deep-winter's slumber, standing guard outside its cave, its twitching nostrils smelling out for the intruder that had disturbed its sleep but was now long gone. What was left of the late-November daylight was receding rapidly from the depths of the shop, leaving a gloomy half-light within.

'Hello,' Victoria greeted the man cheerfully. 'We've been given your address. It's about something that was bought from here.'

'The shop's closed.'

The man stepped back to close the door with the same surprising agility of a bear, but Lynnford was alert and his foot shot forward, blocking the door before it closed, wedged in on the threshold.

'Oi! What do you think you're playing at? We're closed,' the man snarled.

'There's no need for you to worry at all, sir.' Lynnford eased the door open with his weight.

'Please, sir,' continued Victoria, 'we've driven a long way and it'll only take a minute of your time.'

Lynnford had by now pushed his way into the shop, the man reluctantly, despite his size, relenting and releasing the door handle, and taking a step backwards. Inside, the shop was damp, old furniture stacked everywhere with little to suggest the sale of expensive antiques, and Lynnford's first impression was that the man could only be a fence for stolen goods. 'Can we ask you a couple of questions?'

The man turned his back on the unwelcome visitors, shrugging his large, round shoulders under the shapeless cardigan, and ambled back into the interior of the shop as if disinterested in their business, hoping they would tire and leave like two unwanted marauders.

'We've been told that you sold a large blue gem, a replica sapphire, to a dealer from Lincoln about a month ago.'

The furniture dealer simply shrugged his shoulders, ignoring Lynnford, stopping beside a work bench and giving his attention to a lamp that required repairing. Lynnford insisted, carefully taking the lamp out of the man's hands to get his attention. Finally, the man replied, 'What of it? Do you think people bother to tell me where they come from? Where do you two come from? You haven't told me.'

'We know you did,' Lynnford replied.

'Whatever you say.'

Victoria, tired and impatient, pulled out of her coat pocket the photograph of the Duncans' drawing room. She spread it out under the man's nose, pointing to the jewel on the sideboard. 'Look!'

The man shrugged, 'So, what's it to me?'

'A lot,' Lynnford intervened. 'This is not just an expensive trinket, stolen from a London West End jeweller, that you've sold under the counter.'

'No! Nothing stolen goes through my shop.'

The denial sounded more like a challenge. Lynnford cast his eyes around the collections of tables piled with chairs, the backs of armchairs rubbing against the table edges, the empty picture frames, and the crockery sets piled higgledy-piggledy. He shook his head, wondering where it had all come from.

'Probably not amongst all this,' he conceded. 'But certainly through the back door or in the pub next door.'

The man sighed, giving up. 'What is it you want? Police? You don't look it.'

'No. But this large blue gem is going to bring you more problems than you could have imagined.'

'I told you. I've nothing to do with it.'

'Let's look at it from another angle.' Lynnford changed to a softer tone, producing from his wallet five single pound notes, placing them one by one on the work bench. 'We don't want to cause you any problems. All we want to know is the name of the person who sold you the item, or you will have the police at your door.'

'What's to tell me I can trust you?'

'You'll have to take our word.'

'You can't prove anything.'

'You know I can. And be sure the police will be blowing on your doorstep before you've had time to sing Three Little Piggies.'

The man hunched his shoulders in resignation. 'Try Stubb's Coal Merchants in Romford. Ask for Steve. He drives one of the coal wagons. But don't breathe a word about me.'

'You needn't worry yourself on that score. But the next time you might not be so lucky.'

Lynnford and Victoria returned to the car.

'Romford?' Victoria asked, placing her hands on the steering wheel. 'It's just outside London, in Essex, isn't it?'

Lynnford shook his head. 'That's quite enough for one day, don't you agree? Anyway, about the coal merchants – I believe we'll have a better chance tomorrow morning. They've probably all gone home by now. London and Park Mansions will do me fine.'

Lynnford yawned noisily, and Victoria pressed her foot on the accelerator pedal.

*

'Jack! What are you doing here?'

Jack Worth spun round on hearing Lynnford's voice. He was standing in the foyer of Park Mansions talking to the porter, Mr Cobley.

'Mr Lynnford, you're back. Mrs Beaumont, Madam.'

'Hello Jack,' Victoria replied.

'Good evening, Cobley,' Lynnford greeted the porter before turning to the young clerk. 'What's the matter, Jack? Problems with Kombinski or George? Let's go upstairs. That's all right, Cobley, I've put the car away.'

'Just one thing, Mr Lynnford,' the porter detained him.

'Oh yes, Cobley? What's that?'

'A parcel for you. Delivered by hand this afternoon. One moment and I'll get it for you.'

Once the porter had returned with what was a strangely shaped parcel, Lynnford led the way upstairs, accompanied by Victoria. Jack continued talking excitedly. 'There's been a real rumpus.'

'Where? At the museum?'

'Something's gone missing. But, really missing.'

'What?'

'I'll tell you in a minute. When we get inside. The whole place is being turned upside down.'

'What are they looking for?'

Jack ignored the question. 'The alarm went off this

morning and all hell was let loose. The curator held a meeting of all the staff.'

Lynnford dropped his case on the landing and took out his key, opening the door to let them in.

'And so, what are they looking for?' Lynnford repeated his question as he began opening the parcel, removing the wrapping as he spoke. Jack was about to reply when his attention was caught by the contents of the parcel, his face dropping.

'What?' Lynnford prompted, noticing Jack's strange expression.

'That!' replied Jack.

'What do you mean, "that"?'

'That,' Jack repeated, pointing to the opened parcel. 'That's what they're looking for.'

Lynnford stared down at what he was now holding in his hand.

'Napoleon's ceremonial sword!' explained Jack.

'Good Lord! Who on earth sent me this?'

Victoria picked up a small note that had fallen to the floor.

'KEEP AWAY FROM THE ELEPHANT,' she read out. 'But who sent you this, Robert? And why?'

'No idea, but at least we know where it's come from.'

'Mr Philips?'

'Hardly!'

'Why steal an antique from a museum and send it to you, Robert? Why?'

'As I said, Victoria, I don't know. A bribe, a present, a threat? Who knows?'

'A threat?'

'It wouldn't be the first. Coming back from Portsmouth last Friday, someone tried to drive me off the road.'

'Robert! Why didn't you tell me?'

'I've told you now.'

'We've been all the way up to Scotland and back, not to mention Paris, and now you tell me!'

'Well, at least we can give it back to Mr Philips and put his mind at rest.'

'Not before we tell the police,' Victoria cautioned.

'Not yet. Not until we find out what's happened to the Elephant's Sapphire.'

'At least inform your friend at Scotland Yard, Detective Chief Inspector Sheffield.'

'That we can do, Victoria. Just to keep ourselves on the safe side.'

'And what's this?' Victoria asked, picking up the roll of drawing paper that Lynnford had left on his desk after returning from the Matthews' home on Monday evening.

'A portrait.'

'Of you?' Victoria unrolled the drawing that Janet Matthews had done of him, holding the edges of the paper in her hands. 'Oh, Robert!' she exclaimed, mockingly. 'You've got an admirer!'

SIXTEEN
UNDER CHARING CROSS BRIDGE

The telephone rang almost as soon as Jack had left them. Lynnford picked up the receiver.

'Knightsbridge 3434.'

'My name is Grafton.' The voice was rough, gravelly almost, and with a proximity that made Lynnford feel as if the speaker was standing next to him, hovering over his shoulder. 'You placed an advertisement in *The East London Gazette*.'

The long day's drive was forgotten in a flash. 'Yes, that's correct. Can you help me?'

'Possibly.'

Articulate and to the point, Lynnford remarked to himself.

'Perhaps you can tell me who you are,' the caller continued.

'Taylor, Mr Taylor,' Lynnford replied, maintaining his assumed name, the same name he'd given Mr Friedman and

Joseph Matthews. Only Mr Bhat, unfortunately, had his real name.

'Are you a collector, Mr Taylor?'

'No. I can't afford to be. I'm a trader.'

'So your advertisement implies. What are you looking for exactly, Mr Taylor?'

Lynnford recalled the text of his advert. 'Fine quality replicas.'

'Copies?'

'If you like.'

'Why replicas?'

'That's my business.' Lynnford was happy to let the caller interrogate him.

'To be clear, Mr Taylor, I make copies to order, in metal and lead crystal glass. Is that what you want?'

'Yes.'

'Do you have something particular in mind?'

'Possibly.' This time Lynnford replied with his own evasiveness. 'My clients often ask me to find them something of special value.'

'Such as?'

'Perhaps we could discuss this in person?'

Lynnford waited for the reply, which was several seconds in coming.

'Yes, if you like. This evening?'

Lynnford would have preferred the next day, the time to recover from his travels, but the caller did not wait for him to reply. 'The Embankment, under Charing Cross Bridge.'

'That's an unusual place for business,' Lynnford ventured, seeking more information.

'It's the most convenient this evening. Come in by Villiers Street. Eight o'clock sharp.'

'How will I recognise you?'

'Don't worry. I'll be waiting for you. Be prompt. That's all.'

The caller rang off.

'Who was that?' Victoria asked.

'A fish that's taken the bait. A Mr Grafton, to be precise,' Lynnford replied, giving Victoria details of the proposed meeting.

'It's already a quarter past seven. He must be somewhere close by, or he wouldn't have suggested such an odd place,' she observed.

'Odd or not, Victoria, I can't turn it down.'

'No, but you're not going alone. I'm coming with you.'

'Victoria!'

'No questions. Not after the sword and the lorry. I'll keep a discreet distance. What are you doing?'

Lynnford had crossed the floor of the drawing room, and, stepping round the desk, slid open the middle drawer. Sifting through the notepads, ink bottles and loose coins, his fingers touched what he was looking for: a small, moulded, circular cedarwood box. He picked it up, closed the drawer and, standing up straight, showed Victoria the box.

'And, what's inside?'

Lynnford turned the box, splitting it in two. A gold disc shone back at Victoria, reflecting the light of the shaded lamp. 'It's my grandfather's 1887 Queen Victoria Jubilee medal.'

Lynnford passed his finger over the raised bust of the

queen, her head garlanded with a simple crown and a head scarf in the classical Greek style. 'Somebody's going to walk off with it one of these days, lying loose in this drawer,' he added, dropping the box in his coat pocket and switching off the light. 'Let's see what Mr Grafton makes of it.'

Before leaving Park Mansions, Lynnford knocked on the porter's door. Mr Cobley appeared without a tie, the top button of his shirt open, and chewing something in his mouth, which, on seeing Lynnford, he tried unsuccessfully to swallow.

'Sorry to disturb you during your tea, Cobley, but could you inform Mrs Wilson that I've returned, and ask her if she wouldn't mind taking up some supper for me later this evening? I'd be most grateful.'

'No trouble, Mr Lynnford. She already knows you're here. I told her. I'll pass on the message. Interesting story?'

Lynnford tapped his nose with a smile. 'This one's too hot for the moment, Cobley. Don't worry, I'll tell you about it in good time. Oh, and by the way, could you ask your sister-in-law to bring me up some of your old gardening clothes, if you've got any to spare?'

'Old gardening clothes? Are you sure?'

'Yes, Cobley. I need a disguise. The full works, mind! Vests and boots included!'

Twenty minutes or so later, Lynnford descended the steps into Villiers Street below Charing Cross Station, recalling Mr Friedman's office, tucked away in one of the nearby arcades to his left. Villiers Street was empty, filled only by the damp fog drifting up from the river. Victoria had stayed at the top of the road, watching. He kept to the pavement, passing by the shops built into the deep walls that supported the railway station.

The archway under the railway bridge opened up. A cavernous, quiet world protected by the rough brickwork that had been built up to span the passageway under the bridge. It was dark now, the yellow light from the streetlamp penetrating only a short distance into the mouth of the archway, its twin glowing faintly at the other end. Across the road, the gates to the gardens were closed and chained, the dark bushes around the gates still heavy with a late afternoon's rainfall. Some distance further down, intervening before the tide-running Thames, lay the Embankment, and, just before it, the Underground station out of whose maroon-tiled entrance another light was shining.

Lynnford stopped in front of the archway, waiting. Mr Grafton did not delay in announcing himself. A voice from the unlit side of the archway addressed him with the same gravelly sounds that he had heard less than an hour ago. He looked to his right and beheld a man unfolding himself from the wall of the arch. Straightening himself, he advanced a few paces towards Lynnford. His head was bald and uncovered despite the cold evening air, a smooth, clinical dome. A pair of round, frameless glasses were stretched around his ears, their bridge resting on a nose that resembled the beak of a bird. A scarf was wrapped around his neck and the collar of his raincoat pulled up. His hands remained thrust deep in the pockets of his coat.

'Mr Taylor?'

Lynnford nodded, enquiring in his turn, 'Mr Grafton?'

The man ignored Lynnford's question. 'Follow me.'

He turned his back and, stepping into the middle of the passageway, walked towards the other end. A bearded man, stooping under a ragged and torn overcoat, called out to them in a hoarse voice, seeking attention. 'Something for a poor man.'

'Three pence for a whisky,' another voice rasped, and an infectious peel of pleas rang out from the huddled forms seeking shelter under the bridge, none of them seemingly paying any real attention to Lynnford or the man he was following.

'Ignore them,' Grafton advised.

The railway bridge thundered as a train pulling out of the station roared above them and another crossed it on its way in.

'Perhaps you are wondering why I brought you here.'

Mr Grafton had stopped under the lamp post at the other end of the passageway. 'But that's my business,' he quickly added.

'As you wish,' Lynnford replied. 'What can you offer?'

'I can provide you with replicas of almost anything, if you have the money. In metal or lead crystal glass, as I told you.'

'What about this?'

Lynnford took out the cedarwood box and handed it to Grafton, who, removing his hands from the pockets of his raincoat, took it and carefully unscrewed the lid. On seeing the medal, he paused a moment before holding it up to the light, examining it carefully.

'Yes, of course,' he replied, handing it back to Lynnford, his tone matter-of-fact. 'Why should you want this copied? It's of little value.'

'Perhaps not for you. What would you charge?'

The man hunched his shoulders as if the matter was of no real interest. 'The same metal? It will cost you more than the value of the original.'

'And if we copy several thousand?'

'It will lose its collector's value altogether; but if, as you say, you have an order, it's your money.' Grafton's tone was now dismissive.

'But you could set it up?'

'Of course. But I doubt it's worth your while. With too many copies, even abroad, the medal will become worthless. I wouldn't waste your time, or money.'

'I had in mind something else.'

'Yes, of course you did.'

'Something slightly more difficult.'

'Tell me.'

'My client would like to acquire a copy of a jewel in a museum.'

'A perfect copy?'

'Yes, so perfect that he wouldn't know the difference from the original!'

Mr Grafton looked hard at Lynnford. 'Your business is to cheat your clients? That's a dangerous trade, Mr Taylor.'

'I take my risks.'

'There's nothing illegal in making a copy of an old jewel. What you do with it is your business.'

'But could you make such a perfect copy, discreetly, without drawing attention to yourself?'

'It's not easy, Mr Taylor. It's not like a painting. With stones, you first need to feel their weight, the texture of the surface. Staring at them is not enough. Far from it.'

As he spoke, Lynnford could almost feel him caressing a precious stone in his hands, imagining its minute details hidden to the naked eye. His eyes dilated into little black balls, intense, red-shot and feverish.

'I can arrange that. It's not a problem.'

'Good.'

'It's a sapphire, the size of a large egg.'

Lynnford spoke quickly, hoping to catch Mr Grafton off his guard.

'You mean the museum piece from Nepal?'

The twitch of his lips told Lynnford that Mr Grafton already regretted his careless words. Lynnford pounced on him. 'Have you already made a copy of it, Mr Grafton? If that's the case, perhaps it would be cheaper for me to buy a ready-made copy.'

Coldness crossed the bald man's face, and the look in his eyes hardened again. 'I misheard you. I took you to be referring to another piece.'

Lynnford saw that he was clearly flustered, despite his apparent calm. 'What else could it have been? The Elephant's Sapphire is hardly a jewel one can forget easily or confuse with another.'

'Of course not.' Rattled, Grafton's tone was aggressive.

'It was you, then, who made the copy of the Sapphire?'

'Why are you interested in the Sapphire? Making copies of historic jewels is perfectly legal. It's not a crime.'

'So you said before. But it all depends on what is done with them. Wouldn't you agree?'

'That's all you wanted, isn't it? To find out who had made the copy.'

Mr Grafton's eyes opened and his lips twitched again, this time in a thin smile, almost of superiority. But Lynnford sensed fear behind the mask.

'So, who did you make the copy for?'

'I think our little talk has come to an end, if you'll excuse me, Mr Taylor.'

He made as if to walk away. Lynnford stretched out his hand as if to detain him, but Grafton shrugged him off and began walking quickly back under the bridge.

'Hey, come back! Not so fast!'

Mr Grafton now broke into a run, his shoes striking loudly against the pavement. Lynnford started to run too, certain that he would easily catch him up, which he would have done had it not been for the rising figure of the tramp crossing his path and knocking him off balance. Lynnford's face touched the cold pavement stone, his hands having broken his fall.

Frustration infused his mind as he got back onto his feet, his grazed hands stinging painfully, and saw Grafton escaping from him, running out into Villiers Street. Turning involuntarily towards the bedraggled vagabond, now standing at full height, he was surprised to see him holding out his fists menacingly and coaxing him in a mocking demeanour. Worryingly for Lynnford, he was a giant of a man and no easy match for him. More importantly for him though, he had no time to waste on a pointless scuffle under the bridge, so he started running again, still hoping that he might catch up with Grafton.

Tumbling out of the archway, he looked up and down, but there was no sight of him. Where had he gone? The pounding steps of the bearded vagabond behind him, however, gave him little time for reflection. He sprinted down to the river and along the Embankment, taking the big man with him until he was sure that he had lost him. He then headed back another way to rejoin Victoria at the top of Villiers Street, cursing his bad luck, the large man tugging at his memory all the while.

As he walked, his thoughts turned to Mrs Tunn, Jack's mother's acquaintance in Hoxton. Maybe, with her special knowledge of who's who in London, she would be able to help Lynnford look for Mr Grafton. But first, he was going to see what he could learn from the coal merchants in Romford. If, he reasoned, Grafton had indeed made the replica of the Elephant's Sapphire that was in the Queen's Fine Art Museum, then most likely Grafton had also made the one bought by Councillor Duncan, and the coal merchants might just lead him more quickly to Grafton than Mrs Tunn. But, to follow this lead, he would need to be up at the crack of dawn, if not earlier, the next day.

SEVENTEEN
STUBB'S COAL MERCHANTS

The next day, Lynnford was up early before daylight and, without having had breakfast, had left home and crossed London. It was now just past eight, and the air was cold and frosty. He was standing on the pavement opposite the entrance to Stubb's Coal Merchants in Romford, with his hands in his trouser pockets, waiting for the gates to open.

He had been there since half past six. Around seven-thirty, he'd been joined by three men, one of whom – Gary – it turned out was in Steve's crew; and from whom he learnt that Steve was not a driver, as the furniture dealer in Ipswich had told him and Victoria, but in fact Gary's crew master. When Lynnford had offered him a pound to spend the day at home, he had become suspicious and was reluctant to accept, telling Lynnford that his wife would not want him hanging around at home under her feet. Yet, he'd readily accepted another ten shillings to spend the day around several glasses of stout in The Masons' Arms, and, with the coins in his pocket, the coal man had left.

The high, wooden gates were still closed. Some of their grey weather-worn boards, having lost their fixing, hung loosely from the gates' top rail. An arched sign spanned the entrance, bearing the merchant's trading name in faded yellow and red lettering. Not only had Lynnford foregone his breakfast, he had also left home without a shave or a wash, apart from some cold water splashed over his face. He was wearing some of Mr Cobley's old gardening clothes: a collarless shirt, the open neck revealing a dirty yellow vest, a loose pair of trousers rolled up around his boots, and an old, lined-grey jacket. His outfit was completed with a grey cap that he wore straight on his head. Without thinking, he yawned, his mouth opening with tiredness. He passed a hand over the rough stubble on his chin and whistled a tune. As he stood watching, more men, similarly attired for work, began to gather outside the gates, quietly drifting along the street and assembling like birds on an empty washing line strung up in a back yard.

At a quarter past eight, the gates opened, sucking in the men standing outside. Lynnford followed them, picking out straight away the man he was after. A stocky man dressed like the others – heavy boots, roughly cut thick jacket over baggy blue overalls – but slightly shorter. With four others, the man went over to one of the coal sheds, an open construction filled with heaps of black coal. As he walked, he spoke rapidly, giving out instructions. Yet it was clear that they all knew what had to be done. Picking up rough bags of sacking, and setting up in twos, they began shovelling up the coal.

'Where's Gary?'

Steve had now realised that he was missing one of his team.

'He's laid up at home,' Lynnford called out over their heads. 'His back's got him.'

Steve and the other men stopped what they were doing and looked up at Lynnford, noticing him for the first time.

'Who are you?'

Lynnford assumed a dumb expression. 'Gary sent me over. He can't work. His back.' Lynnford made a gesture to his back, indicating the pain the absent coal man must be suffering.

'So, who are you then?'

'Like I said, Gary sent me.'

'How come he knows you?'

'I'm his cousin, Taylor.'

'News to me. I never heard he had a cousin.'

'I've come down from Ipswich.'

'What do you do there?'

'Nothing. I was laid off. I'm looking for work. That's why Gary sent me along. Said I might find something if you let me fill in for him.'

'If he's not coming, it's all the same to me. You can take his place. You can sort out the wages with him.'

Lynnford nodded his agreement and the crew master continued, 'But if he's still on his back tomorrow we'll have to sort something else out. Take this shovel and muck in.'

Steve threw the shovel he was holding over to Lynnford, who caught it with both hands.

'You'd better get hold of some rubber gloves or those

fair hands of yours will be torn to pieces by the end of the day,' he added with a rough laugh that was echoed by the others.

'Done this before?' asked the man holding open the sack in front of Lynnford, already half full. Coal dust covered the man's hands. A curl of brown hair stuck out over his forehead from under the woollen bobble hat covering his head. His frame was thin, as were the fingers that held hard the sacking.

Lynnford let the black coals slide off the tin shovel into the bag. 'No, I was a beer man for Worthington's, delivering beer.'

'So, what happened?'

'I fell out with the gaffer, didn't I? Like a fool.'

'You want to watch yourself here. Stevo doesn't like trouble.'

'Robbie! Go and bring round the lorry.'

At Steve's command, a wiry lad wearing a red and blue neckerchief detached himself from the group and scampered over the coal heap. He returned shortly, sitting high up in the cab of a coal lorry and grinning like a Cheshire cat, as if it was all a big joke. He stopped the lorry alongside them and jumped down, the engine rumbling and his driver's door left open.

'This should be easy work for you, Taylor. A coal sack and a beer barrel, there can't be much difference.'

Lynnford picked up a sack and launched it onto his back, and straight away he felt himself wobble under the strange weight, with the rough coals digging into his back. It took some twenty minutes to load the coal lorry. Once done, they drove off, crammed inside the cabin with Robbie at the wheel, still smiling, his elbow poking into Lynnford, stuck between him and Steve, sitting next to the window.

The morning passed by quickly, the crew walking alongside the coal lorry, down one street and into another, unloading sacks of coal and carrying them round to the backs of the houses according to a delivery pattern they all seemed to know by heart. As they moved along, Lynnford began to see a pattern in Steve's behaviour. He rarely left the lorry, spending most of his time ensuring that the others did not slack behind, and that they did not mess up the deliveries. Occasionally, he would slip off the lorry and walk down a side path between two houses, but, Lynnford noticed, never houses to which a delivery of coal had been made.

At the back of one house, Lynnford had just emptied two sacks of coal into a coal bunker when he spotted Steve's khaki woollen hat bobbing about on the other side of the fence that separated the adjoining houses. Through a slit in the fence, he saw him disappear inside the house, closing the back door quietly behind him. Outside in the road, Lynnford struck up conversation idly with Robbie whilst keeping an eye on the side path, waiting for Steve to reappear, which he did shortly; but, to Lynnford's surprise, without anything in his hands. *What has he been doing, then?* he wondered.

'Another two sacks at Number 38 and that's us finished here. Brunswick Street next, Robbie,' Steve called out, walking ahead of the lorry.

As the morning came to an end, Lynnford turned over in his mind several options to the enigma of Steve's seemingly unofficial sallies, which he continued to make as the coal lorry completed its round. The last sack of coal was taken off the lorry, and the men scrambled back into the driver's cabin.

'Not bad for a first morning, Taylor.' Steve gave Lynnford a begrudging smile. 'We knock off for lunch now. A second round this afternoon. Are you coming back to the yard?'

Lynnford shook his head. 'No, I'll catch up with you. Drop me off on the main road.'

'As you like. Get back for two.'

Lynnford watched the coal lorry drive off, the empty back covered only with coal dust and a pile of flat, empty sacks tied down behind the cabin. Once it was out of sight, he turned back, quickly retracing their route that morning, and hiding down one of the side alleys to one of the houses that Steve had visited. He found a place behind a sparsely leafed hedge that separated the back yards of the houses from some forlorn garden allotments, and waited. He did not have long to wait.

Somebody had entered the side alley, walking carefully but speedily. Through the hedge, Lynnford spotted Steve as he turned the corner and ran along the path behind the houses, towards the spot where he was hidden. He was carrying a rucksack. Without hesitation Steve picked out a house, lifted the latch of the back gate, opened it sufficiently to reach the metal dustbin next to it, lifted the lid of the bin and stretched inside, pulling out a small package that he dropped into the rucksack. *So much a poacher making the round of his traps*, exclaimed Lynnford to himself. *So that's it! I guessed right. He's picking up whatever he's stolen from the houses in the morning.*

Lynnford stood up, pushing his way through a gap in the

hedge and coming out onto the path in time to block Steve before he could escape. The coalman looked at Lynnford, his face fixed with surprise, and then flushed with anger. 'You! What the hell are you doing here?'

Lynnford ignored his question. 'Couldn't get back quick enough, could you, Steve? Collecting what you've left behind on your morning round? Let's see what we've got in here.'

Lynnford pointed to the rucksack, smiling. The coalman hesitated. His eyes hardened and he made a lunge at Lynnford, wielding the rucksack like a weapon, hoping to catch Lynnford off his guard. But Lynnford was too quick, side-stepping and tripping his aggressor, who fell headlong on the dirt path. Lynnford knelt on his back, pinning down his arms. He opened the rucksack. It was full of silverware. He alighted on a large bowl, which he pulled out, reading out loud the inscription, 'Essex Crown Green Bowling Cup. Well, Steve, it looks like you're on the losing side this time.'

His prisoner said nothing.

'What's this worth? Not so much as the blue sapphire-like gem that you picked up on one of your rounds, I bet.'

He sensed the man underneath him listening attentively.

'Yes, that's right, that's what I'm looking for. I'm not interested in your petty burglary, although this cup and the other contents of your bag are going back to their owners, somehow. We'll see how.'

The man lying on the ground still did not say anything.

'Did you hear me? You've got a choice, Steve. Either I turn you over to the police or you tell me where you picked it up from.'

'I don't know what you're talking about.'

'What's that? Oh yes you do. Don't waste my time. I've followed its trail all the way from Scotland back to your mucky hands. You couldn't resist it, could you? Where was it? In a drawer? You should've been more careful.'

'Who are you?'

'That doesn't matter. All you need to do is show me the house where you found the blue jewel. That's all I need to know.'

'Tresham Gardens.'

'Where's that?'

'Round the corner.'

'Where, round the corner?'

'I can't remember the number.'

'That doesn't matter. You're going to take me there anyway.'

So saying, Lynnford lifted the coalman to his feet. 'I wouldn't bother running off,' he warned.

The coalman shrugged his shoulders submissively, and Lynnford followed him out into the street, carrying the rucksack in his hand. They turned into a crescent, with larger semi-detached houses replacing the brick terraces, their pebbledash facades set further back from the street, rising gradually as they curved round the crescent. Seemingly tamed by Lynnford's authority and accepting that Lynnford was no longer one of his crew members to be ordered about, the coalman ambled passively alongside him, doing no more than indicate from time to time with a dumb movement of his arm the direction to take.

'This is it,' he finally muttered, signalling the house in front of them. He said nothing more, his hands in his pockets, as if waiting to be dismissed.

'Are you sure? Don't fool with me. It could be any of these for all I know.'

Lynnford stared coldly at the man in his khaki woollen hat, and then at the house. It was shabby and in some disrepair. The paintwork on the window frames and the timbered porch was peeling in places, and the house numbers one and five were hanging loosely from the wall. The windows looked unwashed and the garden was overrun. *He could be taking me for a ride, but then why should he?* reasoned Lynnford. 'It looks empty,' he commented.

'Go inside and see for yourself. No one's here. He's out at work.'

'You know who lives here?'

'Not personally, but I know he lives by himself.'

'Where did you find the jewel?'

The coalman burst into a coarse laugh. 'Well, that's a good one. Believe it or not, I didn't even know I'd nicked it. Sometimes you're better off not trying.'

'What do you mean?'

'I found it in the bag when I got home.'

'A bag! You took a bag?'

'It was a leather briefcase, stuffed behind a chair. I picked it up to carry out some stuff. The jewel was a bonus. I found it when I got home, see? I didn't know I had it, like I told you. So, you can't accuse me of taking it.'

'Have you still got the case?'

'Are you joking? Anyway, have you got want you want? I've got to get back to the yard. I've already wasted enough time.'

'If I haven't, I know where I can get hold of you. Go on, beat it.'

The man didn't move.

'What is it?'

'Don't I get anything for my trouble?'

'Your trouble! Just remember you're lucky you're not sitting in a police cell.'

'I thought you said you weren't the police.' A look of alarm crossed Steve's face.

Lynnford swung a loose fist at him. 'Hop it, before I change my mind.'

The coalman needed no further encouragement and left Lynnford, swearing loudly at him as he walked quickly back the way they'd come. Lynnford pushed open the garden gate and walked up to the front door. He knocked loudly. Nobody answered. Protected as it was from the wind, dry leaves, brown and brittle, lay scattered on the floor behind the porch wall. A bottle of milk left by the milkman that morning was the only sign of life. Pushing open the flap of the letter box, he picked out a single envelope lying where it had fallen on the carpet. So, clearly, the house was lived in. He decided to return in the evening to see who lived there.

Back out on the main road, Lynnford headed towards the high street. The lunchtime trade was beginning to trickle away. After spotting the Romford local police station, and discreetly dropping off the rucksack with Steve's stolen silverware in the entrance, he stopped off at the fish and chip shop next door, catching it before it closed for the afternoon. He was famished after the long morning's heavy lifting. Inside, a woman took his order and a man smoking a cigarette casually shook the handle of the basket he held submerged in the tank of hot oil below the counter. The chopped potatoes in the wire basket sizzled in response. Walking out of the shop, a steaming pile of chips in an open paper nestling in his hand, Lynnford popped a piece of hot dry fish into his mouth, letting his teeth break through the crust of batter.

*

'Oi! Where do you think you're going?'

The voice, although familiar, was loud and hard. Lynnford turned round. George, his blood vessels a livid purple, had run out from behind his glass-panelled counter and into the lobby of *The London Herald*, his parade-ground decorum lost, and his hands raised on either side as if to stop a runaway locomotive; giving Lynnford the impression of a gorilla about to seize him by the scruff of the neck, and lift him off his feet.

'Good afternoon, George,' he replied mildly. 'What on earth's wrong?'

George paused in mid-motion, the deep purple flush in his face cooling to a pink-tinged greyness as he realised who it was standing before him. He lowered his arms. 'Mr Lynnford?'

'Of course, George. Who else?'

George did not reply immediately, and Lynnford observed him to be uncharacteristically ill at ease.

'What is it, George?'

George coughed lightly. 'Well, sir, if you don't mind me saying, you look a disgrace.'

'What a cheek!'

'I don't know what you've been up to, sir, but I really cannot allow you upstairs in your present state. You really should take a wash, sir.'

'George, don't be impudent.'

Then it dawned on Lynnford that the clerk was trying to dissociate the grime-faced coalman, badly attired and dishevelled, from the urbane gentleman and respected member of *The London Herald*'s staff of journalists. Whatever respect George held for the former pilot, decency had also to be respected, and the house rules obeyed. Lynnford's expression registered shame and apology.

'Yes, of course, George. I must look a mess. I'd forgotten! A wash and a change of clothes will do me the world of good, I know, but first I really must make a telephone call, and then I'll be out. In a jiffy! I promise.'

As the clerk still appeared reluctant to let him pass, Lynnford added, 'It's an important story, George. We can't afford to waste a minute.' His words were coated in sugar, as if to say please. He needed to speak to Edwin Philips and inform him of his discovery.

The clerk relented. 'It's a good job there's no one else like you here, sir! Otherwise, I don't know where we'd be.'

As Lynnford headed towards the stairs, the head clerk added with a friendly smile, 'I wouldn't hang about upstairs too long. The editor's having a bad day and he's been looking for you for some time.'

EIGHTEEN
WHO ARE YOU, MR TAYLOR?

Refreshed and in clean clothes, and after having met Jack for his daily report in the Lyons Tea House in Piccadilly, Lynnford returned to Romford. Back in Tresham Gardens, he walked up to Number 15. A yellow light shone through the frosted-glass panel set in the upper part of the front door. He rang the bell. Nobody answered. The bottle of milk had gone. Someone was at home. It was seven-thirty in the evening. The clap of nailed boots hitting stone suddenly broke the silence. Lynnford spun round to see a large-framed figure in a heavy overcoat, running out from the side entrance. Caught by surprise, Lynnford was left standing as the man ran away down the road.

It's him! The vagabond from under Charing Cross Bridge. And Lynnford now knew where he'd seen him before: he was the dockhand in Alexandria Wharf. Lynnford stepped out of the porch, following the fading sounds of the man's footsteps. He didn't bother giving chase, dismissing the idea that it was the dockhand's home. Still, it occurred to him that, quite possibly, the dockhand had left open the back door in his haste, whatever had been the reason for his visit.

A wooden shed and a square patch of heavily soiled grass filled the garden at the rear of the house, the back fence lost in the darkness. A grey metal coal bunker, its roof dented, leant against the bare brick wall of the house, lit up by the light from the window overlooking it. The kitchen door was open, poking out over the concrete step that led up to it. The man in the overcoat had certainly left in a hurry. *What had spooked him?* Lynnford wondered as he walked towards the door, and as he stepped cautiously inside, he saw the reason why. A man sat slumped over a kitchen table, his back to the window.

The man did not move as Lynnford approached the table, his face staring at him. Lynnford felt his pulse. He was alive. A deep cut ran above his right eye – the knuckles of the man in the overcoat, he assumed, but it was too late now to catch him, and the unconscious man slumped before him required attention. Lynnford looked quickly around the room. Behind a copper-wire fireguard, red-bottomed coals nestling in a bed of grey ash smouldered in a grate. *So, he's been home for some time now*, mused Lynnford. An empty armchair was drawn alongside the tiled fireplace.

He winced as Lynnford dabbed the wound with a wet tea-towel. His eyes opened, and he stared up at Lynnford at first without comprehension, his mind trying to recollect what had happened and who this stranger was until recognition dawned upon him.

'You again!' he cried out, snatching the damp cloth roughly from Lynnford's hands. The man's gravelly voice finally removed any doubt in Lynnford's mind. It was Grafton! So this was his home.

'Careful!' Lynnford took a few steps backwards. 'I'm not going to hurt you. I want to help.'

Grafton looked suspiciously at him.

'You need to sit by the fire and put your feet up. Here, on this stool.'

Lynnford helped him to get to his feet and walk across the kitchen, easing him into the armchair and placing the stool in front of it, Grafton, this time, acquiescing in silence.

'What are you doing here?' he asked once he was comfortably seated. 'How did you find me?'

'Let me clean up this wound first. And it needs bandaging. Have you got anything?'

Grafton indicated a cupboard next to the sink.

'Your last visitor doesn't appear to have left on good terms. Who was he? An angry customer?'

Grafton said nothing in reply, dabbing the wound above his eye from time to time. Then he asked with a start, 'How did you get in?'

'Your visitor left the back door open.'

Grafton nodded, as if he understood why. 'So, what do you want?'

'The Elephant's Sapphire.'

'You're still on about that?'

'I know it was you who made the replica.'

'Did I? How did you know I lived here?'

'I didn't, as a matter of fact.'

'So, how did you end up here?'

'Because I followed a very long trail here, all the way down from Scotland. I know you must have made a second copy. I've seen it myself. It's in a private house in Dundee.'

'So, you think I made two copies now! What's to say I didn't make more – hundreds, even?'

'The copy I'm talking about was stolen. Then passed on. And the man who stole it has admitted to me that he took it from this house.'

'Did he? And you believe him?'

'He told me that, when he broke in here, he picked up a briefcase that was lying around and used it to carry away what he'd come in to steal. Only later did he find the replica gem in a bag at the bottom of the briefcase. It sounds credible to me. But you didn't report the burglary to the police, did you?'

'No, I didn't because there wasn't one!'

'There can't be many forgers living in this road or nearby.'

'I'm not a forger! I make copies. It's not a crime.'

'With clients like the angry one who was here just a few moments ago, I don't think the police would quite see the distinction the way you do.'

'Well, that's what I do. I make copies.'

Lynnford looked through the window into the back garden. 'Do you work out there, in the shed?'

Grafton shook his head. 'I have a workshop in East Ham.'

'And why did you make a copy of the Elephant's Sapphire? Not for your own amusement, surely.'

'Who are you, Mr Taylor, to be asking me such questions? That's your name, isn't it? Now I remember.'

'Because I have a client who would very much like to acquire it – the real one, of course – and for that I need to find who has it, but that doesn't seem to be so easy. Not with so many copies confusing the trail.'

'So, you're not going to pass him off with a copy as you suggested last night,' replied Grafton, recalling the explanation Lynnford had given him the day before.

'No.'

'The Sapphire is still in the Queen's Fine Art Museum. How could it be anywhere else?'

Lynnford stared back at Grafton, a poker face hiding his thoughts. *We both know that's not the case, don't we, Mr Grafton?*

Grafton took a breath as if making a resolution. 'Mr Fields commissioned me to make a replica of the Elephant's Sapphire.'

'Mr Fields, the curator of the Queen's Fine Art Museum?' Lynnford allowed a little surprise to filter into his voice.

'Yes, Sir Christopher Fields. It was all above board.'

'Was it? Why should he have wanted a replica made?'

'He said the museum was going to loan out the Sapphire for an exhibition and he wanted to have a replica to display in its place, so that there was at least something for the visitors to see.'

'I see. And you believed him?'

'Of course, why not? And it wasn't the first time.'

'You mean, he'd asked you to make replicas of other museum exhibits?'

'Yes, occasionally.'

'And how long had that been going on?'

'You make it sound as if it was a trade.'

'It's what you make it sound like, Mr Grafton. And, to make the copy of the Elephant's Sapphire, did Sir Christopher give you official access?'

'Naturally, he didn't want the Sapphire removed from its display, so he let me go in on Sundays and late in the evenings during the week, whenever I needed.'

'And that didn't make you suspicious?'

'Suspicious about what?'

'Oh, Mr Grafton, really! And he paid you for it?'

'The museum paid me.'

'Really? With a cheque?'

Grafton shifted uncomfortably in his seat without replying.

'I see. How much, Mr Grafton?'

'Two grand.'

'Two thousand pounds and in cash.' Lynnford gave a soft whistle, recalling the thousand pounds paid by Gordon Duncan to the dealer in York and thinking, *If only Duncan realised what a bargain he'd made!*

'That's not cheap, Mr Grafton.'

'Skill has a price. It took hours of work, and it was a perfect copy.'

'And so why did you make a second replica?'

'It wasn't perfect enough – the first one I made, that is. The blue wasn't deep enough. That's why I made a second. I should have ground the first one down.'

'But you didn't.'

'No.'

'Instead, you left it in a bag in an old briefcase and forgot about it.'

'I didn't forget about it, Mr Taylor.'

'And your angry visitor, what did he want? Lucky for you that I called here when I did, otherwise your beating might have been a lot worse.'

'The same as you, Mr Taylor.'

'The Elephant's Sapphire?'

Garston nodded.

'But he's a dockhand in London Docks, I believe, if it's the same man. What would he want with it? Where would he get the money? And how does he know that the Sapphire has been stolen?'

'What is it to you?'

'I like to know who my competitors are.'

'Don't imagine, Mr Taylor, that if the Elephant's Sapphire is out there, you're the only horse in the race.'

'But how does he know that the original is no longer in the museum and that you made the copy that is being displayed in its place?'

Garston took another long breath, as if making a second, even more important, resolution. 'Who are you exactly, Mr Taylor? I've been in this business a long time, and I don't believe for one minute you're interested in buying or stealing the Sapphire, even for a client.'

'Maybe I'm not.'

'Then who are you or what are you? Police?'

'No, Mr Grafton, I'm not the police.'

'Well, then?'

'I'm a journalist.'

'A newspaper reporter?'

Lynnford nodded. 'For *The London Herald*.'

'I see. You're looking for a story, then?'

'I already have a story, Mr Grafton, and the report is almost ready to file. I'm just trying to see how it all ties up. And finding the real Elephant's Sapphire would help. So far, you've told me Sir Christopher commissioned a replica from you. The replica is now exhibited in the Nepalese Room of the Queen's Fine Art Museum in place of the original. I believe you know that, but what did he do with the original? Sell it? He certainly didn't loan it out to another museum.'

Grafton remained silent, then said, 'All I know is that it was supposed to have been sent out on loan, to a museum in Paris. I don't know anything more than that.'

'But your visitor, the docker from the London Docks, thinks otherwise. Why is that?'

'I don't know. You should ask him.'

'I will. What's his name?'

Again, Grafton took a deep breath before replying, almost sighing with lassitude. 'His name's Bosworth. He's a dockhand in London Docks, as you said. So, you must know him.'

'I've seen him working in Alexandria Wharf.'

'So, you've seen the *Martaban*?'

'Yes.'

'And if you're any good at your job you'll already know what it carries, Mr Reporter, or whatever your name is.'

'Only duty-free tobacco and illegal visitors for the moment, apart from, of course, what's legally in its hold.'

'Bah! That's nothing. It's what it takes when it sails out of London that's important.'

'Tell me.'

'That would be putting my life at risk.'

'I need to find the Elephant's Sapphire, Mr Grafton. That's all I'm interested in. You can trust me not to disclose my sources or to pass on information that might reveal your identity.'

'Stolen paintings, jewels, sculptures, books, antiques. And not just from here, but from all over Europe.'

'And that's where you think the Elephant's Sapphire may have gone? Aboard the *Martaban*?'

'No, that's where it will go if Bosworth can get his hands on it.'

'And you don't think the curator, Sir Christopher, was mixed up somehow with this traffic?'

Grafton hesitated uncomfortably before replying. 'Sir Christopher asked me to make a copy. That was all.'

'But you know Bosworth. Couldn't Fields have also known him? Through you, maybe, Grafton.'

'Listen, all I know is that the Sapphire was stolen after Sir Christoper had removed it from display and that the replica I had made was already in its place at the time.'

'So, this all happened in August, is that right?'

Grafton nodded.

'And so, the Sapphire has been missing since then?'

Again, Grafton nodded.

'And do you think that's the reason why he killed himself, the curator? Because he couldn't bear the shame of having lost one of the museum's treasures?'

'Word is that he didn't kill himself.'

'That is interesting. What do you know?'

'I heard that he had an argument with Bosworth.'

'Over the Elephant's Sapphire?'

'Possibly. It seems that, according to Bosworth, Mr Fields had gone back on an agreement to hand over the Sapphire to him.'

'Simply hand it over, not even sell it?'

'I don't know, exactly. What I've heard is that Bosworth believed Sir Christopher had double-crossed him, that the theft was just a ruse, and that he was trying to get Sir Christopher to tell him where it was. He overplayed his hand with the result that Fields ended up at the bottom of the stairs, dead.'

'That's most interesting, Mr Grafton, and I wouldn't be surprised if it was true, but it's not what the coroner concluded.'

'No, it's not. But sometimes suicide is an easy conclusion for everyone to accept. I'm only telling you what I've heard.'

'Of course.'

And almost as if he had found a confessor, Grafton continued, 'You may find a lot of other things are missing from the Queen's Fine Art Museum, and from other museums too, if you look carefully. Sir Christopher had quite a business.'

'And all shipped out on the *Martaban*?'

Grafton nodded.

'Why does Bosworth think you're somehow mixed up in stealing the Elephant's Sapphire from Sir Christopher Fields?'

'He has to find the stone so, of course, he's knocking on every door, not just mine.'

'And you think you're safe? After his attack on you, alone in this house.'

'It was just frustration.'

'I'm not so sure.'

'I made some copies and I was paid for the work, nothing more.'

'Still, you need to be careful, Mr Grafton. My advice is that you take a long holiday, somewhere away from London. Somewhere far.'

*

Travelling back home on the Underground, Lynnford was more than usually apprehensive. At least two parties were chasing him for the Elephant's Sapphire: Chandra Bhat and now this Bosworth. He also knew there was a man out there trying to sell it, who had slipped through his fingers in Paris, and Lynnford had no clue as to who he was. So far, he'd found Grafton, the copier or forger, depending on which side of the law one stood, and through him he had discovered a traffic in stolen works of art on a massive scale, about which he needed to alert Mr Philips and the police. Indeed, it was the very information he'd been searching for in his, until then fruitless, visits to Alexandria Wharf and his night-time vigils with the tobacconist, Eddie Campbell. But as to the actual whereabouts of the Elephant's Sapphire, Grafton had been a dead end. There was also the death of Sir Christopher Fields to consider. The former curator of the Queen's Fine Art Museum, had he in fact been murdered as Grafton had told him? Certainly, there was more than enough for Lynnford to discuss with Detective Chief Inspector Sheffield at Scotland Yard. There was also the mystery of the Napoleonic sword, stolen from the museum and sent to him by special delivery. So many stories, they seemed to be sprouting like mushrooms in the dark. Lynnford needed to write them up soon, or at least some of them, and get them out on the front page of *The London Herald* before Kombinski lost patience with him and found someone else to write the newspaper's crime stories!

He got off at Hyde Park Underground Station. The escalator took him up into the open vestibule of the station, the tiled walls reflecting the yellow lamplight that accompanied his ascent. Stepping off the clanking metal plates, he walked towards the ticket collector and handed him his ticket, wishing him a good evening as he walked past, the tired man yawning in reply. The kiosks inside the station foyer were closed, their lights off. In the late evening, the place was no more than an empty walk-through passageway. Outside, the evening air was cold. Lynnford turned up the collar of his coat and headed towards Park Mansions, leaving behind the ticket collector, now alone in the deserted station.

NINETEEN
AN UNWELCOME VISITOR

Park Mansions was quiet. Lynnford climbed the stairs to his apartment and inserted the key in the lock. It was already unlocked! Cautiously, he opened the door. A polite, familiar voice greeted him, 'Mr Lynnford, please come in.'

The tone was more ironic than pleasant. Lynnford opened the door fully. Mr Bhat was sitting comfortably in Lynnford's armchair beside the fireplace, the yellow bars of the electric fire glowing hotly. The intruder had removed his overcoat, and it lay folded on the chair seat in front of him. One leg crossed over the other, his hands resting loosely from the arms of the chair.

'Mr Chandra Bhat,' he recalled his name. 'I've been waiting for you, Mr Lynnford.'

Lynnford closed the door. 'Who let you in?'

Mr Bhat smiled politely. 'I didn't think it necessary to trouble the porter and took the liberty of allowing myself in – or should I say, ourselves.'

As he spoke, two younger men, looking almost like twin brothers, appeared, one from the direction of the kitchen and the other from the bedroom. They were fashionably dressed in black slacks, jackets and pullovers. With a wave of his hand, they returned to what they had been doing.

'You weren't expecting me, Mr Lynnford? Well, that is odd.' Mr Bhat continued in his polite, ironic tone, his words falling slowly and carefully into place, one after the other. 'I understood that we had an agreement.'

'An agreement?' Lynnford questioned. 'And what agreement exactly are we supposed to have made?'

Whilst he spoke, Lynnford removed his coat and hung it in the cloakroom.

'Your memory can't be as poor as that, Mr Lynnford. You know very well what I want – the Sapphire!'

'That's something we both want, but your two friends won't find it here.'

'Really, Mr Lynnford? I believe otherwise.'

'Perhaps I could offer you something whilst we wait?'

'Thank you, but it will not be necessary.'

Lynnford collected his visitor's coat in his hands and placed it across the back of the chair.

'If I remember correctly, you asked me to give you first offer on the Sapphire once I had secured it. Wasn't that it, Mr Bhat?'

'Indeed, and I have come to ensure that you make that offer,' his visitor confirmed. He raised his eyebrow and lengthened his smile slightly, adding, 'And to ensure that you make it on such terms as I consider satisfactory and acceptable.'

'Well, I couldn't make it to you the other day and I'm still not in a position to do so, but look around as much as you like.'

Lynnford sat down opposite Mr Bhat, hiding his annoyance by meeting his visitor's ironic smile with his own look of amusement.

'That's not what I've been led to understand, Mr Lynnford.'

'And what is that exactly?'

'That you have acquired the Sapphire since our last meeting.'

'Really?'

The man in the kitchen re-emerged, distracting Mr Bhat's attention. He shook his head. Mr Bhat motioned him to the front door, where he took up guard, his arms folded across his chest. Lynnford continued to make light of the occupation of his apartment.

'You've made good progress, I see. You must have arrived early. How did you know I wasn't in?'

'It wouldn't have made much difference.'

'And why do you believe I have the Elephant's Sapphire?'

'I am fairly certain you have it.'

'But not one hundred per cent sure?'

'No, not one hundred per cent, as you say. But I'm not usually wrong.'

'I doubt you'll find it here.'

'We shall see. I am sure that you didn't come back

empty-handed from Paris. How you obtained it I don't know, but it was on sale there, that I know.'

'But that was last weekend. If I had it on Monday when I came back, do you think I'd still have it now?'

'As I said, we shall see.'

Mr Bhat closed his eyes as if he had no further wish to pursue the conversation. A moment later, however, he reopened them, the irony now lost from his smile. The second man had reappeared from the bedroom.

'So, what have you found, Amrit?'

Lynnford looked at the man. *The man on the boat train!* The man who'd been searching through his luggage. Lynnford recalled and recognised the reflected image of his face in the compartment window before being knocked to the floor of the boat train back from Dover.

Amrit shook his head.

'So, that must conclude your visit,' Lynnford interjected, and made as if to rise to his feet by way of encouragement. A pair of hands, however, thrust him back roughly into the chair and remained, resting heavily on his shoulders.

'That will do, Mohan,' Mr Bhat warned. 'Careful with my coat.'

Mr Bhat did not move or raise his voice, all the while speaking calmly and with self-assurance. 'You see, Mr Lynnford, my business is still not finished, and likewise, nor is my visit. It seems that the Sapphire is not here, or at least we've not succeeded in finding it yet. Perhaps you need a little persuasion. Mohan, or even Amrit, will only be too pleased to assist. You know, like tigers that lie in the shade and lazily stretch out their huge limbs, they are beautiful creatures until hunger makes them get up and prowl the land. They are no friends of elephants, I can assure you.'

'You must desire it a lot, the Elephant's Sapphire, Mr Bhat,' Lynnford tried to joke, but his visitor's reply was serious.

'That is correct, and I intend to get it. So, Mr Lynnford, please tell me where you have put it before I lose my patience. Where is it?'

'But I've already told you, if only you would listen.'

'Mr Lynnford, we've been very patient. We have been waiting a long, long time, too long. Now we are impatient. I will give you thirty seconds to reflect. Please do not disappoint me.'

Suddenly, with a jump, Bhat got to his feet, as if to release the nervous energy that had been building up within him, and took several paces around the room. He stopped next to the desk, his attention caught by the object that Lynnford had still not had time to return to the museum: the Napoleonic sword.

'A beautiful weapon,' Mr Bhat observed, 'and from where was it taken?'

'It doesn't cut as a weapon—' Lynnford began.

'Perhaps not, but even so, it's dangerous enough.'

Chandra Bhat lifted the sword off the desk, balancing it lightly in his hands, meditating, as if he were about to pronounce a professional opinion on its value. He began to pace the floor again. Without warning he sprung across the room, the sword stretched out in front of him. The blade's point touched lightly the tight skin of Lynnford's throat. He had thrown back his neck, anticipating the blow. The pair of hands resting on his shoulders strengthened their grip, pinning him firmly down in the chair.

'And so, now, if I were to ask you again?' his visitor taunted him, menacingly.

Lynnford glanced up along the length of the blade. The violence of the scene rendered incongruous the orange domesticity of the radiator bars glowing warmly in the hearth. The steel tip of the blade pricked his skin.

'I did not hear your reply, Mr Lynnford?'

'You make it difficult to speak.'

'Don't waste my time.'

'What can I say?'

'Where have you put the Sapphire?'

'Why can't you listen, for once?'

'If you don't have it now, you still must know where it is. Speak!'

Lynnford felt the blade press harder against his throat. 'That's not going to help you anymore.'

'No, but the satisfaction will.'

Lynnford closed his eyes, but felt the pressure on his throat ease, and opening his eyes again, saw Mr Bhat raise the sword and, stepping away, angrily throw it aside. It fell on the floor.

'Mohan!'

The hands on his shoulders released their hold, and Lynnford sensed the man's weight move from behind the chair. Lynnford was ready for him. Mr Bhat had turned his back on Lynnford, assuming that their superiority in number and skill placed him out of harm's way. However, despite his jocular tone, Lynnford was desperate, realising only too well the danger he was in and the need to act before it was too late. Mohan was now standing in front of him, confident and relishing his task, and so the reaction from Lynnford must have been even more surprising and unexpected for him. Lynnford's foot shot up, striking the henchman on the chin with a blow that sent him reeling backwards several steps. Lynnford sprang out of his chair and followed up the kick with another blow to the man's chin, this time knocking him further backwards and off balance. Mohan fell and struck the back of his head against the edge of a low table placed under the window.

Chandra Bhat and Amrit rushed towards Lynnford, but he was already ahead of them. He grabbed hold of the second henchman and pulled him forward, his momentum bringing him down and making him hit the radiator. The fireguard stopped him from falling on the electric bars, but not his outstretched fingers that slipped through the guard, their scorching making him scream with pain. Yanking hold of an ornamental metal poker, Lynnford had time to strike him across the head before Bhat crashed into him, the two of them falling to the floor, gripping onto each other but neither able to secure an advantage.

Lynnford felt Chandra Bhat's hold relax, and then his own grip was snapped open as his assailant scrambled free to his feet. Turning his head, Lynnford realised immediately the reason, seeing Bhat lunge for the sword, still lying abandoned where he had tossed it only moments before. Bending down, Bhat had it in his hand when the electric buzz of the doorbell caught them both by surprise. The doorbell rang again, impatiently. Getting to his feet, Lynnford raced to the door, pushing off Bhat as he tried to stop him. The bell rang once again, this time long and loud. Lynnford's hand fell on the door handle. Grasping it, he pulled it down. The door opened with his falling weight.

'For heaven's sake, Lynnford! What on earth's the matter with you?' The outraged voice of *The London Herald's* editor rang in his ears. '*Kombinski!*' Lynnford muttered to himself and looking up, saw with relief the editor's stocky figure in the doorway. Stepping over Lynnford, Chandra Bhat, coat in hand, elbowed the surprised editor out of his way, and escaped onto the landing.

'What on earth? Damn you!' exploded the editor, momentarily and unusually lost for words. 'Lynnford, who the devil's that?'

The editor's question trailed after the heels of Lynnford's unwelcome visitor, as he swung round the banister and down the stairs, taking two at a time, followed closely by Amrit nursing his scorched fingers.

'Don't worry about them, Paul. Here, help me with their friend.'

Lynnford had got back to his feet, and holding Mohan's upturned heels in his hands, was dragging the prostrate body across the carpet.

'Is he dead?'

'Almost. Don't worry, we'll wake him up.'

So saying, he dropped the man's legs on the landing and went back into the apartment, returning a few seconds later with a basin of water that he emptied over the unconscious man's face.

Spluttering, Mohan opened his eyes, staring at the two figures standing over him.

'The visit's over, you can go home now. The others have already left.'

A look of disgust passed over the man's face as he picked himself up. 'We'll be back!'

Lynnford closed the door and turned to his new guest.

'What's all this about, Robert? They look like dangerous men.'

'I can handle it. It's not their first visit.'

'Not from what I've seen. You seem to be damn lucky I turned up. You don't want them coming back.'

'I can't do much to stop them, but they're mistaken. They won't find what they're looking for here.'

'And what's that?'

Bearing in mind Mr Philips' desire for discretion, although recent events seemed to be making it increasingly untenable, Lynnford gave the editor an abridged account of what had just happened, not mentioning the Sapphire, as he went around the room straightening the rug, replacing the chair, picking up the fallen sword – and, once he had finished, brushing down his clothes. Kombinski watched as he listened, ensconced in Lynnford's armchair beside the fire. He accepted the glass of whisky that Lynnford proffered, sipping it quietly as Lynnford cast an eye around the rest of the apartment.

'So, what brings you out of Fountain Street, Paul?'

As usual, the editor started with a secondary issue. 'You've had one of the messenger boys spend over a week in the Queen's Fine Art Museum, Lynnford.'

'Jack Worth wasn't missed, and the museum is covering his wages.'

'If he wasn't missed, then what am I doing with him on my payroll?' the editor huffed. 'And, for that matter, what are you doing for me? Your story of this missing bauble doesn't seem to have produced any copy yet. At least, nothing's crossed my desk.'

So Irvine has told him about the missing Sapphire, Lynnford inferred from the editor's words before declaring, 'I'll find the Sapphire. But there's more to it.'

'Such as?'

'Suspicions that the museum's previous curator didn't kill himself.'

'Sir Christopher Fields, you mean? Clear evidence of suicide. The coroner found as much, although not sufficiently to make it a formal conclusion, I agree. But there's no story there, Lynnford,' Kombinski declared, dismissively taking a gulp of whisky before adding, 'Anyway, Lynnford, it's all taking too long. How many days have you been on this?'

Kombinski didn't give Lynnford time to reply. 'Whilst you've been chasing up and down the country, and amusing yourself in Paris, you've been missing the real stories here under your nose.'

Kombinski jabbed his finger at the folded newspaper that he had brought with him and had lying on his lap. *So this is it*, thought Lynnford. 'Is it tomorrow's paper?' he asked.

'No, it's today's, damn you, Lynnford! It's today's, and it's almost yesterday's news! And worse, it's in *The Daily Chronicle*.'

'There's nothing there of interest, I checked earlier. Just the story on the Corbitt hanging at Strangeways Prison. And that was on Tuesday.'

'Nothing there! Look for yourself, and don't be so cocky.'

The editor spun the paper out of his hand like a boomerang, letting Lynnford catch it. Lynnford spread out the front page. It was the late afternoon edition of *The Daily Chronicle*. He must have picked up the lunchtime edition. The late extra column had a large print heading in red, announcing the theft of several paintings from a private collection. "Turner and Constable among the masterpieces stolen from Westlake House" ran the subtitle.

'When did this happen?'

'What does it matter? You should have been on to it, and would have been if you hadn't been seduced by this damned sapphire. What was Joseph Irvine thinking in agreeing to you taking on this assignment? And worse, not telling me about it until I wormed it out of him.'

'Do you want me to follow it up?'

'No! It's too late! I want a scoop, Lynnford, and soon. *The Daily Chronicle* has got one in ahead of us. Now you get on and find me one. Don't waste my time and money. You're a journalist. And on my payroll.'

Kombinski raised the glass of whisky to his lips and took a large gulp that drained the glass. 'I'll be off. It's getting late. You keep an eye out for yourself. Victoria will see to it, I hope. Where is she, by the way?'

'At home.'

'Well, give her my regards.'

Lynnford shut the door. It had been a long day. His muscles were still aching from the strain of humping coal sacks around the back streets of Romford earlier in the day.

TWENTY

A ROLLERCOASTER RIDE!

Early the next day, the telephone rang in the offices of the Queen's Fine Art Museum. The curator answered. 'Philips here.'

'Good morning, Mr Philips. It's Robert Lynnford.'

'Mr Lynnford! Any news? You're very early this morning. It's only just gone eight.'

'I need to talk to you, Mr Philips. Can I come over? There's a lot to discuss and I wanted to catch you before the museum opens.'

'Certainly. As you can see, I'm already in. Mrs Fellows won't be in until much later this morning.'

'Good.'

'You know your way up? The night guard is still on duty and will let you in.'

'Understood. I'll be over shortly. I'm at home in Park Mansions.'

Less than twenty minutes later, Lynnford was outside

the museum offices, high up above the lobby. He knocked respectfully on the outer door, doubting that Mr Philips would hear him from inside his own office at the end of the corridor. He knocked again, and, without waiting for a reply, pressed down the iron handle and entered the white-walled reception area. As the curator had led him to expect, it was empty. The back of Mrs Fellows' chair was pushed neatly against the edge of her desk, and her typewriter hidden under a black cover. Lynnford closed the door behind him and proceeded along the corridor towards the curator's office. He knocked and a distracted voice beckoned him in. Bent over a package that he had opened, the curator turned his head to face his visitor. 'Ah, Mr Lynnford, it's you. Splendid, come in. You must look at this. It's what I came in early to examine.'

The curator straightened his back. Before him, amidst a pile of brown paper, string and blond wood shavings, stood a finely decorated blue and white porcelain vase, twelve inches or so in height, slender and elegant. 'What do you think? Charming, isn't it?'

'What is it?'

'Early Victorian. In fact, it's of little value. There must be hundreds of them littered all over the country. But still, I like it. Quaint.'

'For the museum?'

'Heavens, no!' Edwin Philips laughed out loud. 'It was sent to me by somebody from out in the country somewhere, I forget where. Anyway, it's not important. What have you got to report? My life's on a knife's edge with this damned visit of the Prime Minister. What dreadful luck!'

'May I?' Lynnford indicated the chair in front of the curator's desk.

'Yes, of course.'

Lynnford sat down, placing on his lap the parcel in which he had wrapped the Napoleonic sword.

'So?' The curator looked expectantly at Lynnford.

'Mr Philips, what do you actually know about Sir Christopher?'

If Edwin Philips was surprised by the question, he didn't show it.

'Christopher Fields? What should I know? He was the curator of the museum and had been since before the War. A distinguished antiquarian, a classics scholar from Cambridge and a family man. What else?'

'Nothing suspect?'

'Certainly not.'

'But did you know him personally?'

'Only by reputation. I never met him. What are you suggesting? That he stole the Sapphire?!'

Lynnford simply shrugged, and his momentary silence brought down the curator's veil of light-heartedness, leaving him aghast. 'You're not serious, surely?'

'Didn't you say yourself that you were surprised to find the business card from Wheeler, Chambers & Son in amongst Christopher Fields' affairs in his desk?'

'Yes, that is true, but there could be any number of reasons to explain that. As I said at the time.'

'Mr Philips, have you had a chance to complete your inventory of the museum? You mentioned that you were in the process of making one.'

Embarrassment flashed momentarily across the curator's face before replying, 'Not exactly. It's rather a mammoth task.'

'And what have you found so far? Or not found?'

Edwin Philips pursed his lips. With difficulty, he restrained a nervous facial twitch. He looked hard at Lynnford. 'Indeed, there are at least five replicas of what should be authentic exhibits, and in the vaults, I counted eight missing pieces. But nothing quite as valuable as the Elephant's Sapphire.'

'And you haven't finished?'

'No, not yet. That's what I said.'

'Have you informed the museum's trustees?'

'I'm preparing my report, but I've already had an informal word with the chairman.'

'And what was his reaction?'

'What do you expect, Mr Lynnford? Still, he was surprisingly sanguine. He is prepared to accept the discrepancies as unavoidable consequences of the wartime storage.'

'But not the Elephant's Sapphire, surely?'

'He doesn't know anything, yet, about the Sapphire. He is waiting for me to complete my inventory.'

'And, since you were appointed as the acting curator of the museum, has anyone approached you about borrowing or acquiring exhibits from the museum? Illegally, I mean.'

'Most certainly not!'

'And the *S.S. Martaban*, does that mean anything to you?'

'Where are you leading with this, Mr Lynnford?'

'The *Martaban* is a cargo ship bringing in whatever it can pick up from around the world, usually on her route from Southeast Asia and ports in the Indian Ocean.'

'A tramp ship?'

'Yes, if you like.'

'What of it?'

'It's a story I've been investigating for a good part of this year without really getting to the bottom of what's going on. Until yesterday, all I'd been able to get evidence of was smuggled tobacco and the odd illegal passenger. Nothing more.'

'Is this relevant? What has it got to do with the museum?'

'Please hear me out, Mr Philips. I have good reason to believe that the real and very lucrative business of the *Martaban* is to ship out stolen art treasures. It usually docks in Alexandria Wharf, here on the Thames in London.'

'How extraordinary!'

'Quite so. There is also a newspaper article in yesterday's *Daily Chronicle*.'

'About what?'

'The theft of masterpieces from Westlake House in Theydon Bois. It included several paintings of Turner and Constable. I have a real hunch that it could well be the same criminal gang at work. People with contacts and access to keen buyers outside Europe. I strongly suggest, therefore, that you consider tightening the museum's security. Otherwise, you might find that the museum will be missing further valuable items.'

'Yes, of course. I shall see to it immediately. But what is your conclusion, so far? Could the Elephant's Sapphire have been shipped out aboard the *Martaban*?'

'No Mr Philips, I believe that it's still very much here in the country, hopefully in London itself.'

'Why is that?'

'Because there are several different unsavoury people actively looking for it here, and all the indications point to the sapphire that was being hawked in Paris last week being the genuine Elephant's Sapphire.'

'Which you believe was brought back to London, is that correct?'

'Yes, on the boat train last Sunday. It's the lead I'm working on. Expert French antiquarians on the *Île St-Louis* in Paris examined the Sapphire in the light of day. They wouldn't have been fooled by a replica.'

'Why, then, didn't they buy it?'

'I believe because either the price was too high for them or, most likely, it was too low for a jewel of its size, and this made them worry about its provenance. That it was stolen. These are reputable dealers. They wouldn't touch anything that had been stolen.'

'No, of course not. Do you know how much he was asking for it?'

'No, I don't. It was not something the Parisian antiquarians were willing to disclose.'

'I see. And, of course, we know now that the blue stone in Dundee is a replica.'

'Correct. A genuine replica of the Elephant's Sapphire.'

'So, if your theory is good, this means that our man, the man you saw in Paris, is looking for a buyer here in London, or somewhere in the UK. So, we still have a chance of recovering it, is that what you're saying?'

'Yes, it is. And we also have a description of him to go on, but—'

'But, what?' the curator interrupted, impatiently and nervously.

'There's still the matter of the *Martaban*.'

'What of it?'

'And its connection with Sir Christopher Fields, your predecessor.'

'The poor chap is dead.'

'True, but he left a debt.'

'A debt? Aren't you digressing, Mr Lynnford?'

'Let me finish telling you what I have managed to put together about him and the *Martaban*.'

The curator nodded, and Lynnford continued, 'I think that Sir Christopher must have had some sort of arrangement with the *Martaban*, or rather with the people using her to smuggle out stolen works of art. It is more than likely that the unaccountable items in the museum were not somehow simply lost during the War, but rather sold or handed over to them by Sir Christopher.'

'It's unbelievable! How could a respected scholar like Sir Christopher do such a thing? It's slanderous.'

'He's dead now.'

'Still, there's his family. They have feelings. But go on!'

'The Elephant's Sapphire was to be disposed of in the same way. Sir Christopher had commissioned a replica to be made to take its place in the Nepalese Room—'

'Incredible!' the curator interrupted, dumbfounded.

'But somebody, it seems, was a step ahead,' continued Lynnford, 'and stole the original Sapphire for themselves from the museum before Sir Christopher could actually pass it on to the *Martaban* gang.'

'And do you have any idea who this person might be?'

'I think that it is most likely the man I saw in Paris. If I'm right, then it means that he's probably working alone. Someone without the necessary contacts to be able to find a buyer for a very valuable but stolen jewel.'

'I see, that seems plausible.'

'But it also means that whoever is behind the *Martaban* has not given up on obtaining the Sapphire. That's why I mentioned Sir Christopher having left a debt.'

'So, word has got out?'

'I'm afraid so. At least, that is, in the small world of international fine art thieves. If it's any consolation for you, I believe they probably knew well before you stepped into the museum and took over as curator.'

'Nevertheless, I am the one who is responsible for the museum now. Tell me, how have you found out all this?'

'I'm sorry, Mr Philips, I appreciate that it must be difficult for you, but please understand that I can't disclose my sources. At least, not at this stage.'

'Well, until you give me some hard evidence about Sir Christopher's involvement, I'm not going to alter my report to the museum trustees.'

'Of course not. It's far too soon to let the cat out of the bag. We need to find the Elephant's Sapphire first.'

'Precisely! And how does all this help us to find it?'

'More so than you think. I'll explain.'

'Go on.'

'It seems clear enough from what my source has told me

that the genuine Sapphire was stolen from Sir Christopher after he'd had the replica made. In which case, I'm fairly certain that the thief must then be someone who knew there was a replica.'

'How's that?'

'Because it meant that it was safe, if you like, for the thief to steal the genuine Sapphire.'

'Safe?'

'Yes, because this person must have known that the reason for having made the replica was to steal it from the museum. This person knew that Sir Christopher intended to display the replica in the museum in place of the Elephant's Sapphire, and that he wouldn't, therefore, or couldn't, report its theft to the police by someone else.'

'I don't know how you've done it, but it all seems plausible to me. Do you have any ideas as to who this thief might be?'

'There are several possibilities. I'm not excluding any of them, but it must have been someone who needed the money, or at least wanted to make their fortune. What about someone in the museum?'

The curator shook his head. 'It can't be. From what I gather, Sir Christopher was a stickler for class and didn't believe in fraternising below decks, so to speak. Nobody in the museum would have known about the replica. He would never have associated himself with them, not if, as you say, he was defrauding the museum.'

'What about somebody who observes what's going on, especially in the Nepalese Room?' And changing tack, Lynnford asked, 'Tell me, Mr Philips, who was it that told you about the elephants in the antiquarian's shop in Portsmouth? You know, the place I drove to last Friday. Strange that someone should call you out of the blue about something you were looking for at that precise moment, don't you think?'

'We were looking for the Sapphire, not the elephant.'

'Yes, but the caller was able to persuade you that it would be worth your while taking a look.'

'It seemed like a lead that needed to be pursued. It was all we had to go on then. I don't know who it was who called.'

'So, you didn't recognise the voice? I recall you told me that you considered the information was reliable. It wasn't someone who works here, was it, by any chance?'

'No.'

'I see. Then what do you know about the warder in the Nepalese Room, Mr Philips?'

'Joseph Matthews?'

Lynnford nodded.

'Well, obviously he's got his eye on the Elephant's Sapphire all day long, or did have, but I wouldn't credit him with the gumption to steal it.'

'Maybe not, but for some peculiar reason he tried to drive me off the road on my way back from Portsmouth that day, after following up the lead you had been given there, and it nearly got me killed.'

'Good Lord!'

'So, he knew that I'd gone down there, and that I'd be driving back to London at that time of day.'

'I can assure you that it wasn't his voice on the telephone, Mr Lynnford. I would have recognised it.'

'Well then, as you said, maybe he doesn't have it in him to steal from the museum.'

'So, coming back to Sir Christopher, he jumped to his death when he realised that someone had stolen the Sapphire from him and he couldn't face the public shame, is that it?'

Again, Lynnford shook his head. 'It's not that simple. Why would he have taken his own life for that reason? He was going to steal the Sapphire anyway, for himself, wasn't he?'

'True, I suppose.'

'No, Mr Philips, it wasn't suicide at all.'

'How's that? It was the coroner's verdict, wasn't it?'

'It's how the death was reported. I'm still waiting to see the verdict itself.'

'I see, you must know what you're doing. But what is the evidence that he didn't take his own life?'

'So far, it's only what I have been told. I'm waiting for corroboration, as I said. From what I've been told it appears there was an altercation between Sir Christopher and another man that led to Sir Christopher being found dead in the museum's lobby at the bottom of the stairs.'

'An altercation! With whom?'

'A man called Bosworth. He's a member of the *S.S. Martaban* smuggling gang. My source says that he had come to collect the Elephant's Sapphire from Sir Christopher. When he was told that he no longer had it, that in fact it had been stolen from him, Bosworth thought that he was being double-crossed and, in a rage, pushed the curator to his death. Deliberately or accidently, I don't know.'

'Surely whether Sir Christopher jumped or was pushed would have been made clear in the autopsy report?'

'Indeed. That's why I've taken the liberty and asked Detective Chief Inspector Sheffield at Scotland Yard to look again at the file and the autopsy report. I contacted him this morning before coming here to discuss matters with you.'

'So, you spoke to the police? I expressly told you not to.' The curator almost spluttered with indignation.

'Mr Philips, you no longer have the luxury of tiptoeing around the loss of the Elephant's Sapphire. Surely, that must be clear to you by now, and even more so with the Prime Minister's visit in only a matter of days. And, if your predecessor was indeed killed, the police must open a murder inquiry. However, rest assured, I know DCI Sheffield. He will be discreet.'

'And where is the evidence Sir Christopher was murdered? Your unidentifiable source?'

'As I told you, it appears that there was an argument between the two men that turned violent.'

'So, it's only a rumour then?'

'But one that should be taken seriously. It may even be that Sir Christopher had double-crossed Bosworth, and rather than the Sapphire having been stolen from him, he had in fact sold it himself.'

'But to whom? We're going round in circles, Mr Lynnford. And running out of time.'

'You are right, but I'm afraid there's worse, Mr Philips.'

'Can that be possible?'

'There's someone else actively searching for the Elephant's Sapphire. Someone who is possibly far more dangerous than the *Martaban* crew.'

'Who?'

'His name is Chandra Bhat. I believe he's some sort of Nepalese nationalist. A political agitator who believes the Sapphire should be taken back to Nepal where it rightly belongs. He's got wind that the Elephant's Sapphire is no longer in the museum – at least not the genuine gemstone – and he wants to get his hands on it. And he's not shy as to how he'll go about achieving that.'

Mr Philips let his face fall into his hands as Lynnford continued. 'He broke into my apartment yesterday evening, believing I had come back from Paris with the Sapphire. He was there when I returned home, and the party got a little violent. Let's say I'm lucky to still be in one piece. I recognised one of the two men with him. The man who I caught searching through my suitcase on the boat train on Sunday night. Have you come across Chandra Bhat before?'

'No, I haven't had the pleasure,' Mr Philips sighed. 'And as if the Nepalese Prime Minister's visit wasn't enough!'

'Well, if we haven't recovered the Sapphire before he arrives in London, we should advise the Foreign Office, as well as the Home Office.'

'Must we?'

'There are political and security implications, Mr Philips, but I'll see what I can find out about him, first. He could well lead us to the Sapphire. You never know. He, of course, is hoping that I will lead him to it! You know, we need to keep going, even if it feels as if we're going round in circles.'

'You could always try the Nepalese Embassy here in London.'

'Yes, I'll do that.'

'But for heaven's sake, don't mention the Sapphire!'

'I won't. I do know how to be diplomatic, Mr Philips.'

'Yes, I'm sure you do, Mr Lynnford. Forgive me. The strain is getting to me.'

Lynnford waved aside the curator's concern as if he had nothing for which to apologise. The curator changed the subject. 'Do you mind telling me what you have on your lap? I've been curious ever since you sat down.'

'Oh, this!' Lynnford smiled. 'I believe it's something you have been missing.'

Lynnford placed the parcel on the curator's desk.

'What is it?'

'Take a look.'

Edwin Philips' face twitched momentarily with annoyance at Lynnford's theatrics, but caught by his own curiosity, quickly unfolded the cloth wrapping. His impatience was lost in a flash of astonishment as soon as he revealed the Napoleonic ceremonial sword, the bare blade sparkling in the light.

'The sword! But how did you find this?' His eyes questioned Lynnford in wonder, whilst his fingers caressed the handle. 'Where did you find it?' he repeated.

'I didn't find it. It was sent to me.'

The curator released his hold of the sword, astonishment transforming into disbelief. 'It was sent to you! We've been turning the museum upside down looking for it since Wednesday.'

'Yes, it was sent to me.'

'What do you mean? How?'

'Exactly that, it was sent to me. At Park Mansions.'

'But why? Who sent it to you?'

'I've no idea. It must have been someone with easy access to the museum and able to slip out valuable exhibits without being noticed.'

'It wasn't being exhibited. It was in storage. It was whilst I was doing the inventory on Wednesday that I spotted it was missing.'

'Still.'

'Someone in the museum!'

'And someone with some connection to the theft of the Elephant's Sapphire, which is why I believe that it was someone from the museum, or connected with it, that stole the Sapphire in the first place. This is the note that came with it.'

Mr Philips read out the simple message, written in bold capitals, 'Keep away from the elephant.'

'As you see, it's anonymous. I've had it checked for fingerprints, but of course there are none. But it really is most interesting.'

'It's impossible to make anything from it. Is it a threat?'

'One can find cheaper blades for that. But it's true, that's what I thought at first.'

'And now?'

'Given its value, and the risk whoever it was took, I'd say it was more of a bribe or a gift.'

'A gift!'

'From someone most likely in the museum, as I just said, but naïve enough to think that I would accept one antique in consideration for renouncing my search for another.'

'And do you have someone in mind?'

'The warder, Joseph Matthews. He is my top suspect.'

'Matthews! Do you have any reason to suspect him? Should I inform the police?'

'No, wait a little. Give my lad, Jack Worth, a chance to see what he can uncover. It could be someone else.'

'Fine, but I shall keep an eye on Matthews anyway.'

'There's something else that's been teasing my mind about the Elephant's Sapphire.'

'What's that?'

'It's only two weeks now to the winter ball at Straw House Farm. Isn't that right? And you told me that this year the Stocktons are eligible to have the Sapphire back for their ball.'

'That's right.'

'Have they been in touch with you yet about the arrangements for getting it there?'

Mr Philips hesitated slightly before replying, 'No, not yet.'

'Isn't that odd, don't you think? Shouldn't it be planned well in advance? It's not exactly a routine removal job, is it?'

'No it's not, but I expect to hear from them any day now, although, to be quite frank, I'd much prefer that I didn't, and that somehow, they forgot all about it. And given the economic situation we're all in, I'd quite understand if they decided it was not appropriate to organise a ball at all this year.'

'I understand, but shouldn't their silence make us suspicious?'

'What do you mean? Suspicious of what, exactly?'

'I'm doing no more than speculating, Mr Philips. We can't overlook any possible lead.'

'No, of course not. So?'

'It could be that the Stocktons haven't contacted the museum about the return of the Elephant's Sapphire for their winter ball for the very good reason that they already have it. What if they took it from Sir Christopher?'

'What?' The curator almost flew out of his chair. 'You mean they stole it? You can't be serious?'

'Why not? They might consider that they couldn't be accused of stealing what is already theirs.'

'The Sapphire's not theirs at all. It's held on trust, a charitable trust.'

'Indeed, but nonetheless I should follow it up.'

'What do you intend to do?'

'Pay them a visit. I was thinking of driving up there this afternoon. Straw House Farm, it's in Norfolk, isn't it? I believe that's what you told me.'

'Yes, near Norwich. I can give you the address, but above all, be discreet.'

'I will be.'

'I must remind you that her husband is on the Board of Trustees. I'll call and let them know you're on your way over.'

'To write a piece on the Elephant's Sapphire. Please, mention this.'

'Indeed. I shall also call Mr Joshi, the First Secretary at the Nepalese Embassy, and tell him you'd like to see him this morning. He's a good acquaintance of mine. In fact…' Mr Philips looked at his watch, 'It's not yet nine-fifteen. You might be able to see him straight away. I'll tell him you're on your way.'

Mr Philips returned to his office after seeing Lynnford out, his thoughts whirling as if he'd just stepped off a rollercoaster ride at a fairground.

Downstairs, Lynnford was held up from leaving the museum by a small group of schoolchildren squeezing in through the now-open double-entrance doors, excitement agitating their movements. Their teacher, a moustached man wearing an old blazer patched at the elbows with leather, was shepherding the children. He gave Lynnford a curt nod as he passed through after his pupils, politely acknowledging the adults' shared toil during a not-so-distant wartime service, before imposing a respectful silence on the children, and leading them off, past a line of Greek and Roman gods, distant and silent, unimpressed by their presence, child or adult.

TWENTY-ONE
ANOTHER COMMON THIEF

The Nepalese Embassy in London occupied a building on Kingsway at the Aldwych end. Mr Joshi, the First Secretary, was a proud, feline-looking man, who seemed to purr with satisfaction as he spoke. The diplomat welcomed Lynnford into his office, sitting behind his desk, the polished surface reflecting the splendour of the richly decorated room, including the chandelier suspended from the ceiling above. A place designed to humble. It was easy to forget the cold street outside.

'And how can I be of help to you, Mr Lynnford? Mr Philips at the Queen's Fine Art Museum has asked me to see you this morning but please understand I am very busy.'

'Yes, I do appreciate it is very short notice. Thank you. I will be brief.'

'So?'

'I was wondering if you could give me some information about someone, a Nepalese subject.'

The First Secretary raised an eyebrow, as if in warning. 'Mr Philips indicated that it was a matter of some urgency. Why is this person of interest to you?'

'He broke into my apartment yesterday evening, accompanied by two of his friends. The visit turned rather unpleasant. They left, but I fear they may return.'

'Surely, it is a matter for the police?'

'They didn't take anything.'

'But still, they were unpleasant?'

'Yes, but for the moment I'd prefer not to involve the police.'

'I see.' And the look of warning turned subtly to one of suspicion. 'So, you know his name?'

'Yes. Chandra Bhat.'

'I see, so your intruder introduced himself.' The First Secretary almost smiled. 'Bhat is a common name.'

'It may be an assumed name. This is his business card: Everest Art.'

Mr Joshi took the card, examining it without comment.

He knows him, thought Lynnford, interpreting the placid expression.

'And how is it, exactly, that you know this man, Mr Lynnford?'

'As I mentioned, he decided to pay an uninvited call. It was his second visit.'

'A second visit?' But the diplomat was no longer humouring Lynnford, and his ironic tone had vanished. 'You must have something he wants. Otherwise, he would not waste his time.'

'You do know him, then? Who is he?'

'Yes, Mr Lynnford, unfortunately I do. Chandra Prasad Bhat is a notorious art thief. His interests extend all over the sub-continent: Bombay, New Delhi, Calcutta and, of course, Kathmandu.'

'I see!'

'Precious stones are his speciality, although his expertise allows him to handle almost any art form. His clients are very wealthy and numerous. I didn't know he was here. This is news to me. I wonder how he got into the country because his name is known to the British authorities, including the Metropolitan Police. He must have come in illegally.'

Suspicion smouldered once again in the diplomat's demeanour. *He must think I'm somehow involved with him*, Lynnford thought, *but I can't tell him about the Elephant's Sapphire. That would be worse!* Mr Joshi did not express his thoughts, limiting himself after a few moments' silence to some words of caution.

'My advice to you, Mr Lynnford, is to keep well away from Chandra Bhat. He is a dangerous man. You know, as a matter of fact, he was a distinguished officer in the prestigious Gurkha regiment before he turned to criminal activities. Now, unfortunately, he is just a common thief.'

*

So much for nationalist politics! reflected Lynnford as he strode past the Aldwych with the idea of dropping in at *The London Herald* before driving up to Norwich in the afternoon. *Just like Bosworth and his friends aboard the Martaban!* He knew now that he had two criminal gangs in competition with him to find the Elephant's Sapphire. Were they aware of each other? Most likely they were.

Still some distance from Fountain Street, a voice across the street called out, 'Hey, Lynnford! Stop a minute.'

Lynnford looked over the road and beheld Eddie Campbell standing on the opposite pavement, slightly breathless. 'Eddie, what's up?'

'Wait there,' shouted the tobacconist, looking for a gap in the passing traffic to cross the road.

'I was on my way to *The London Herald*, hoping to catch you,' he explained once he was safely across the road.

'Why? What's up?'

'The docker from Alexandria Wharf.'

'Bosworth?'

'You know his name now?'

'Yes.'

'Well, I spotted him heading towards Tower Bridge and decided to see where he was going, in case you might be interested.'

'You did right, Eddie. Where did he go?'

'I followed him across Tower Bridge and then along London Wall. He's just gone into the Italian coffee bar, just back there,' and Eddie pointed some yards back along the pavement he had been walking along. 'I thought if I could let you know, you'd have time to get down here before he left.'

'Indeed! Thank you, Eddie, I could do with a coffee right now.'

'Do you want me to hang around?'

'No, thank you, Eddie. I'll let you know if I find out anything.'

The coffee bar had recently opened and was already very popular with both East End bank clerks and wide boys looking for casual jobs. Lynnford stepped inside. The smoke and noisy bustle enveloped Lynnford as he looked for Bosworth amongst the cramped rows of tables and chairs, lost under the heaving clientele escaping the cold of the first day of December. At the far end of the room, he spotted him in deep conversation with another of Lynnford's recent acquaintances, Jeremy Friedman. Somehow, since his talk with Grafton, Lynnford wasn't surprised to see the two men together. Seeing the table immediately behind the dockhand suddenly become free, Lynnford pushed his way forward quickly and sat down. Neither of the two men had noticed Lynnford, who made himself as discreet as possible. He took out *The Times* newspaper from his pocket and lost himself in the crossword whilst straining his ears to catch the half-whispers of his two neighbours. The first words he could pick out were a reference to something familiar.

'You can see them, but they're meant for export. If you want them, you must decide quickly.'

'I'll not be rushed, Bosworth. The newspapers are full of nothing else. I need to be careful.'

The Westlake House paintings, guessed Lynnford. *So, Grafton was right about Bosworth and his gang.*

'Fields could have dealt with them, no problem.'

'He could have if he hadn't gone over the banister last summer. Remember, Bosworth?'

'That wasn't me.'

'But everyone thinks it was, Bosworth. Who else could it have been? Officially they put it down as a suicide, but who the hell believes that?' Silence, and Jeremy Friedman's voice resumed, edged with scorn, 'And, if you hadn't, we wouldn't be in this mess now.'

'But it was Fields who messed up, letting someone take the Sapphire from under his nose. Well, that was his story. I still think he double-crossed us.'

'It was a mistake to shove him over, Bosworth.'

'You aren't listening, Friedman. I didn't do it.'

'Whatever!'

'Easy for you to wash your hands, Friedman. I must get the stone back at any cost. Our people in Hong Kong are getting impatient. They want the stone delivered or it'll be me who pays the price!'

'Well then, you had better find it, Bosworth, before someone else does. For now, we'd better get going if I'm to see these paintings.'

The chairs behind him scraped on the floor, and Lynnford felt himself being squeezed against his table as, it must have been Friedman, got to his feet and followed Bosworth outside. Quickly Lynnford got to his feet, not bothering to order a coffee, and rushed towards the door.

'Mind!' a waiter snapped, holding up the tray he was carrying almost to his chin, just to let Lynnford get past.

Outside on the pavement, he spotted Friedman and Bosworth. They had crossed over the road and were walking quickly in the direction of St. Paul's Cathedral. A double-decker bus passed him by, halting temporarily because of the traffic a short distance further on, and hiding the two men from Lynnford's view. When it moved off again Lynnford saw, to his frustration, that Friedman and Bosworth had both vanished, as if waved away by a magician's cloak. *They've jumped on the bus*! He started to run, hoping the bus would have to stop again but the traffic melted away and the bus picked up speed, leaving Lynnford further and further behind. He stopped. He had a better idea. Gambling they were heading for Alexandria Wharf, and it was as good a guess as any, he hailed a taxi, hoping to get there before them.

*

Alexandria Wharf on the River Thames in London's Docklands was hidden in a maze of warehouses. The black cab dropped Lynnford off outside a public house he knew, The Bunch of Grapes. He hadn't been down this way to the wharf for a long time, but as he hurried along the narrow and twisting roads it came back to him, and he soon arrived at one of the entrances, a brick-lined tunnel under a tall warehouse, similar to the one he had been standing in with Eddie Campbell the other day. The smell of rotting waste filled his nostrils. There was no sign of life and, as the warehouses masked completely the dock sheltering behind them, but for the smell, for want of indication, the passageway could have led anywhere.

Lynnford slowed down and walked carefully through the tunnel. He didn't want to risk colliding with either Friedman or Bosworth, if they had indeed come to the wharf and had surprisingly arrived before him. If they had, they could be anywhere, inside one of the warehouses or on the quay itself. Although it was more than likely that he had arrived ahead of them. Carefully, he approached the end of the passageway. The *Martaban* loomed up in front of him, its huge size seemingly even more immense in the stark, wintry daylight.

The ship was quiet, and the familiar quayside empty. Peering out from under the arched entrance, Lynnford looked around the wharf, so far as the ship's hull would allow him. Open entrances led into the interior of the warehouses and above them, shuttered casements. Higher up still, short protruding platforms, equipped with block and tackle, were fixed into the walls. A rat scurried across the cobbled quay, disappearing over the side and plopping into the water.

The paintings could be stored anywhere, if they're here at all, even on the ship, Lynnford reflected, looking around him, before starting to search systematically the insides of each warehouse, going from one end to another before climbing to the next floor.

Suddenly, Lynnford caught the sound of footsteps shuffling on dry wood, echoing in the hollow spaces and carried down from floor to floor. He stopped. An open arch a few steps ahead of him brought in a slight breeze from the water. He tilted back his neck, looking up the flight of steps, trying to pinpoint the source of the footsteps. They seemed to come from the uppermost floor. Now he could make out the sound of voices, dull and hushed, their identity lost in the planks of dusty timbers. It could be them. He stepped cautiously onto the first step, letting his weight fall before taking another step, and so he proceeded upwards until he reached the fourth floor. Now he could clearly distinguish the voice of Jeremy Friedman. So, he and Bosworth had finally arrived and, somehow, gained the top of the warehouse without Lynnford seeing them – or, he hoped, more importantly, them not seeing him.

Some way up the stairs, he placed his foot down too quickly, not giving it time to test the strength of the stair. The loose timber squeaked horribly, disclosing his presence immediately to the men above him. They stopped.

'What's that?' the voice of Jeremy Friedman ran down the stairs. 'Quick, take a look.'

The other man obeyed, stamping across the floorboards. Retreating softly, Lynnford quickly slipped back down the flight of stairs to the floor below, where he had time to step off the stairs and duck out of sight before Bosworth reached the open stairwell. Staring down, the dockhand saw nothing but the stone slabs of the passageway below, filtered through the criss-crossing timber stairs.

'It's nothing. A rat.'

Jeremy Friedman's reply was indistinct, but Lynnford got the impression that he was not convinced and wanted to finish up as quickly as possible. Carefully, Lynnford regained the stairs and, descending to the bottom of the warehouse, hid in the next section of the building, where he waited for the two men to follow him down. Whatever they were up to, he would soon find out. He leant against the brick wall, breathing slowly and listening for their movements. Some ten minutes went by before he heard their footsteps on the stairs. They were coming down quickly and easily, so they were not carrying anything, he guessed. He waited for them to pass outside and onto the quay and, rushing to the open archway, he was in time to see them walk round the other side of the *Martaban*.

Lynnford returned to the stairs and climbed back up to the top floor, unconcerned now about any noise he might make. The dusty floor stretched out in front of him as his eye level reached the uppermost floor. Tea chests filled the space, lining the walls on all four sides, but it was easy to see what had occupied the attention of Jeremy Friedman and Bosworth. Their footprints were scattered in the dust that covered the floorboards and led Lynnford's search to a pile of sacking in one corner. Pulling aside the sacking, he revealed a tea chest full of cylindrical boxes. He picked up one and, taking off the end cap, looked inside: a roll of thick protective paper. With his fingers, he carefully brought out the paper, unrolling it just enough to see what it was protecting. It looked to him like a Constable landscape. Opening another tube, he pulled out a second painting. He counted the boxes: twelve in total. *The stolen Westlake House paintings! It must be them, and perhaps some other ones besides!* Replacing the paintings and throwing the sacking back as he had found it, Lynnford descended the stairs for a second time, thinking to himself that to leave such a hoard unguarded, the thieves must be very sure of the place indeed. Still, he realised that the paintings could all be shipped out at any moment, or removed to another hiding place. He had to alert Inspector Sheffield at Scotland Yard without delay.

TWENTY-TWO
THE END OF A BUSY MORNING

'Ah! Lynnford, I was just going to call you.'

Lynnford closed the door to Detective Chief Inspector Sheffield's office in Scotland Yard and sat down in the chair opposite the police officer; his discovery of the stolen paintings pushing hard in his thoughts but caught by the police officer's greeting. 'Something on the coroner's findings?' he asked. The inspector had agreed to review them, as Lynnford had informed Mr Philips earlier in the morning.

'Possibly. Nothing conclusive, though. But you look like you've got something burning on your mind, Lynnford. You go first; the coroner's report can wait.'

'Well, you'll be pleased, Chief Inspector. I've got a gift for you! I can tell you where the Westlake House haul has been stashed.'

'What! The stolen paintings?' The inspector hid with difficulty his incredulity.

'Yes, and there's probably much more there, besides.'

'Where?'

'Alexandria Wharf, down in the western docks. But you need to be quick.'

'Are you sure?'

'One hundred per cent. I've just come from there.'

Without hesitation, the inspector reached for the telephone on his desk. 'I'll get a team of officers down there right away.'

'If I may, Chief Inspector, for the moment it might be wiser to just have your officers keep an eye on the place,' Lynnford suggested, adding, 'With a little bit of good timing you might catch the whole ring.'

'Seems a good idea. Wait here whilst I sort out a surveillance team.'

Some minutes later, the inspector returned to his office. 'Well, that's done,' he remarked as he sat down again. 'So, what else can you tell me about these stolen paintings?'

Lynnford explained about the *S.S. Martaban* moored in Alexandria Wharf and gave the names of Bosworth and Jeremy Friedman whilst the inspector took notes. 'Still, I suspect that the operations are being directed by people outside the country, in Hong Kong, possibly.'

'Do you? I suppose you're not going to tell me where you've got all this from, are you?'

Lynnford smiled. 'It's what I've heard, that's all I can tell you, Inspector.'

'Nothing else?'

'No, Inspector, not really.'

'Well, what you've told me is certainly more than

helpful. Thank you, Lynnford. Perhaps then you might want to hear what I've got to say about Sir Christopher's death and the coroner's report?'

'If you don't mind, Inspector. You've got the file, then?'

Inspector Sheffield nodded.

'What then, exactly?'

'As I said when you came in, nothing conclusive. More a question of interpretation.'

'I see. What was the conclusion?'

'It wasn't suicide, contrary to what the newspapers reported, and everyone, it seems, believes.'

'What then?'

'Death by misadventure.'

'So, why the idea of suicide?'

'Because that's what everyone thought at the time, but there was nothing to prove conclusively that Sir Christopher had deliberately taken his own life. There was no clear and compelling evidence. So, the coroner had to conclude death by misadventure. I believe it was also partly in deference to his widow, to alleviate her suffering a little. To avoid the public shame. And besides, there was no suicide note or letter explaining the reasons for him having taken his life. Although at the time, you press people didn't concern yourselves overmuch on that score.'

'Suicide makes good headlines.'

The inspector nodded grimly, keeping silent.

'So, what is there in the post-mortem report that makes you think it wasn't either suicide or an accident?'

'I didn't say that.'

'No, but as good as.'

'Well, to be clear, the injuries are all consistent with a fall from a height of approximately fifty or sixty feet.'

'Which would be about the level of the landing on which the museum offices are located,' Lynnford confirmed.

'Indeed. It was a clean fall, directly to the ground floor, clearing all the intervening flights of stairs. The head hit the marble floor and the consequent trauma killed him, the fractured skull causing internal bleeding. So, he could have simply slipped and fallen.'

'Come on, Inspector! Was he supposed to have been standing on the balustrade? Did your coroner take him for an acrobat?'

Inspector Sheffield ignored Lynnford's dry humour. 'But now, if, as you suggested this morning when you telephoned, there was someone else there with him, and I would remind you that there isn't any actual evidence at the moment to support the idea – quite the contrary – some of the pathologist's findings could be given a different interpretation.'

'To support the idea that he was pushed?'

The inspector nodded.

'For example?'

'Firstly, the injuries sustained by Sir Christopher's body suggest a headlong fall, a dive, which is more consistent with a push, or a suicide for that matter, but not with someone falling by accident.'

'Agreed.'

'Secondly, and if we discount the idea of a suicide because of the presence of another person, there's the location.'

'Yes, indeed. Wouldn't someone wanting to end their

life jump from the tallest point on the outside of the building rather than from a few floors inside?'

'Most probably. Thirdly, the height of the fall. From fifty feet, or sixty at most, there are good chances that somebody simply jumping or falling would end up seriously crippled without the fall being fatal.'

'So, evidence that he was pushed, or thrown.'

'No, just another indication of the possibility.'

'Except Sir Christopher fell headfirst.'

'Exactly.'

'Anything else?'

'His broken arm.'

'His arm was broken?'

'Yes. Again, it could have been broken by the fall, but it could just as well have been broken before the fall.'

'So, what did the autopsy find?'

'The autopsy report doesn't indicate one way or the other. In which case, most likely it was considered that it was broken by the fall. The pathologist would, otherwise, have drawn attention to it.'

'But, on the assumption that there was another person present and that a struggle took place, surely, on balance, the inference should be that the arm was broken before the fall?'

'There's no mention in the report of bruising, Lynnford, to the arm or elsewhere, to support the suggestion of an aggression before the fall, and no defensive wounds.'

'Could it not have been overlooked?'

'It could have been, but unlikely.'

'Inspector, consider then this question carefully. Was

Sir Christopher such a pillar of the Establishment that it was inconceivable at the time that someone might have murdered him, and that this influenced the finding?'

The inspector smiled, as if in tacit agreement, before declaring, 'Nevertheless, the fact is that there was no evidence that my colleagues could find at the time to suggest that it was anything other than an accident, or a suicide at most. According to the night guards, there was no one else in the museum at the time. Who do you think could have pushed him over the balustrade? And why?'

'Bosworth.'

'The same man tied up in the Westlake paintings?'

Lynnford nodded.

'And for what reason?'

'Because, according to my information, Sir Christopher, contrary to his very respected public reputation, was heavily mixed up in the same traffic of stolen art as Bosworth. The two of them then had a falling out, so I understand.'

'Over what?'

'A very precious jewel.'

'I see, but you know perfectly well that this is all hearsay. Let's see what Bosworth has to say for himself when we catch him. Now, if there's nothing else—'

'There is one more matter.'

The inspector looked enquiringly, although a little impatiently, at Lynnford. 'Yes?'

'I'll be quick.'

'Go on, then.'

'The Nepalese Embassy tells me that a certain Chandra Prasad Bhat is known to the London police. Is that correct?'

The police officer didn't need to search his memory. 'He's an infamous international crook, Lynnford. Something tells me that you're onto a very big story.'

'Because of Chandra Bhat?'

Inspector Sheffield nodded. 'Is he here in London?'

'Yes. He's already paid me a visit in my apartment. Twice.'

'Has he indeed? Then you're lucky to be sitting here in my office right now.'

'Is he that dangerous?'

'He's very dangerous, Lynnford. He's wanted in Europe, in North America, in Southeast Asia, and in the UK. Do not go near him, Lynnford. I'm very serious.'

'That's what the Embassy's First Secretary told me, but the man's intent on following me.'

'Be very careful, Lynnford. That's my advice. In fact, it's a warning.'

'I will, Chief Inspector. Thank you.' Lynnford got to his feet, picking up his hat, adding, as he walked towards the door, 'Don't forget to tip me off when you're about to make the arrests in Alexandria Wharf. I wouldn't want to miss that.'

Outside Scotland Yard, Lynnford flagged down a cab, instructing the driver to take him to Park Mansions as quickly as the traffic would allow. He looked at his watch. One o'clock. He should still have time, he calculated, to pick up his car, drive to Straw House Farm and arrive there before dark. *It's been a long and busy morning*, he reflected. *Let's see now what the Stocktons have to say about the stolen Elephant's Sapphire, if anything.*

TWENTY-THREE
STRAW HOUSE FARM

The front wheels of the Morgan spun on the loose, chalky gravel. Lynnford released the accelerator. It was close to four o'clock in the afternoon, and the light was beginning to fail. He'd pressed hard to arrive before the winter darkness closed in, the country roads and villages of East Anglia slowing his progress. He'd just passed through a lifeless hamlet on the road south of Norwich, the flat fields stretching out around him, meeting nothing but the shortening sky. He pulled up gently and switched off the engine. Straw House Farm.

The building appeared to date from the 1700s, a low-built stone edifice. Looking out over the car's polished mahogany dashboard, the house in front of him appeared drab and lifeless, or was it simply the failing light that made it so? The grey stone was scoured with green and white scaling, the large, deep-stone window openings were fitted with leaded glass, and the entrance was marked by a stone canopy resting on two pillars. It had only one upper floor. The slated roof, running down to the guttering, was damp in places, stained here and there with patches of dark green moss.

What had Colonel Urquardt thought eighty years or so ago, standing in this very spot after returning from all those years spent abroad in the British Army, the Elephant's Sapphire in his hand? Had he been pleased to be back? *Most likely not, if it had been a cold and damp winter's day like today*, mused Lynnford as he studied the scene, tapping the steering wheel with his fingers. As for the farm, he couldn't see anything to warrant the title.

He climbed out of the car and walked up to the entrance. A holly bush, red with its berries hanging amidst the dark green leaves, flowered out from one side of the entrance. A wrought-iron boot scraper had been fixed into the stone pavement. The oak door was inset with a small coloured-glass panel. Lynnford pulled the doorbell. He heard nothing, and rang again, waiting. The silence persisted, broken only by the lonely chirp of a blackbird's winter song. The bird was perched on the ledge of the window nearest to him, scraping and fidgeting its feet on the cold stone. The door opened. A woman in her forties greeted him. 'Mr Lynnford?'

Lynnford nodded. 'I'm sorry if I'm a little late. I didn't leave London until gone one o'clock.'

'Well then, you've done very well. How do you do? I'm Mrs Stockton, Helen Stockton. Mr Philips said that you might be delayed.'

She stepped aside, adding, 'Please come in before the cold beats you to it.'

'It's kind of you to see me at such short notice.'

'Well, it's a little out of the blue. But it's not as if I'm terribly busy this afternoon. Mr Philips said that you're a journalist. You want to write about the Elephant's Sapphire. Is that right?'

'That's part of it.'

'Oh?' His host hesitated.

'I'm sorry, what I meant to say is that I'm really more of an historian, and that what I want to tell the readers about is the history behind the jewels that have been brought back to Britain from the four corners of the globe, not just describe them.'

'The globe doesn't have corners, Mr Lynnford,' she replied, teasing him, a strange sense of relief in her voice.

'You're right, Mrs Stockton. You see how journalists can get confused with their own images. One cliché after another until the very sense is lost.'

'I hope you'll write about the Sapphire better than that, but at least you're honest enough,' she replied, laughing lightly and adding, 'Unusual enough for a journalist, if one judges from what they write.'

'I wouldn't say that we're as bad as that. Bad news is bad news whichever way you paint it.'

'There you go again!' Her light voice pealed out in laughter once more. 'Please follow me. We'll be more comfortable in the drawing room.'

Mrs Stockton led Lynnford through a spacious, oak-panelled hall, pausing in her stride to bend down and collect in her fingers a dried brown leaf that had fallen on the rug. Continuing, she stopped again, a whimper catching Lynnford's attention.

'Nelson!' Mrs Stockton's mocking voice combined affection and admonishment. A Great Dane padded into the hall, reaching up to her waist, its ears drooping around its head, and its big eyes staring up at its mistress, appealing. The hound moved forward, forcing Mrs Stockton to recoil a pace or two simply to avoid being pushed over by its weight.

'What is it, Nelson? It's too early for tea.' She spoke in soothing tones, rubbing the dog's muzzle vigorously in her hands and lifting its large ears in amusement. Her laughter rang out clear as crystal. 'Go back to the kitchen. We have a visitor. Now, don't be jealous.'

She steered the animal back down the passageway, giving it a final push to help it on its way. 'He should be outside, but he's getting old. With the short winter days, he likes to be inside, in the warmth. Only he gets bored.'

'Like the best of us.'

'Here we are.' Mrs Stockton opened a door and led Lynnford into a large south-facing drawing room, the warmth of the long-lost summer sunshine replaced by a crackling fire. Lamps and wall lights transformed the window into a blackened curtain, reflecting the interior through the broad expanse of leaded glass. 'I'll draw the curtains. It's suddenly gone dark outside, hasn't it?'

The drawing room was long and comfortable. Large, shaded table lamps and drapes decorated the room. A large Chinese vase, filled with dried flowers and grasses, stood on a low, circular walnut table, its curled polished feet resting on the carpet. An open magazine and a pair of clear-rimmed reading glasses had been left on the table, as if in passing, and as she walked past, his hostess picked them up. Closing the magazine and folding the glasses, she placed them to one side.

'Please, Mr Lynnford, take a seat.' Mrs Stockton smiled, indicating the sofa in front of her, next to the fire. She sat down on the sofa opposite, brushing her tweed skirt underneath her and adjusting her cream-coloured cardigan. A diamond brooch sparkled on her blouse. 'So, you like history, Mr Lynnford?'

'Yes, very much,' he replied. 'Do you mind if I take notes?'

'Of course not. And in stolen jewels?'

Lynnford was taken aback despite the teasing voice. Was she reading his mind?

'The Elephant's Sapphire!' Mrs Stockton explained.

'Oh yes, of course, but I understood it was given to your grandfather as a present, a reward from a powerful Nepalese nobleman. Isn't that right?'

'Yes, of course. But still, was he right to give away such a priceless national treasure, and let it out of his country?'

'The colonel had saved the son's life, and that of the father.'

'That's so. But still, its history is one of greed and envy, as much as one of pride and pleasure.'

'Well, yes then, I suppose I am interested in stolen jewels, if you put it like that. In their history.'

'The Elephant's Sapphire is quite an exhibit. I suppose you've seen it. Of course, you must have. The Elephant itself, although a replica, is also a fine sculpture.'

'A replica?'

'Yes, you know. The Sapphire was worn by a real,

ceremonial elephant, not a bronze imitation. Did the new curator tell you the history?'

Lynnford nodded.

'That was a dreadful matter, the death of Sir Christopher last summer. Oh, but where are my manners?' Mrs Stockton interrupted herself. 'Can I offer you some tea?'

'No, thank you. I'm fine,' Lynnford declined hastily.

'Nonsense. You've driven a long way. You must be starving, and you certainly can't go back without some refreshment. A sandwich and a cup of tea?'

'Well then, if it's really no trouble.' Lynnford held up his hands in surrender.

'Not at all. It won't take me a minute.'

Ten minutes or so later, Mrs Stockton returned with a tray, apologising for the delay. 'The staff have gone home. Friday afternoon. I let them off. It's very quiet, as you can see, and there's little for them to do.'

'I'm sorry. I didn't mean to take up your time.'

'I'm pleased for the interruption, Mr Lynnford. It was a long, dreary afternoon anyway.'

'And your husband, Mr Stockton?'

'Leonard? He's away on business,' she replied quickly.

'And Straw House Farm, has it always been in the family?'

Before replying, Mrs Stockton lifted the teapot and gently tipped it, releasing a finely scented golden liquid into one of the cups on the tray, which she offered to her guest.

'A distant ancestor, Geoffery Urquardt – that's my maiden name – bought it at a good price from someone who'd lost his fortune in the South Sea Bubble.'

'So, where does the name come from? Its very solid for a house made of straw.'

'The original building had a thatched roof.'

'Was it a farm then?'

'You really are interested in the past aren't you, Mr Lynnford?' Mrs Stockton commented with emphasis before explaining, 'It still is, although the house is no longer part of it. The farmland is rented out, barley fields, mainly, and flowers. Our neighbour farms it along with his own land.'

'I couldn't see any sign of it when I drove up.'

'You wouldn't. The farm's on the other side, and Jefferson, our neighbour, has a direct access from his own land. I don't think Leonard would have made much of a farmer.'

'That's Major Leonard Stockton, is it?'

'Yes,' Mrs Stockton replied crisply.

'The Sapphire… I suppose you rarely saw it?'

'How's that?'

'Well, if it's been in the Queen's Fine Art Museum in London all the time.'

'Oh, I see. No. My mother was extremely proud of it. She always talked of it as grandfather's sapphire, his Nepalese prize. My grandfather, that is.' Mrs Stockton laughed, the memory bringing back the warmth in her voice. 'Whenever we went to London, it was always to see the Sapphire. I'm sure mother invented excuses just to go up to London and see it, and she always took me along with her.'

'It must have been exciting for you, as a young girl.'

'Marching through the museum, past all those cold statues, reaching the gallery with its rich drapes and fineries, and then seeing the Elephant's Sapphire! It transported me to another world, and another time. It was magical.'

'Still, it must have been some time since you last saw it.'

'Before the War. That's when we last had it here for our winter ball. With the War, I lost the habit of going to London, and my mother died.'

'I'm sorry.'

'Some more tea?'

'Yes, please. And what about the future?'

'The future?' Mrs Stockton asked, surprised.

'The winter ball. You must be looking forward to having the Sapphire back home once again, so to speak.'

'Yes, of course, if all goes well. I can't wait.'

'Speaking of which, Mrs Stockton, Mr Philips was wondering whether in fact you were going to request its release for the ball. It's only two weeks away and he would need to make the necessary arrangements. He still hasn't heard from you.'

'A couple of weeks? So soon! Although to tell you the truth, this year I don't think it'll be much more than an informal party for a few friends. Cocktails, you know. We seem to have got a bit behind with the preparations for a full-blown affair. Oh, how dreadful!'

Somehow, Mrs Stockton had knocked over the milk jug and its contents were beginning to drip steadily from the edge of the tray onto the carpet. Lynnford got to his feet to help.

'Heavens, what a stupid thing to do!' she exclaimed.

Mrs Stockton picked up her napkin, scattering crumbs onto the floor as she did so, and started mopping up the milk as best she could. 'I'll go and get a cloth from the kitchen. Please don't worry. I'm so sorry. How clumsy of me.' And she disappeared, hurrying out of the room.

Mrs Stockton returned a few moments later, apologising, her calm little restored. She offered Lynnford the cup of tea that she had intended to give him, the cup rattling in its saucer.

'Where was I? Oh yes…' She paused, seeming to bite her lip.

'Is there anything the matter, Mrs Stockton?'

Mrs Stockton shook her head. 'Oh, nothing, nothing at all. We seem to have forgotten the Elephant's Sapphire, haven't we? I must be wasting your time.'

'Not at all, Mrs Stockton. It's clear that it still has an important place in your life—'

But before Lynnford could finish his sentence, Mrs Stockton had got to her feet and turned her back on him, her hands to her eyes, sobbing. Lynnford leapt to his feet. 'Mrs Stockton, what's wrong? If there's something troubling you, I can leave if you would prefer to be alone.'

She held out a hand to the fireplace, as if for support, turning her head to face Lynnford. 'It's nothing. Nothing at all. It'll pass.'

'Are you unwell? Is there something I can get for you?'

'No, no thank you. I'm fine. I'm just sick of this ghastly house,' she exclaimed suddenly, hitting the shelf of the fireplace with her clenched fist.

'A glass of water?'

'No, really. I'm fine now.'

Mrs Stockton took a deep breath, flicking back a loose

curl of hair. 'I'm sorry that you should have to see me like this, but I don't know how much longer I can go on.'

'What are you talking about, Mrs Stockton? Please don't distress yourself. Can I help in any way?'

Lynnford guided her to the sofa and sat down opposite her.

'Where is your husband? Can I call him for you?'

'Oh goodness, you might as well know. I haven't seen him for over a week. He's run off again.'

Uttering these words, she lowered her head, a convulsion whipping down through her body, from her head and shoulders to her waist. 'I'm sorry, please excuse me.' And she fled the room, leaving the door open, her steps fading along the corridor.

Lynnford wondered what to do. He disliked being caught up in a domestic row. Mrs Stockton was clearly taking it badly. He got to his feet, absentmindedly picking up a sandwich from the abandoned tray. Perhaps in the circumstances, he reflected, it wasn't surprising that the formalities for bringing the Elephant's Sapphire over to Straw House Farm had been overlooked, whether it was for a ball or not.

'I do apologise, Mr Lynnford.'

Lynnford looked up and saw his hostess passing through the doorway, pale but composed.

'Have you any idea where he might be, your husband?'

'I tried his club in London. They hadn't seen him. Since our son was killed in the War, it's been difficult.'

'I'm sorry. Is there anything I can do before I go? Do you want me to call the police?'

'No, that's very kind of you,' Mrs Stockton smiled weakly. 'I'm fine. I'm sure he'll be back in a day or so. I can manage until then. I'm so sorry, I don't seem to have been much of a help for your story.'

'Don't worry, Mrs Stockton. I can come back another day.'

Mrs Stockton appeared relieved. 'I'll get your coat.'

A few moments later, Lynnford was turning out of the drive of Straw House Farm, and back onto the Norfolk Road. But only a few minutes later he felt the front wheel turning heavily and the steering wheel tugging sharply to the left. 'Blast! A flat! Damn it!'

He stopped the car on the grass verge, got out and walked round to the front nearside wheel. The wheel hub was sunk into the deflated tyre, the flattened rubber hidden in the damp grass, pulling the car's wing down at an odd angle. Without wasting time, he had the wheel axle jacked up and was slipping on the spare wheel, the hard rubber tread dry in his hands.

'Evening,' a rough voice spoke out from the dark.

Lynnford looked up, surprised at not having heard the man approach. He was tall and dressed in a worn jacket and corduroy trousers.

'Need any help? It's a cold place to have broken down.'

'Thank you,' replied Lynnford. 'I'm almost done, but you could hold the torch, if you don't mind. At least I'll be able to see what I'm doing.'

The man placed the sack he was carrying on the ground and took the torch. Lynnford quickly tightened the nuts and was soon finished. 'Well, that's done.' He gathered together his tools and fitted the old wheel to the back of the car. The man handed back the torch and picked up his sack.

'Smartly done for a gentleman. If you don't mind me saying so.'

'Can I give you a lift?'

'I'm only going as far as the village.'

'It's on my way.'

'Well then, if you don't mind. Graham Pike's the name.'

'Robert Lynnford.'

The man got in beside Lynnford, placing the sack on his knees. 'Potatoes,' he explained.

'You dug them up? It's a bit late in the season, isn't it?'

'Wages. Well, sort of. I've spent the day making good some fencing on the farm back there.'

'Straw House Farm?'

'That's right. Do you know it?'

'I'd only just left there when the tyre burst. I was visiting Mrs Stockton.'

'The Stocktons don't run the farm. It's rented out. But Mrs Stockton's a fine woman.'

'Do you know her?'

'My Ellen does; that's my missus. She's the housekeeper.'

'It's a bad business, the husband running out,' Lynnford commented.

'He'll be back.'

'Really?'

'Of course, he doesn't have any money, and doesn't know how to make it. She has all the money, what's left of it.'

'Why? They seem to be comfortably off.'

'They were some time ago. The shops in the village have refused them any more credit. But it's worse than that.'

'Really? I had the impression she had a sizeable staff helping her run the house.'

'Don't you believe it! He's walked off with an overdraft of several thousand pounds and a mortgage on the house that hasn't been paid for the last year.'

'A mortgage on Straw House Farm? Surely not, it's been in the family for over three centuries – at least, that's what I was told.'

'Well, somehow he took out a mortgage.'

'I see.' Lynnford let him go on speaking.

'It was all for gambling, and big losses, so I've heard. He's in France right now, I believe. Most likely in Paris and Deauville. Probably trying his luck on the horses there, I suppose. She's best rid of him, but as I say, he's bound to come crawling back. Anyway, here's my stop, if you don't mind, The Red Lion.'

Leaving Mr Pike outside the inn, Lynnford pulled away, waving him a friendly goodbye. He drove on to the next town where, stopping at a junction in the high street, his attention was caught by the lights of a hotel shining back in his wing mirror. The traffic at the crossroads cleared, but the idea of the long drive back to London made up his mind. Twisting back in his seat and looking backwards, he put the car into reverse and edged back slowly until he was alongside the hotel. *This'll do*, he said to himself. *I can get back to London tomorrow. It's still only Friday. And I need some time to think.*

Mrs Stockton's distress seemed to him real enough.

Certainly, something was wrong, but could it just be that he was being made the dupe of an elaborate hoax? The Stocktons were in debt, a lot of debt, if the labourer was to be believed. And could it have been Mr Stockton he had seen in Paris, hawking the Sapphire? Thinking back, he wished he had got a description of the missing husband from Mrs Stockton or tried to get hold of a photograph. Still, how could they have stolen the Elephant's Sapphire? Grafton had made the replica for Sir Christopher, not for the Stocktons. Unless, of course, the Stocktons had learnt of the replica and stolen the jewel for themselves. There was much for him to ponder. He locked his car and walked through the hotel entrance.

TWENTY-FOUR
A COLD AND WET NIGHT

'Jack. Good evening. It's Lynnford.'

'Mr Lynnford! Did you want my report?'

Lynnford was standing in the lobby of the hotel, calling Jack Worth at home from the public telephone fixed to the wall. He now realised he'd forgotten to cancel his daily meeting with him before leaving London, but it wasn't the reason for his call.

Jack continued, 'I waited at the Lyons Tea House until six-thirty, but as you didn't show up, I decided to come home. Should I have stayed longer?'

'No, Jack. I had to leave town. It's been a busy day and I didn't get round to leaving a message for you.'

'Are you onto another story?'

'No Jack, I'm afraid not. Still the same one. I'm up in Norfolk. What'd you say to a spot of camping?'

'Camping? It's the middle of winter! Where?'

'Norfolk, near Norwich. I know it might be a little cold.'

'Sounds sort of all right, but what about my job at the museum? And shouldn't I be back at *The Herald* next week?'

'Don't worry about that. I'll square it with the curator and with George.'

'But what is this story? I'm completely in the dark. You haven't told me anything.'

'I'm sorry, Jack, it's highly sensitive. It's had to be like that. I'll explain what I can when you come up.'

Pride and astonishment vied for control of Jack's emotions. 'What do I have to do?'

'Keep watch on a house. Someone's gone missing, and I want to know as soon as he comes back.'

'A stakeout!'

'Yes, Jack, that's it. Are you up for it?'

'Right now?'

'First thing in the morning.'

'And I won't be back for Sunday?'

'I doubt it, why?'

'I go to church with my mum. She won't like me missing it, but I suppose she'll let me off this once. I'll see with her. I should be back before next Sunday, right?'

'Yes, of course, Jack. But what about your mother, won't she worry about you sleeping out alone? Could your cousin come with you?'

'Norman works weekends at the hotel. Mum won't mind. Sleeping out in a field isn't the same for her as walking around the city at night.'

'Fine.'

'Where do I meet you?'

'Newmarket. Catch the ten twenty-eight from Liverpool Street. I've checked the times. Can you get hold of a tent?'

'A tent? Yes, there's my dad's old one.'

'You'll need some warm clothes. And bring a pair of binoculars.'

'No problem. I've got a Swedish primus stove from before the War. Mrs Sharp, one of our neighbours, gave it to me. I'll bring it with me. Anything else?'

Despite the weather and the late hour, Jack's excitement was mounting rapidly.

'No, that's it. Just don't miss your train. And give my regards to your mother.'

*

Just before noon the next day, Saturday, Lynnford pulled up on the grass verge, about a mile past Straw House Farm. 'Come on, Jack, this is where you get out.'

A light rain had already begun to fall as he opened the Morgan's rear door and took out the two rucksacks that Jack had hastily packed on Lynnford's instructions, together with his father's old hiking tent.

'Try and get onto the fields over the road from the house. Ask the farmer if you can pitch your tent there for a couple of nights. You can tell him you're hiking around the parish and you want a base. He won't say no. At this time of year, he'll be glad of some extra money.'

'I can't walk up carrying all this,' Jack objected. 'Who would believe me, hiking with two rucksacks and a tent?'

'No, you're right, Jack,' Lynnford agreed. 'I'll tell you

what. I'll keep one of the bags. Once you're set up, come down to The Red Lion inn in the village, back down the road. You can pick it up there.'

*

The landlord was ringing last orders for the afternoon in The Red Lion when Jack walked in. Lynnford greeted him. 'Everything all right?'

Jack nodded. 'The farmer was a bit surprised to see me, but he agreed, and let me choose wherever I wanted. I can get fresh eggs and milk, and even eat with them if I want.'

'Good. This is what you need to do, but remember, it's strictly confidential. Don't tell the farmer what you're doing.'

'Agreed.'

'Good. The Stocktons live in Straw House Farm, that's the building just across the road from you. They're linked to one of the museum's most valuable and important jewels.'

'The Queen's Fine Art Museum?'

'Yes.'

'I see.'

'It's a sapphire, Jack, but you must absolutely keep this information under your hat. The museum's sapphire has been stolen and a replica left in its place.'

'Gosh! Which one?'

'The Elephant's Sapphire. That's why we went to Paris – to trace its whereabouts and bring it back to London, but we didn't succeed.'

'And the man you asked me to follow off the boat train had it?'

'Yes, Jack.'

'And I lost him!'

'It happens sometimes. It wasn't your fault.'

'And you think that Mrs Stockton's missing husband might be that man? That's why we're here?'

'Very good, Jack. Yes, it's possible. We've got several other leads so we're keeping an open mind for the moment. The Stocktons and Straw House Farm are one of them. I need you to keep a record of the comings and goings. Write it all down and let me know as soon as you see anyone who looks like he could be Mr Stockton. His full title is Major Leonard Stockton. I'll be back up on Tuesday, or Wednesday at the latest. Mind you don't catch a cold. Here's some cash to keep you going. Don't forget to call me immediately should you need help.'

He gave Jack a friendly pat on the back before leaving him to walk back to the farm, and he drove off, heading back to London.

*

Lynnford rubbed the sleep out of his eyes and sat up, pushing the pillow behind his back. He had fallen fast asleep with the bedside light still on. The telephone was ringing loudly in the drawing room in his apartment. He looked at the clock. Two o'clock in the morning. Who could it be at such an hour? Dragging on his dressing gown, he hurried out of the bedroom, tying the belt around his waist as he did so. The telephone continued ringing, the clatter disturbing the quiet darkness of his home.

'Knightsbridge 3434.' He held the receiver to his head, stifling a yawn.

'You have a reverse call.' It was the operator. 'Will you accept the charges?'

'Yes.'

'Go ahead, caller.'

'Mr Lynnford.'

It was Jack, excited and impatient.

'Jack! What's happened?' His attention awakened, Lynnford's sleepiness slipped away, imagining Jack some hundred miles away in a lonely telephone box. 'Where are you?'

'In the farmhouse.'

'Straw House Farm! What are you doing there?'

'No. I'm at Mr and Mrs Jefferson's. The farmers across the road. Don't worry, they're outside. They've let me use their phone.'

'What's that noise?'

'The wind! It's already whipped off part of the barn roof. They're trying to stretch out a sheet of tarpaulin to protect it from the rain.'

'Is it raining, then?'

'Buckets! The tent's a shambles. The farmer's offered me a bed here for the night.'

'You'd better get out there and help them.'

'I will as soon as I put the phone down.'

'What else?'

Jack sneezed loudly.

'What's wrong?'

'Nothing. I've just got soaked. It's no joke. It's really raining hard. It hasn't stopped all evening.'

Jack sneezed again, this time muffling the noise in a handkerchief.

'You'd better look after yourself. Get into some dry clothes.'

'I'm all right. The farmer's lent me some of his.'

The image of young Jack standing lost in a grown man's old clothes whilst holding the telephone would have made Lynnford laugh but for his concern for Jack. 'What about Straw House Farm? Has anything happened?' Lynnford was now wide awake.

'Everything, or almost. The husband's here. He's come back; at least I guess it's him. And there's a car parked outside in the road with two men inside. They look like they're watching the house.'

'What, they turned up together?'

'Almost.'

'Tell me what happened.'

'Right.'

Lynnford could hear Jack rustling through the pages of his notebook. He'd done well to keep it dry if it was raining as hard as Jack had said, Lynnford thought.

'At about eight o'clock, a car stopped outside Straw House Farm and dropped someone off. I couldn't make out who it was, but I guessed it was the husband as he walked straight up to the front and let himself in.'

'What does he look like? Is it the man from Paris?'

'I can't say. It was too dark to see his face properly, but he seemed to be. Same sort of clothes and walk. It had already started to rain by then. Mrs Stockton had been in the drawing room since six o'clock. At least, the light was still on and I had seen her draw the curtains. I rushed across the road and up the drive, and crouched under the window, but I couldn't hear anything. And the curtains were too closely drawn to see anything inside. Anyway, I decided to go round to the back of the house and there was a real argument going on. They must have been in the kitchen. They were shouting at each other something rotten. Sparks everywhere. The husband seemed to be getting his marching orders. Several plates were smashed against the wall. One almost came through the window. One of them must have got the lightbulb as suddenly it went dark. They still carried on, screaming at each other until the door banged shut. I guess it was the husband, but nobody left the house. They just wore themselves out, I suppose. At that moment the wind picked up and a real storm set in. I was getting soaked, so I decided to go back to the tent. It was then I almost ran into the others.'

'Who are they?'

'Two Indian men, I think.'

Bhat! It must be him, thought Lynnford before replying, 'Nepalese, most likely, Jack.'

'You know them?'

'Yes. Go on.' *So, Bhat must also think the Stocktons have the Sapphire, or at least could have*, Lynnford continued musing. 'Did they see you, Jack?'

'No, not then anyway. But they might have seen me before when I walked round the house. It depends when they arrived. I just saw their car parked in the road. They must have been following behind the husband.'

'Why do you say that?'

'Because there was no other traffic on the road, and they must have turned up very shortly after him. Anyway, I stepped back just in time. I had to cut back and walk round the back of the house, and then it took ages to get round the hedge that runs along the road and come out behind them. They were sitting in the car looking up at the house, so I was able to get up close to them. One of them came back to the car whilst I was hiding behind the back of it.'

'Maybe he had been watching you up at the house,' interrupted Lynnford.

'I don't think so. Otherwise, he'd have followed me. No, I think they just missed me.'

'Are they still there?'

'Yes. Well, at least up until midnight, they were. That's when I got back to the tent, or what was left of it. It had almost blown away, and the farmer had come out to see if I was all right. When he saw the mess the tent was in, he told me to come back to the house. But just as we were crossing the courtyard, the front of the barn roof came off in the wind.'

'You'd better get a warm night and keep an eye on Straw House Farm. We need to know what Major Stockton is up to.'

'What about the men in the car?'

'Don't worry about them. I've got something in mind. Did you manage to get the registration number?'

'Yes. I'll read it out.'

Lynnford took down the number.

'You'd better also give me the telephone number you're calling from, just in case. Call me first thing in the morning if you see that the two men have gone. And Jack, see if the Jeffersons can put you up for another night or so.'

'Are you going to come up, sir?'

'Not straight away. I need to sort out some business here in London first. Good work, Jack! Keep me posted, particularly if anyone leaves.'

Lynnford replaced the receiver. The low light from the bedside lamp shone out from the bedroom. Was he at last getting close to the Elephant's Sapphire? he wondered. If Chandra Bhat had located Straw House Farm and sent his men there, then he must think the gemstone is there. So, did the Stocktons have it after all? Whether they did or did not, it was too dangerous for them and Jack to have Chandra Bhat and his accomplices sitting in a car outside the farm, watching and waiting. Somehow, he had to lure Chandra Bhat away, and already he had the inkling of an idea.

TWENTY-FIVE

A FRUITFUL SUNDAY

Standing at the window at the top of the stairs along the corridor from his apartment in Park Mansions, Lynnford looked down on Hyde Park. Jack had just telephoned to report that the car was still parked outside Straw House Farm. He'd spotted two men walking down the road, away from the car, in the direction of the village and he'd followed them all the way to The Red Lion inn, where he had found out that they and another two men were staying. 'They must be sharing shifts sitting in the car,' he had suggested to Lynnford. It was now ten o'clock in the morning, and time was pressing. Major Stockton was still inside the house, according to Jack, but Lynnford realised that he and his wife could leave at any moment, and if he could not get rid of Chandra Bhat and his men before then they would certainly get to the Elephant's Sapphire before Lynnford. Certainly, the Stocktons would be no match for them. A few hours' restful sleep had matured his plan to lure Bhat away from Straw House Farm and he had awoken with a clear idea of what he had to do. He could only hope that he had time enough for it to bear fruit and that the Stocktons wouldn't do anything to precipitate matters before then.

Lynnford looked down along the pavement on his side of the road, opposite the park. It took a while to pick out the person he was looking out for, and he'd almost given up, but, yes, he was there. This time, from his bandaged hand, it looked like it was Amrit, one of the two men who had accompanied Chandra Bhat when he had broken into the apartment on Thursday evening. Amrit had positioned himself further along the pavement than usual, passing up and down briskly, trying to keep warm in the early-winter morning's cold. Since their visit, Lynnford had been aware of a constant watch being kept on his apartment, just like on the Stocktons in Straw House Farm; Mohan and Amrit being replaced by two or three others during the day and night. *A dull job for not much reward*, thought Lynnford, smiling to himself, but this morning he was going to give them something to bite into.

Back in his apartment, he put on his coat and hat and picked up a briefcase, in which he'd placed some papers relating to other stories he was working on of no real value, except that on top he'd added the magazine with the photograph of the replica sapphire in the Duncans' drawing room, the page clearly indicated and annotated with several misleading notes in Lynnford's handwriting for Chandra Bhat's attention. This was going to be his present for Amrit. He descended the stairs and walked through the lobby.

'Morning, Cobley,' he addressed the porter.

'Have a good day, sir.'

Outside, he crossed the road and stood next to a woman waiting at the bus stop. He smiled at her in recognition. She was also a resident of Park Mansions and he greeted her, tipping his hat. Behind them, on the other side of the park's railings, they could hear the pounding canter of horses' hooves approaching them through the pale grey air of the empty park.

'They're out early,' the woman remarked.

Lynnford glanced over the railings. Two riders appeared in sight, slowing their mounts to a trot, one following the other. They were standing up in their stirrups, the horses' reins in their hands, their faces flushed. 'Beautiful animals, don't you think?' Lynnford returned.

'Not really!' she retorted. 'They just leave a lot of mess. And to think people complain about the pigeons!'

Lynnford smiled. Looking down the road he observed the red bus taking shape some distance away. 'At last, here's the bus. It's a Number 52. Is that fine for you?'

The woman nodded. 'And about time too, with this cold!'

She climbed onto the platform of the bus, walking into the lower deck with Lynnford following her. Sitting down and glancing behind out of the window at the disappearing bus stop, she suddenly tugged at Lynnford's sleeve.

'Sir, I believe you've left your briefcase behind.'

Lynnford looked sharply round, following the woman's pointing hand.

'Oh, dear me, yes,' he remarked, smiling to himself,

having spotted Amrit, now clearly recognisable, hurrying across the road towards the bus stop. 'Not to worry, somebody's just picked it up. I'll get off at the next stop.'

Indeed, Lynnford stopped the bus at the next stop, but once on the pavement he made no attempt to walk back, leaving Amrit to make the most of his spoils. Lynnford smiled, congratulating himself, but wondering how long it would take for the magazine, with its photograph of the replica sapphire and his notes, to end up in the hands of Chandra Bhat. Not too long, he hoped.

*

Arriving back home an hour or so later after a stroll in the park, Lynnford was stopped by a police officer standing beside his car, which was parked in front of Park Mansions.

'Mr Lynnford?' the officer asked.

'Yes, what is it?'

'Detective Chief Inspector Sheffield is in Alexandria Wharf and thought you might like to join him.'

Is he going to make an arrest, already? Lynnford wondered whilst replying to the police officer with a cheerful smile, 'Let's go then, officer.'

*

Detective Chief Inspector Sheffield was standing outside a large warehouse. The grey water of the River Thames could be glimpsed slipping by between two buildings at the end of the road. He opened the door of the police car for Lynnford.

'Just in time, Lynnford.' He spoke softly. 'Come on up, everything's in place.'

The two men entered the warehouse and hurried up the stairs and out onto one of the platforms high up above the wharf.

'What's happening?' enquired Lynnford, looking down.

'The *Martaban* is about to sail so we had to bring forward our raid.'

A shrill, dry whistle broke their conversation. The call, loud and commanding, echoed around the brick-walled wharf with its alarm.

'There he goes. After him!'

The fall of heavy boots rang out in succession as a group of blue-helmeted police officers surged out of the arched entrance below them. The policemen headed across the quay, their quarry already swinging up the gangway to the *Martaban*.

'He can't escape going that way,' observed the inspector.

The police officers were already clambering up the gangway onto the ship. Bosworth had, however, disappeared.

'Can they see him?'

'It doesn't look like it,' replied Lynnford, holding onto the rope from the pulley.

'Well, he can't have gone very far, unless he's going to jump ship. Let's go and see who we've managed to catch so far, and also how many paintings have been recovered.'

Up on the top floor of the neighbouring warehouse, they found Jeremy Friedman, his hands handcuffed, about to be escorted downstairs.

'Well done, men. That's one in the bag. Take him back to the station,' ordered Inspector Sheffield.

A man in an open overcoat, assisted by a police constable, was carefully examining the contents of the various cylindrical cardboard boxes that Lynnford had spotted on his previous visit.

'Professor Gibbons, from the Royal Academy,' explained the inspector, indicating the man. 'He's making sure that he can identify the paintings that were stolen from Westlake House and attest to their authenticity.'

The inspector addressed the academic. 'Are these the paintings, Professor?'

Professor Gibbons looked up. 'So far, all correct, Chief Inspector. And there are several others besides. All authentic.'

'From other burglaries?' enquired Lynnford.

'I'll check the professor's list once I get back to the station, but it's just as likely that they've been stolen from storage and that the owners aren't even aware yet that they've been taken.'

'How's that?'

'You'd be surprised,' answered the professor. 'The insurance can be so expensive that some people prefer to keep the paintings in storage and instead hang a replica in their homes.'

'That's correct,' confirmed the inspector. 'So, you were right, Lynnford. We've got more than just the Westlake House haul. A very fruitful Sunday's work.'

The inspector walked over to the open window to check on the progress of the pursuit of Bosworth. A small group of handcuffed men were already penned in at one end of the wharf by several police officers. The inspector scanned his eyes impatiently around the ship's decks, looking for the dockhand, only to shake his head dismissively. 'It looks like Bosworth has given them the slip. He's left them chasing his shadow inside the boat! The clot heads!'

'He'll turn up, Inspector.'

'I guess so, Lynnford.'

'And for the moment, congratulate yourself on a good day's work, Chief Inspector.'

'A job's not done until it's done. We shall have the ship impounded. It won't be allowed to sail until further notice and that'll certainly put a spanner in the works.'

'And no mistake!'

'Can you make your own way back, Lynnford? I need to accompany this lot to the police station. And make sure my officers don't make any more mistakes.'

'Certainly, Inspector. I need to get back to Fountain Street anyway. I've got a story to write up for tomorrow's paper. Many thanks for the tip-off, Inspector.'

'Don't mention it.'

TWENTY-SIX
LYNNFORD HANDS OVER A SCOOP

'You, again!' Walter Duff, the editor of *The East London Gazette* exclaimed as he bustled into his office and beheld Lynnford sitting in a chair opposite his desk. It was Monday morning, the next day, and Lynnford had already been waiting fifteen minutes or so for his friend to return. 'So, did anything turn up from your advert?' he asked, dropping his bag beside the desk.

'Yes, the fish took the bait.'

'And so?'

'And so I've got another line baited, so to speak, and I thought you might like the scoop, Walter.'

The editor's eyebrows arched up and the furrow on his forehead deepened. Suspicion clouded his eyes. 'You're not giving me a story, are you now, Lynnford?'

'Well, I can always take it somewhere else if you're not interested.'

'I didn't say that. What is it?'

'Nothing big.'

'I thought you said it was a scoop.'

'Well, it is. You're the only one to get it.'

'Yes, but does anyone else want it?'

'It's a burglary.'

'That's not exactly news around here.'

'No, but as you're going to know about it beforehand, you'll be ready to get some exclusive pictures of the burglar caught in the act, or at least being taken away by the police.'

'Well, that's something different at least. A bit unusual, though. What about the police?'

'They'll be there.'

'And they have agreed to this?'

'Well, to be honest, not exactly. They will probably be as surprised as the burglar.'

'So, what's the story?'

'There's a very smart international jewel thief wanted across Europe who has targeted a particular item. The police will be tipped off and ready to arrest him the moment he comes out of the house with the jewel in his hand.'

'So, why me?'

'I need someone I can rely on and who can keep quiet until everything is in place.'

'This sounds like a trap, and one that has not yet been set.'

'That's right. I'm setting the trap. And I will tip off the police once it is ready. They haven't been told yet.'

'Why don't you want it?'

'I'm tied up with another investigation.'

'It sounds fishy, Lynnford. What's so special about this person?'

'As I said, he's wanted across Europe, and indeed in many other countries. There are international warrants for his arrest but he's extremely elusive. His name is Chandra Bhat. Quite by chance, he's come across my path, and I know exactly how to entice him. I've let him know exactly where he can find the gemstone he craves. Except it's not the genuine item, it's a replica. But he won't know that until it's too late. There's one more important thing...'

'What's that?'

'You mustn't mention the actual object of the theft.'

'Uh? What's the point of that?'

'It's essential. You can mention that it's a jewel, but without describing it or giving its name.'

'Why not? It's only a replica, you said?'

'Yes, but discretion concerning this particular jewel is absolutely vital. There must be no suspicion that the original might have been stolen or could be stolen. That's why I need someone I can rely on.'

'Why not send someone from *The London Herald*?'

'I'd rather keep the paper out of it, just like myself. Let's say there are conflicting interests, but only for the moment. Once this fellow is arrested, everything will be fine.'

'And when's this going to take place?'

'Soon, any time this week, but I can't say exactly when. The thief will probably move very quickly once he learns about the jewel's whereabouts.'

'How much is this jewel worth?'

'The replica is worth a couple of thousand.'

'That's not bad. And the real thing?'

'At least a million, Walter. So, you understand now the importance of this?'

'Is whoever owns the replica of this jewel going to be informed beforehand?'

'No. It's too risky. He might spoil the show. Anyway, Chandra Bhat will know how to get in and out of the house without the need for any violence. I'm sure of it.'

'Okay, Lynnford, you've convinced me. Let me know, and I'll get someone to cover it. Where's this all going to take place? What's the address of the house?'

'Edgar Terrace. Number 17.'

'Where's that? South of the river?'

'Dundee.'

'Dundee! You must be joking. Dundee, that's in Scotland, Lynnford.'

'It's a bit of a trip, I admit.'

'Lynnford! I'm running a local newspaper, not Reuters. We're not made of money, you know. What's a burglary north of the border to do with my readers?'

'It's an international scoop, Walter! This man has evaded police forces all over the world. And as you told me many times, Walter, a good story's a good story. The location's not important.'

'For *The London Herald* maybe, but not for *The East London Gazette*. Why don't you get in touch with a reporter up in Dundee?'

'No, I need somebody I can trust. Who do I know up there? And besides, if it goes right, it will make you some money.'

'All right, Lynnford, you win. For you, I'll do it. I've got a photographer I can send up there at short notice. He can take the night sleeper train to Edinburgh. But it's *The Gazette*'s story. We'll print it and then sell it. A Scottish daily's bound to take it. Let's just get all those details down.'

Walter Duff turned over a fresh page of his notepad and, stretching down, picked up the pencil from the floor, where earlier it had dropped in his surprise.

TWENTY-SEVEN

MRS TUNN'S TIP-OFF

Lynnford waved goodbye to his friend, Walter Duff. Standing on the pavement outside the offices of *The East London Gazette*, he noticed the sky above was filling out with heavy, grey clouds, blowing south from the fenlands of East Anglia and threatening snow. Jack had called again earlier in the morning from the comfort of the Jeffersons' farmhouse, catching Lynnford just as he had been about to leave Park Mansions. There'd been no change, and Chandra Bhat's men were still outside Straw House Farm, keeping watch, just like Jack. An icy gust of wind snapped around Lynnford. He pulled up the collar of his coat. He had some spare time then to help Inspector Sheffield in the search for Bosworth, who was still evading the police. Lynnford had a source he could turn to: Mrs Tunn.

He crossed the street and jumped on the first bus that would take him to Hoxton and the Marsh Street Junior and

Primary School where Mrs Tunn served school dinners. It was already lunchtime, and by the time he arrived the dinner ladies in the school canteen would be clearing up. The possible whereabouts of somebody on the run from the police after the raid in the London Docks was just the sort of information that Mrs Tunn was good at picking up and giving to Lynnford; and for which, it is true, she did have a price.

The children were still in the playground when Lynnford walked across the concrete courtyard and into the white-tiled kitchen. A sense of aftermath pervaded the space as the dinner ladies cleared up after the lunchtime service, disinfectant pushing away the lingering smells of boiled cabbage and sweet powdered custard. A diminutive woman, wearing thick glasses too large for her face, looked up on seeing him. 'Oh, so look who the wind's blown in! If it isn't my knight in shining armour come to rescue me from this drudgery.'

Lynnford smiled. 'Good afternoon, Mrs Tunn. How are you?'

'As you can see, working.'

'And Mr Tunn?'

Mrs Tunn's husband was the school's caretaker. He had lost his hearing during the War.

'As well as can be expected,' Mrs Tunn replied. 'Are you still working young Jack Worth to the bone?'

'He's in Norfolk, camping.'

'Camping in the middle of winter! How the working class suffers.'

'Working for a newspaper isn't a holiday, Mrs Tunn.'

'No, but you don't actually work, do you, Mr Lynnford? Not like me, or Jack, whose mum needs the money he earns.'

Lynnford knew where Mrs Tunn was going with this and kept quiet. Although she had a soft spot for him, having lost her job on the London buses when the men had returned from the War, he knew she begrudged Lynnford and his class the ease with which he had been parachuted into what she considered a cushy job after being demobbed.

'No, you don't work like the rest of us, Mr Lynnford. You enjoy yourself. Admit it. I know you do.'

'I'm not here to argue social politics with you, Mrs Tunn.'

'No, of course not. You would like some information, I'm sure.' And, despite the hard words, her face softened, charmed as always by Lynnford's manner, pleased with the attention he gave her.

'A dockhand in Alexandria Wharf, in the western docks. Bosworth. A large giant of a man.'

'What about him?'

'I'm looking for him.'

'Why?'

'A story. Smuggling stolen goods out of London through the docks. He escaped a police raid in Alexandria Wharf on Sunday and he's still on the run.'

'I know who you're talking about. I've seen him around, but not since Sunday. If he's a docker, then the docks are your best bet.'

'You don't know where he lives?'

'No, but you wouldn't find him there anyway, not if he's hiding from the Old Bill. More likely than not he'll be in the Tube.'

'In the Underground?'

'Best place to be in winter and for keeping out of sight, and also for getting out of town quickly, if needs be. He'll be cadging money.'

'Begging?' Lynnford shook his head. 'It can't be him then. He's not short of a bob or two, I'm sure.'

'No, but he likes to play the accordion, so why not pick up some coins whilst he's at it? Gives him something to do in his free time. Try Aldgate East Station, that's one of his favourite haunts. Best place to be if his home's not safe from the police.'

'Thank you, Mrs Tunn.'

'Terms as usual, Mr Lynnford,' she replied, smiling.

*

The flat-fronted train rattled out of the tunnel, sliding along the length of the platform, filling the dirty empty space, through which, moments earlier, the metal rails had vibrated in anticipation. The carriage doors opened and Lynnford got in. Standing, he braced himself ready for the train to set off again. He had spent some time in Aldgate East Station, exploring its platforms and passageways, and making discreet enquiries of the staff, but without finding Bosworth or anyone admitting to having seen him. So, he had decided to stop for the time being and go back, instead, to Piccadilly and the Queen's Fine Art Museum with the idea, after what Mr Grafton had told him, of speaking to Joseph Matthews again. This time, going over with him the precise circumstances of Sir Christopher's death.

Looking back through the shaking window of the

carriage, the arched tiled walls retreating along the platform, Lynnford recognised with a start the solitary figure left on the platform, who until then had been hidden from him by the crowd. Bosworth! The dockhand from Alexandria Wharf was staring back at the departing train, an accordion slung over his shoulder, his teeth grinning through his rusty-red beard. The fugitive from the police raid on Alexandria Wharf drew Lynnford's attention like a magnet whilst the train, now picking up speed, rattled back into the darkness of the Underground.

He has nerve, mused Lynnford. The next station glared yellow as the train shot out of the tunnel. Jumping out, Lynnford ran along the platform, up the stairs and along the winding tunnel that took him back down to the platform on the opposite side. A train heading eastwards hurtled out of the tunnel just as he arrived at the bottom of the stairs. Back once more at Aldgate East Underground Station, Lynnford let the train pull away, revealing the opposite platform across the rails. It was empty. Bosworth had disappeared. 'Of course!' he muttered.

Don't waste any more time, he told himself. He had to inform Inspector Sheffield without further delay. Racing back up the escalator, he found a public telephone in the hall of the Underground station entrance. Furiously, he pulled round the numbers on the dial, and almost barked when the police officer picked up the receiver. 'Sheffield? Lynnford here.'

'Morning, Lynnford, what's up?'

'I've just spotted Bosworth.'

'Where?'

'On the Tube. Aldgate East Underground Station. I'm in a phone box, just inside the station.'

The opening doors of a lift behind him and the rush of voices and footsteps pouring out of it made him turn round and, as chance would have it, head and shoulders above the others, he spotted once again the giant dockhand. Lynnford jerked back quickly, hiding himself in the telephone cabin as best he could.

'What's wrong?' Inspector Sheffield's voice came down the line.

'He's just come out of the lift.'

'Who? Bosworth?'

'Yes.'

'I'll be right over.'

'He's not going to hang about.'

'Just keep him in sight. I'll catch up with you.'

When Lynnford turned round again, Bosworth was already out in the street. Instinct must have made him look back that very instant, and he recognised Lynnford. Speaking a few quick words to a man selling newspapers, he slipped off the accordion and handed it to him, and then he began to run, not bothering to look back. Lynnford hurried after him, surprised at the pace of the big man who, this time, despite his heavy boots was able to gain distance on Lynnford.

How Sheffield would catch up with them, Lynnford had no idea. He just had to keep sight of the fleeing man. As the streets wound one into another, and he crossed yet one more road, it became clear that Bosworth was heading for the River Thames, and the place that Mrs Tunn had first suggested would be his natural refuge: the docks and their warren-like warehouses.

As Lynnford was about to cross a street, a horn blared out loudly and voices yelled at him. Stepping back just in time, a lorry rolled past and a bus crossed in the opposite direction, blocking both his passage and his view. Hopping impatiently from one foot to the other and stretching up on his toes, he tried desperately to see where Bosworth was going, the seconds ticking by. Once the bus had gone he shot across the road, almost colliding with a cyclist, who screamed at him. Safely on the other side and with the river in sight, he sought out the fleeing man. And there he was, darting behind a closed freight wagon in a row of wagons left abandoned at the end of a set of rails in the concrete quayside.

'Have you seen him?' A policeman joined him, breathless.

'Where's Inspector Sheffield?'

'He's on his way.'

'How did you find me?'

'It wasn't easy!'

'He's behind that freight wagon.'

'Then we've got him!'

'He's a big man.'

'Not a problem. We'll keep him blocked in there until the inspector arrives.'

Bosworth was hiding between two freight wagons. He scowled on seeing Lynnford and turned round to escape, only to see the police officer blocking his way with a truncheon in his hand. Assuming an air of resignation, he sat down on one of the connecting buffers. They had him boxed in, but to Lynnford, it was as if they had trapped in a wild tiger, which with a single swipe of its paw could take out either him or the policeman and leap to freedom. *How long before the others arrive?* he wondered. Somehow, to gain some time, he had to make Bosworth talk, and keep him talking.

'Bosworth, isn't it? Dockhand at Alexandria Wharf?'

The dockhand didn't deign to reply, not even raising his head to look at Lynnford.

'I wonder what it was that you were doing in the Queen's Fine Art Museum in Piccadilly on the night that Sir Christopher Fields fell to his death?'

The big man laughed, coarsely. 'Do I look like someone who visits museums?'

'Well, that would depend on the reason you were there.'

'And I tell you, I've never set foot in a museum in my life.'

'Well, you were there that night, long after the museum had closed to the public. I wonder why?'

'You can scratch your head as long as you like.'

'But he was killed, Sir Christopher.'

'I wasn't there.'

'But you surely left your fingerprints.'

'With the rest of London! You won't find anything now.'

'The police will match the ones that were taken with yours, once they've got you safely in custody. That will prove it. And then there's Jeremy Friedman.'

'What's he been saying? He's lying.'

'He says that you killed Sir Christopher. Why would he think that if you weren't there that night?'

Another voice spoke out. 'Lynnford!'

The inspector's call was accompanied by the sounds of several pairs of pounding boots.

'I didn't kill him!' Bosworth almost shouted out the denial as he turned and, catching him by surprise, leapt at the policeman standing behind him, knocking him down flat, and then raced to the waterfront.

'After him!'

A splash of water followed the command.

'He's dived in!'

Lynnford and Inspector Sheffield joined the line of policemen along the waterfront, watching the fugitive resurface and, with his legs and arms methodically thrashing the water, head straight out towards the middle of the river, and the bank on the other side.

'He's going to need some iron to make it,' one of the officers commented with grudging respect.

'Well, what are you waiting for?' a sergeant among the policemen asked dryly.

'Sarge!'

'Go on, jump in.'

'You're kidding me, Sarge. Sir?' the policeman appealed to Inspector Sheffield.

'Well, we're not going to get far with you all standing in a row like a line of penguins,' quipped the inspector. 'Sergeant, go back to the car and call the river police.'

'Sir!'

'I'll leave you to it then, Inspector. I'm sure you can fish him out of the river without my help.'

Inspector Sheffield smiled at Lynnford's remark as he,

along with the sergeant and his men on the edge of the quay, watched the progress of the lone swimmer. *He must be cold out there in the water*, Lynnford thought to himself as he headed for the nearest Underground station.

With Bosworth located and almost under arrest, Lynnford didn't doubt that Chief Inspector Sheffield would soon wring out of him his involvement in the theft of the Westlake House paintings. There was, nevertheless, the death of Sir Christopher Fields to resolve. He was sceptical about Bosworth's role in his killing. His impression of the dockhand was that he was a man who could control his violence. He wouldn't have killed Sir Christopher by mistake, and he had no reason to kill him. On the contrary, so long as the Elephant's Sapphire was missing, he had needed the curator alive, Lynnford reasoned. And he also remembered overhearing Bosworth vigorously deny that he had killed the curator when speaking freely to Jeremy Friedman in the Italian coffee bar near London Wall.

TWENTY-EIGHT
THE MUSEUM WARDER'S STORY

Lynnford stepped out of the Piccadilly traffic and into the calm of the museum foyer, heading directly towards the Nepalese Room.

'You, again!'

Joseph Matthews had been sitting on his warder's stool, lost in his thoughts, until the arrival of Lynnford had thrown him onto his feet.

'I'm working,' he cried out, as if wielding a weapon.

'Mr Philips can spare you for a moment or two.'

'So you're working for him now, are you?'

'Let's find somewhere quiet to talk, shall we, Mr Matthews?' And Lynnford took the warder by the arm, coaxing him towards the exit.

'I know all about you, Taylor. You never wanted to make a copy of the Sapphire and steal it, did you? You're a newspaper hack. I saw through you from the very beginning!' And with a feeble laugh, he added, 'You're a phoney!'

'Come along, Mr Matthews. As I said, let's find somewhere quieter to talk.'

'It's quiet enough here. There's no one but us.'

'More private, if you like.'

'What do you want me to say?'

Lynnford didn't reply. He was now propelling the warder more firmly and they passed into an adjoining room, and through into another.

'Hold on! Where are we going?'

'You'll see.'

They stopped finally at the top of the great stairs that led down to the main foyer, almost outside the curator's office and those of the administration.

'So you want to know about the sword?' the warder asked weakly. It had occurred to him that this must be the reason for his quasi abduction at the hands of this man.

'So it was you, Matthews. I thought as much. No, it doesn't really interest me,' replied Lynnford. 'Tell me instead where you hid the night Sir Christopher fell to his death at the bottom of these stairs.'

'What are you talking about?' The warder looked around nervously. 'Why are we here?'

'You must have been hiding somewhere inside the museum because the police didn't find you, and they must have looked everywhere. But you know this building and its secrets inside out, don't you?'

'I wasn't here.'

'All the time you used to spend here in the evenings, walking around alone,' Lynnford continued, ignoring the warder's protests. 'I guess you have your favourite secret places that only you know about. That's what finally put me onto you.'

Now the warder was just staring blankly at Lynnford, who continued, 'If the curator was killed, and as no one was seen, it had to have been someone who didn't need to come in or go out of the museum because they knew where they could safely hide and sit out the storm, so to speak. And that person was you, Matthews.'

'It was Bosworth.'

'Ah, so you know him, then?'

'Of course I know him.'

'And how do you know it was him?'

'I saw him.'

'But he didn't kill the curator.'

'How do you know?'

'Because he was out of the building before Sir Christopher fell. He must have been. But you were here.'

'No! It was Bosworth. He hadn't left the building.'

Lynnford took no notice of the warder's protestations. He continued, 'You must have been watching, somewhere around here. I can't see where, but you know, don't you, Matthews?'

The museum warder looked to be in a cold sweat, and Lynnford saw the fear of cowardice in his eyes. 'Why did you kill Sir Christopher, Mr Matthews?'

'I didn't kill him.'

'Exceptionally for Sir Christopher, he appears to have had a lot of time for you. Were you friends?'

'Friends! I hope he's burning in Hell.'

The museum warder's screech cut short, as if it were

a screaming kettle taken off the heat, and he fell silent, his lowered head and shoulders rocking backwards and forwards. Lynnford thought he was crying, and he recalled the words of Grafton. 'I've been told he was an evil man. Is that why you killed him, Matthews?' he asked.

'I didn't kill him. How many times do I have to tell you?'

'You pushed him over the balustrade, didn't you, Matthews?'

'No, I never!'

'After Bosworth had given him a beating, is that right?'

'No! What are you talking about?'

Lynnford continued, 'But the three of you seem to have known each other. How was that? What did Sir Christopher do to you that made you push him to his death?'

Joseph Matthews stared at Lynnford, amazed at his lack of understanding and horrified at the memories he had now unknowingly evoked.

'What didn't he do? He took my boy and girl away from me, turned their minds and then threw them away like empty carcasses. You know what happened to them. You told me when you came to my house last week. But I didn't push Sir Christopher over the balustrade.'

The warder's sudden emotion shocked Lynnford. 'So, tell me, how did your son and daughter become involved with Sir Christopher?'

Joseph Matthews leaned down, taking a seat on the stairs, his hands holding his head as he continued his story, speaking almost to himself.

'He took them over. Not straight away, mind. Oh no,

too clever for that. At first, he was very friendly, wanting only to help, especially with their education – and then snap, he had them in his web. Before the War I was a carpenter, and if it wasn't for the War, I'd still be one, I suppose. When I was demobbed, somehow I landed myself this job at the museum, and here I stayed. It's easy work. The two little ones loved their drawing and painting. They were very artistic. I don't know where they got it from. Perhaps their mother. First James and then Janet secured scholarships at St. Martin's School of Art. I was so proud of them. For some stupid reason I got Sir Christopher to meet them. I thought that he could help them with contacts and that sort of thing. He took a fancy to them straight away. I don't know how it happened. Perhaps because they could talk the same language about art and paintings. Looking back, I feel as if they left us almost the very day they met him.'

The warder paused, staring blankly down the stairs.

'Go on,' prompted Lynnford.

'I don't know what he promised James, but he hooked him up good and proper. I suppose I didn't have the sort of money he needed to live the life he wanted.'

'Perhaps you pushed the boy too hard?'

'No!' The museum warder's reply was violent, his words trembling with emotion as he continued. 'He had an eye for art but not as much as his sister. She could paint. She can paint. I don't know what they were doing, really. I'm a fish out of water when it comes to art. So at first, I just thought that they were doing well. Sir Christopher was able to offer them something I could not, so I just accepted the situation. A year ago, as you know, Janet's brother was stopped by the

Belgian police a few miles from the Dutch border. He was carrying stolen paintings in the back of his van. Stupidly, he panicked and ran. They opened fire and that was it. The police, you know, are armed on the continent. Well, that's what the curator told me.'

'What did the police tell you?'

'I don't remember.' The museum warder lowered his eyes.

'Didn't you go over there?'

'What was the use? He was dead, wasn't he? Anyway, I couldn't face it. His body was sent back.'

'How long had your son been working for Sir Christopher?'

'I don't know.' The museum warder seemed reluctant to recall the painful details. 'Three or four years, maybe.'

'And your daughter?'

'They used to pay her in kind. Opium! It's supposed to be fashionable. God knows why, she couldn't work any better for it, that's for sure. It just spoilt her. Evil, that's what they were, getting her so that she could never leave them.'

'What does she do for them?'

'Did! She's completely useless now. Her poor mother died of despair. She painted. She painted copies. Anything, or practically anything she could. As perfect as the original. The curator spotted her talent straight away and worked on her brother to drag her in.'

'And what did they do with the money?'

'They weren't paid much. Not in cash. The profits went back to Hong Kong, always. That's who pulls the strings and collects, every time.'

'I see. And you knew what was going on?'

'And didn't I know! Couldn't help but know. Sir Christopher pushed it in front of me every day. Laughing at me, patting me on the back and thanking me with his sardonic grin. That gave him a kick.'

'So he had a hold on you too?'

'Of course he had a hold. He knew I wasn't going to do anything that would put them in danger. It was a cruel, easy sport for him, which he enjoyed.'

'So you killed him?' Lynnford's sudden question struck home with the skill of a champion fencer.

'No, I didn't. He fell. Bosworth pushed him. I keep telling you.'

'And Bosworth, what did he want that night?'

'The Sapphire.'

'If Bosworth wasn't Sir Christopher's accomplice in stealing it, who was?'

'There wasn't an accomplice.'

'So, who stole the Sapphire? Do you know?'

Joseph Matthews had kept this information to himself for so long but now, after putting all his resolve into denying Lynnford's accusations, his resistance had finally drained away. Staring back at Lynnford, he said, 'One of the museum's trustees, Major Leonard Stockton. Can you believe it? They're all as bad as each other. Now, will you leave me alone?'

The question was almost a plea. Lynnford smiled to himself, but all he said in reply to the museum warder's revelation was, 'Is that so?' before adding, 'Rest assured, Mr Matthews, the police will get to the bottom of how Sir Christopher died, evil man or not.'

TWENTY-NINE
SURPRISE IN STRAW HOUSE FARM

B ack in his office in Fountain Street, and after having immediately gone round to Scotland Yard to see Detective Chief Inspector Sheffield and report in person his conversation with the museum warder, Joseph Matthews, Lynnford received a telephone call from the inspector. His officers had been unable to bring in the museum warder for questioning. They had gone round straight away, but unsuccessfully, to the museum in Piccadilly and to his home in Borough. Nobody had been able to tell them where he might be found. He was now being actively searched for across the capital and beyond.

Two messages had been left on Lynnford's desk, waiting for him. One from Kombinski, the editor, saying that he wanted to see him. *No doubt wanting to know when he can expect my story*, guessed Lynnford. The second was from Jack. Chandra Bhat was still outside Straw House Farm, or at least one of his gang was. Lynnford's magazine photograph had clearly not yet reached him or, if it had, he had not been taken in by it. So, Lynnford would have to sit it out in Fountain Street, waiting. He began drumming his fingers on the desk.

'Stop it!' cried out Maxwell from behind his typewriter.

'Sorry, Max.'

He got up and walked over to the window, and looked down at Fountain Street below.

'For heaven's sake, Lynnford, go and find something to do or go down to The Golden Fox and have a pint,' suggested Maxwell, Lynnford's impatience disturbing his concentration.

'I'd better go and see Kombinski.'

'Good, you do that.'

*

The afternoon dragged by. Around five o'clock, Inspector Sheffield telephoned. Finally, they'd got their hands on Bosworth. They'd found him rolled up under a boat trying to warm himself around a fire, a stone's throw from Alexandria Wharf. Shaking with cold and with fears of him dying from pneumonia, he'd been taken to Guy's Hospital, where a policeman was keeping watch over him. Lynnford enquired about Joseph Matthews and was told that he still hadn't been located. A little later, he telephoned Victoria to update her.

'And what about the sword? Any news on that?' she asked.

'The museum warder, Joseph Matthews, sent it,' replied Lynnford.

'Why? He could have sold it.'

'Bosworth told him to keep me away from the Elephant's Sapphire.'

'And how did he imagine sending you an antique Napoleonic sword was going to do that?'

'I don't know. It was certainly an odd thing to do. Maybe he just thought that I'd take the sword and walk away.'

'Really?'

'He's a weak and frightened man, Victoria. He's dealing with sophisticated criminals and he's clearly out of his depth. He's a simple man. He's lost his wife and son, and his daughter's addicted to opium. I feel sorry for him.'

'Don't be soft, Robert. He killed a man. That's what you believe, don't you? If he did, then he'll have to pay the price. Come on, shake out of it! Let's think of something else. What about meeting at Oscar's this evening? My treat.'

'I'll see you there at seven.'

*

The next morning, before even having drawn open the curtains, he finally got the news for which he'd been waiting impatiently the previous day. Jack telephoned, breathless, having run back from the road to his temporary lodgings in the Jeffersons' farmhouse. He'd been up before dawn.

'They've gone!' he announced.

'Who?'

'The car, and the people in it.'

So, Chandra Bhat has taken the bait, Lynnford congratulated himself, asking Jack, 'When?'

'During the night.'

'And Mr and Mrs Stockton, are they still there?'

'As far as I know,' confirmed Jack.

'Good, then I can be there just after ten this morning. Get some breakfast down you, and then go back to Straw House Farm as quickly as you can. Don't let Major Stockton or his wife out of your sight, should either of them come out. Do you understand, Jack?'

'Yes, sir.'

Lynnford cut the line, and telephoned Inspector Sheffield at home. Not a little surprised that Lynnford should have found out about a supposed plan of Chandra Bhat's to steal a precious jewel from a Scottish city councillor in the next day or so, he grudgingly agreed to contact the local police and have them put a watch on the Duncans' townhouse in Edgar Terrace. Lynnford also left a message for Walter Duff at *The East London Gazette* that the planned burglary was on and that he should send his photographer and, if possible, a journalist up to Dundee on the first available train. He then hurried downstairs to the garage and by eight-twenty he was motoring out of London. Less than three hours later he was walking up the drive of Straw House Farm, its mossy-green roof slates and heavy grey-stone walls seemingly sinking into the earth and rendering the house no more than a part of the low-lying landscape. He'd left his car parked on the road, out of sight of the house, after having quickly spoken to Jack.

'Oh, it's you again.' Mrs Stockton pulled back the door.

'Good morning, Mrs Stockton. How are you?'

Lynnford lifted his hat in greeting. He still wasn't sure about Mrs Stockton. Could she be an accomplice to the theft? He hesitated, not knowing what course to take.

'What is it about? Have you come back to finish your interview?' she asked, taking the initiative. 'Unfortunately, now is not a good time.'

'I wondered if I might speak to your husband.'

'Leonard? You might have telephoned.'

Lynnford couldn't help noticing the two brown leather suitcases at the bottom of the stairs and a coat folded neatly on top of them. 'I'm sorry, is this a bad time?'

'If you have come to see my husband, he's not in. I'm waiting for a taxi. It should be here shortly.'

'You're going away?'

'I am, just for a week or so. I have a sister in Cambridge.'

'I see.'

'What do you see?'

'I'm sorry, I didn't mean anything.'

'Mr Lynnford, you're welcome to speak to my husband, but as I said, he's out, and I don't know when he'll be back.'

Her face was drawn, but her voice was still light and pleasant, although now a little impatient. He found it hard to believe she was involved in the theft of the Sapphire. Did she know what her husband had done? He felt inclined to trust her. At least, to take the risk. He wondered why Jack hadn't spotted Major Stockton leaving the house.

'Mrs Stockton, could we talk in private?'

She looked at him, surprised. 'I thought it was my husband you'd come to see.'

'It is, but do you have the time before your taxi arrives?'

'Very well, do come in.'

She led him into a small sitting room, Nelson the Great Dane padding along behind them.

'What will you do with him whilst you're away?'

'Nelson? Oh, he'll be all right. Ellen the housekeeper will look after him.' Mrs Stockton patted the dog's flank whilst inviting Lynnford to take a seat.

'Now, what is it that's so important that you need to speak to me again?'

'Mrs Stockton, I hope I can trust you?'

'What a question!'

'A week ago, I saw your husband in Paris.'

'What on earth was he doing there?'

'You didn't know he was there?'

'Of course not!'

That's odd, he thought to himself. *How can she not know when Graham Pike, her housekeeper's husband, knew that he was in France?* It was what he'd told Lynnford. He made a mental note but showed no sign of his thoughts, saying instead, 'I didn't know who he was at the time. In fact, he was registered in his hotel under an alias.'

'A woman!'

'No, I don't think he was seeing a woman. It was only yesterday that I realised that it was your husband.'

'What are you, Mr Lynnford, a private detective? I thought you were a journalist.'

'Yes, I am a journalist, as I told you. I work for *The London Herald*.'

'So, what's this got to do with you?'

'Mrs Stockton, I'm not interested in your marriage.'

'What then?'

'The Elephant's Sapphire. The man I saw in Paris, if it was your husband, was trying to sell it.'

'Good Lord! But it's kept safely in the Queen's Fine Art Museum in London.'

'I'm afraid that's no longer the case. What's there, at present, is nothing more than a replica of the Sapphire.'

'A copy!'

'Whether or not it was your husband in Paris, the Elephant's Sapphire has been stolen, and at least one finger is pointing at your husband.'

'Leonard? He's too daft to be capable of such a thing.'

'But if it was him that I saw in Paris, as he doesn't appear to have found someone willing to meet his price, then it's quite likely that he returned with it unsold and that he has it with him, or possibly that he has left it somewhere in this house.'

Mrs Stockton's face turned slowly from perplexity to anguish.

'Really, this is dreadful,' was all that she could finally say before getting to her feet and walking nervously to the window for distraction.

'Mrs Stockton, it pains me to say but I have heard that your husband is in huge debt and has dragged you into a miserable situation. Apparently the house is mortgaged and you could lose it and everything you have.'

'How dare you!'

But there was no spirit in her defiance, not even questioning from where Lynnford had got his information.

'All's not lost, Mrs Stockton. If we can just find the Sapphire and return it, I'm sure the museum will be lenient and won't press charges against him. But there's not a moment to lose.'

'I can't believe it. Good grief! But what to do? I've no idea where he might be. He went out very early this morning and hasn't come back.'

'So you've no idea where he might be?'

Mrs Stockton shook her head and took a cigarette.

'What about here, in the house? The Sapphire, I mean. Could he have put it somewhere?'

'Look at the place. It could be anywhere.' Mrs Stockton held out her hands in hopelessness, the cigarette hanging from the fingers of one, a match in the other.

'What about a safe?'

'There's nothing there but papers. Anyway, he wouldn't put it there because he'd know I would find it.'

'Somewhere you wouldn't come across it by chance, then.'

'Ah yes! Perhaps his study upstairs. I never go there, and for some time now he's been sleeping there too.' She put out her cigarette and stood up. 'Let's go and see for ourselves.'

Lynnford followed her upstairs.

'This is his study.' Mrs Stockton spoke dismissively, showing Lynnford into a dark and heavily panelled room with little space for more than a desk and a sofa. The ashes in the fire grate were cold. 'I never come in here. He's been using the interconnecting room. He's put up a bed in there.'

Lynnford cast his eyes around. There was little in the room to hide anything of value. He went methodically through the drawers of the desk and the cupboards that lined the walls, Mrs Stockton looking on as he did so.

'Let's try the bedroom.'

A camp bed had been set up under the window. It was still unmade, the sheets and blanket tussled together, and the pillow squashed up against the wall.

'We have a deposit box at our bank in Norwich. I hardly ever use it.' Mrs Stockton spoke casually, following his movements. 'But with us owing the bank so much money, he wouldn't have left it there.'

'Does he have an account somewhere else? He might have opened one for himself at another bank.'

'Now you mention it, I did notice a cheque book that didn't look to be from our bank. I'll go back and check the desk in the study.'

Before she could move, the bang of a door being closed downstairs caught their attention.

'What's that?'

'It's Leonard! He's back.'

Mrs Stockton rushed to the open door and before Lynnford could stop her she had gone out onto the landing, her husband already halfway up the stairs. 'How could you?' she cried out. 'How could you?'

Joining Mrs Stockton at the top of the stairs, Lynnford immediately recognised the man who had given him the slip in Paris. So he was one and the same man!

'Who's this?' her husband asked.

She didn't reply, her eyes wild with anger.

'Where is it?' she demanded instead, her light voice lost in an angry outburst. 'Where is it?' she repeated. 'Where is it, you damned fool?' And she would have no doubt fallen on him but for Lynnford's restraining hand.

'What in heaven's name are you on about, Helen?'

'The Sapphire! The Elephant's Sapphire, damn you, Leonard!'

'The museum hasn't sent it yet. What are you getting so worked up about?'

Calling her bluff, Major Stockton would have continued up the stairs and onto the landing, but for it slowly dawning on him that the presence of the stranger on the landing next to his wife was not innocent, and his mind began, amidst his confusion, to identify a danger. He turned on his heels and ran back down the stairs, slipping on the rug at the bottom but quickly picking himself up before Lynnford, bounding down the stairs after him, could catch hold of him. Running through the hall, he disappeared down the passageway into the kitchen and out through the back door, slamming it shut. Nelson, barking furiously, filled the entrance to the kitchen with his great body, holding back Lynnford, who was unable to calm the dog.

'Nelson!' cried out Mrs Stockton, running up behind Lynnford. 'Quiet! Down boy!'

Yet, it still took her a few precious moments to calm the dog before Lynnford could finally squeeze past and charge across the kitchen. He yanked open the door, his eyes darting everywhere in search of the fleeing Major.

THIRTY

ACROSS THE NORFOLK BROADS

Empty fields stretched beyond the house. A wooden bar fence, running along to the left, disappeared behind a cluster of trees. Lowering his eyes, the soft grassy soil still showed the fresh impressions of Major Stockton's shoes leading to the fence, and, running up to it, Lynnford spotted his footprints on the other side, set out even more clearly in the muddy track, freshly churned by the recent storm. He jumped over the fence and followed them in the direction of the trees, careful not to twist an ankle in the deep tractor ruts.

Quickly, the track brought Lynnford to a large derelict warehouse, protected by a high, wooden fence that the trees and the bushes behind it threatened to break down and crush under their weight. Long grass filled the intervening space, and here and there a piece of rusting machinery lay abandoned on the ground. All this Lynnford took in with a glance, wondering where the Major had gone. Apart from the entrance where Lynnford was standing, there seemed no other way out. *He must be inside, but what's he playing at?* wondered Lynnford as he approached the building.

The large double doors, still with their green paint, were padlocked, although for little purpose as the wood was surely rotten. And there, immediately as he started to walk carefully clockwise around the building, he came across an opening in the wall. Someone, taking advantage of the building's abandon, had started to remove the bricks, creating a jagged hole in the wall, almost five feet wide. Without hesitating, Lynnford stepped through it. The stench inside caught his breath, almost making him choke: a mixture of stale urine and manure. *Vagrants*, thought Lynnford, *or the local farmers have been using the building as a makeshift pigsty.* Around the broken opening, daylight revealed the charcoal scratchings of numerous intruders. Many of the timbers of the upper floor had been removed, and it was impossible for Lynnford to guess at the building's original purpose.

If he's in here, there's no point in me getting lost in this mess, Lynnford told himself. Nonetheless, he took several paces further inside, treading carefully amongst the litter of bricks, charred wood, straw, lead piping and broken bottles. Suddenly he heard a scrape above his head, and almost immediately a tremendous weight fell over him, knocking him to the ground amidst a cascading noise of falling stones. Stunned, he felt a heavy sack weighing down on his neck and shoulders. Running footsteps amongst the rubble caught his dulled consciousness, but he was too winded to get up and follow, the heavy sack weighing him down. Finally pushing it off, he got to his feet, staggering a little, his feet slipping on piles of ivory-coloured beads. Scooping up a handful and examining them in the palm of his hand, he realised with surprise what they were. *Teeth, false teeth, not stones!* he exclaimed to himself. A sack of false teeth! The idea seemed more revolting than the nauseous stench of the place that he could still smell despite his shock.

The Major! Lynnford threw away the handful of shining teeth and ran out of the building. *I shouldn't have let him drag me in here, I nearly didn't come out.* Back outside, he looked down the track, but saw nobody. Quickly, he made a full circle of the building, noticing as he ran several more sacks left against the wall here and there, some open, their contents spilling out into the tall grass.

The roar of a motor engine broke the silence and drew Lynnford's attention to a gap in the fence that he would not have otherwise spotted. Breaking through the line of trees and undergrowth on the other side of the fence, he had just time enough to see a grey-green Rover Saloon turning onto the Norwich Road. Running out into the road, he saw it shoot past Straw House Farm and disappear out of sight. *Damn! So close!*

*

'It's an old factory for making dentures,' explained Mrs Stockton. 'It's been disused and abandoned for a long time now.'

They were standing outside under the front porch to

the house. Her taxi had arrived and was waiting in the driveway.

'I've known Leonard to park his car over there.'

'Any idea where your husband might have gone?'

'The Midland Bank in Norwich, if he's put the Sapphire in the safe there. That's his new bank. I checked just now.'

'If he stops there, I'll have time to catch up with him.'

'Or maybe Barton Village.'

'Where's that?'

'Past Norwich, on the coast road. There's a piece of land with an old barn and a cottage outside the village. He was never keen to sell it. He didn't think we'd get enough money for it. But it's been abandoned for years.'

'I'll need directions. Couldn't you come with me?'

Mrs Stockton looked hesitantly at the taxi.

'Don't worry, I'll pay it off. You can still go to your sister's in Cambridge when we get back.'

'Fine. I'll get your coat. You left it in the sitting room.'

'With my car keys!'

As they drove off, Lynnford called out to Jack, telling him where they were heading and telling him to stay put and keep an eye on Straw House Farm in case Leonard Stockton should return.

Mr Stockton had not been seen at the Midland Bank, and so they drove out of Norwich in the direction of Barton Village; Lynnford regretting the wasted time, his foot pressed down on the accelerator, the flat fields rushing past.

Anxiety began to eat away at him. Major Stockton could be heading towards a thousand other places. And maybe his wife was just taking Lynnford on a wild goose chase. He was clutching at straws, and the very desperation that had made him accept Mrs Stockton's suggestion now began to make him worry even more. Might not the Major have already doubled back by another road? For every mile eaten up by Lynnford's Morgan, it would mean two more if he had to turn back.

'This is Barton Village,' confirmed Mrs Stockton.

A line of thatched cottages came up quickly, only to dissolve behind them as he pressed down over the low, stone-walled bridge and out of the village, following her directions.

'It's a little bit out of the village,' she told him.

A mile further on, a farm labourer, a torn jacket falling over his baggy trousers and a spade over his shoulders, suddenly stepped onto the road. Lynnford slammed down on the brake pedal, provoking the angry blare of a car horn from the small black Morris Minor behind them. The driver drove past, gesticulating furiously at him.

'We're here anyway.' Mrs Stockton pointed a few minutes later to a barn nestling in a copse of wind-beaten alder trees, which he would most certainly have driven past without seeing.

The grey-green Rover was parked in front of the barn. Pushed back in retreat, the cottage, which had more the appearance of an almshouse, was dominated by the old barn in the weed-covered yard. Lynnford pulled up alongside the Rover and they got out. Mrs Stockton led the way. They approached the buildings, uncertain of what to expect. Despite Stockton's car, there was no sign of life.

The cottage was boarded up and the doors, front and

back, were locked. There couldn't be anyone inside. The slated-timber sides of the barn were in disrepair, pale and dried out by the salt air. The low-roofed entrance was open to the encroaching grass and weeds. Inside, there were two covered carriages, the type that must have carried the post a century earlier, resting on stocks, their wheels lost from sight. A strange air of melancholy filled the barn. *What could the Stocktons want with such a place?* wondered Lynnford, walking impatiently between the carriages. He was about to turn and walk out when a faint movement caught his attention. It came from within one of the carriages. Mrs Stockton stood watching him from the entrance.

Lynnford leant his face against the window of the carriage door, peering through the dusty glass, the darkness obscuring his view. There was certainly something long rolled up on the floor of the carriage. Wiping the glass with his hand, he saw it suddenly move again, rocking from side to side. He pulled open the door, and a man's head and shoulders fell out, his eyes open wide, staring silently up at him, a thick tape over his mouth. His arms and legs were also tightly bound with rope. It was Joseph Matthews, the museum warder!

Mrs Stockton rushed up, and the two of them eased the frightened man out of the carriage and onto the ground. Lynnford removed the tape with care, screwing it into a ball and throwing it away.

'So, this is where you've got to, Matthews! The police are searching for you all over London. Well, now they won't have to look much further, will they?'

'What are you waiting for? Take the rest off.'

The museum warder's lips were still wincing from the pain of the tape. Lynnford shook his head. 'Not until you tell us what you're doing here, as if I can't guess.'

'You think you're so clever,' blurted out the warder.

'At least I'm not tied up like a chicken. How did you get up here?'

The warder did not reply, his eyes glaring at Lynnford.

'So, the prospect of prison, or possibly worse, the hangman's rope, made you try your hand at getting hold of the Elephant's Sapphire for yourself. And somehow you knew enough about Leonard Stockton to know about this place. You thought yourself a match for him? How little you really understand people's character.'

The museum warder remained silent.

'So, when did all this happen? Just now? You were here waiting for him,' continued Lynnford. 'So, he must still be here. Where is he?'

'Cut me out of this first.'

'No chance! I'll find him myself.' Lynnford turned to go.

'Hey! What about me?'

'You can wait here.'

Lynnford hurried out of the barn, followed by Mrs Stockton.

'Do you have any idea where your husband might have gone?'

She shook her head. 'I hardly know this place. It's years since I was last here.'

Lynnford calculated quickly the time that had elapsed since Major Stockton had driven off from the old denture factory. He couldn't be more than twenty minutes ahead of him, thirty at the most. But the museum warder must have delayed him. Tying up Matthews and leaving him in the barn must have been a temporary measure, he guessed. Take off ten or fifteen minutes. Stockton couldn't be far away. Lynnford looked around him and spotted a wicket gate swinging carelessly on its hinges in a break in the trees at the back of the cottage. Lynnford rushed over to the gate, the muddy path dissolving into a grassy field beyond it. Inspecting the ground around the gate, the soft earth revealed a confusion of footprints, scuffling in every direction, but from which it was clear that there were only two separate sets of prints. Behind an alder tree whose branches overhung the gate, he spotted a single set of shuffled footprints, as if someone had been standing there for some time, waiting impatiently for the second person. Two or three cigarette ends confirmed his thoughts. He could not recall whether he'd seen the museum warder smoking, but it had to have been him. He still couldn't guess how Matthews had managed to get himself out from London to such a remote place. Anyway, it was clear that Stockton must have been heading this way, away from the cottage, when Matthews had jumped him. Unfortunately for him, he must have come off second best and the Major had been able to overpower him, tie him up and take him to the barn. Then he must have come back and carried on his way.

'Found anything?' Mrs Stockton was standing at the gate.

Lynnford pointed to the cigarette ends and the footprints, and then to the adjoining field. 'He must have gone that way. Any idea what's there?'

'A lot of water, that's all.'

Indeed, they were standing only thirty feet or so away from a narrow stretch of water that looked cold and grey. Tall yellow-brown reeds covered the bank on both sides, the waterway seemingly running parallel to the road. A white sail could be seen billowing out from a mast above the reeds, suggesting that the waterway joined another, much wider one. The sail was the only moving thing to break the grey shapeless sky that descended all around.

'Should I come with you?' asked Mrs Stockton.

Lynnford shook his head. 'Better you stay and keep an eye on the man we took out of the carriage.'

'What's he done?'

'Killed the curator of the Queen's Fine Art Museum. The previous one, I mean. Sir Christopher. At least, that's what the police want to question him about.'

'Oh!'

'Don't worry. He's harmless enough, but make sure he stays put. Stay by the cars.'

Gaining the waterway, Lynnford wondered whether Stockton might not have taken a boat, but he couldn't see any mooring where the Major might have kept one. That left the path, but had he gone upstream, back in the direction of Barton Village, or downstream, towards the sea? It was unlikely, he concluded, that the Major would have come out to the barn by car only to return to the village by foot. He must have taken the path downstream.

Leaving behind him the protection of the copse around the cottage and the barn, the solitude of the Broads began to envelop him, and the sense of time and place to dissolve in the rustling reeds and the solitary heron call. The ground began also to harden, more exposed to the drying sea winds. And suddenly he found himself on a flat, low-lying headland with grey swathes of water stretched out before him. Looking back, the trees were no more than pinpricks, and the white sail had long since disappeared.

A footbridge allowed him to continue heading downstream. Why did he think Major Stockton had come this way? He couldn't tell. Illogically perhaps, it was the only way that would have taken the Major further and further away from Norwich and Straw House Farm. The long desolate scene continued to unfold before him, and with the time that passed, he began to think increasingly that the Major must have taken a boat otherwise he would have surely caught up with him by now.

A lonely alder tree broke the horizon, as if some secret mechanism had made it pop up, and as he approached, he could see another tree, and then a third growing alongside an old windmill. And there, walking along the path ahead of him, he made out a solitary figure striding out, seemingly unconcerned by time or place. The Major!

THIRTY-ONE

A HERON'S CRY

Leonard Stockton was only some two hundred yards from the windmill. He was walking briskly and upright, as Lynnford now recalled seeing him cross the Seine among the Parisian Sunday morning crowd. Here there was nobody to interrupt his passage. The sea breeze tickled the open water, but in and among the reeds standing along the banks, the water was still.

With a loud frightened cry, a brown-feathered heron rose up suddenly from amongst the reeds, breaking the wintry silence. The bird flew over the Major, seemingly brushing his shoulder, its legs still extended. Startled, he ducked down but straightened up as soon as he saw the bird fly overhead, casually following its flight over the reeds until, surprised, his eyes fell upon the figure of Lynnford, caught exposed on the open path behind him. For a second the Major froze, too far away for Lynnford to discern his expression, but as Lynnford broke into a run, he saw the Major turn and sprint over the remaining ground to the windmill. Losing ground rapidly to the younger Lynnford, he still got there before him, panting heavily. He already had a key in his hand, and the door was open and shut before Lynnford could make up the distance.

Lynnford banged his hands on the closed door. Damn! But for the bird, he would have surprised the Major before being locked out. He looked up. The timber walls of the mill were as impregnable as a stone castle, sloping upwards with nothing to get a grip on. He stepped back, looking round from left to right. The little square windows high up at the top of the mill were well beyond his reach, and there seemed no other way of getting in, which a rapid, circular visit of the base of the mill confirmed.

What to do? The Major was stuck inside the mill like a rabbit waiting for its predators to move away. He would have to do something sooner or later. He couldn't just wait there, but neither could Lynnford, and there was the rub. He made another fruitless tour of the windmill. Then, thoughtlessly, he took a step back without looking and knocked his head against something hard. Looking round, he found himself face to face with one of the mill's large wooden sails, pointing straight down to the ground like a line of lead. Suddenly, he saw a way up to the top of the mill. Using the slats of the sail, he could climb up!

He gave the sail a shake with his hands. It was light, but the frame seemed strong enough to take his weight. Placing a foot on the edge of the frame, he pressed down and lifted his other foot, carefully letting the sail take his full weight.

The frame held, and he took another step, and then another, surprised at the ease of his ascent; and soon he was almost a third of the way up, the sail swinging slightly with his weight. Looking up, his eyes fixed on the large axle that held the four sails suspended in the air, his hands and arms pulling him up. He had the impression of being a trapeze artist, hanging high up in a circus tent. Taking the next step, his foot in the air, the sail shook slightly and then shuddered. Lynnford put his foot down, steadying his balance, wondering what had happened. He took another step up. As he rested his foot and lifted the other, the sail shuddered again, and then again, more violently. Almost imperceptibly, Lynnford felt his feet being lifted to one side and then gradually, more and more, until he realised with a shock that the whole sail was moving, turning slowly upwards. *He's started the sails!* Lynnford gasped to himself. *He hopes to shake me off!*

The sail began picking up speed, and soon Lynnford began to feel the blood rushing to his head as, inevitably, the sail entered its upper quarter, and he found himself looking down onto the axle and onto the carpet of grass below it. The turning axle pushed him higher and higher, and holding on to the wooden baton of the sail became harder. The sail was almost at its apex. He pressed himself flat against the wooden slats, unable to move. Wartime memories flooded his mind, of the time his Spitfire had almost gone into a tailspin over the fields of Kent, with the pale blue sky all around him full of darting planes and bursting shells.

The speed of the sail's movement continued to increase, arching over and then dropping down on the other side, the acceleration making Lynnford's progression along the sail more difficult, and before he knew it, the sail was ascending again, inverting him headlong once again down its length, his hands pressed white against the thin wooden batons. Still, only three or four feet more and the axle would be within his grasp. The sail brought him down for a second time, and he climbed the remaining steps, waiting for the sail to lift him up again, and just before the sail was at its zenith, he let himself slip down onto the axle, leaving the sail to rotate without him.

But the axle was turning also! Countering the moving axle, he pushed himself carefully along its length, towards the roof of the windmill, easing himself along the remaining foot or so that separated him from the opening that held the mechanism that was turning the sails. And then he was inside! He slipped off the still-rotating axle, his feet thudding on the wooden planking. He breathed a sigh of relief, the large flat sails outside continuing to draw their circles in the air.

Seconds later, before Lynnford had time to recover his balance, the Major suddenly appeared and lunged at him, a large industrial spanner held high in the air. The thick nut-shaped end struck down on Lynnford. It fell harmlessly to one side, Lynnford dodging the blow in time. The weight of the spanner almost threw the Major off balance, but he caught himself and, turning to face Lynnford, raised his arm again, the head of the spanner looking ugly against the grey light filtering through the opening. Lynnford sprung forward, charging into the Major with his shoulder and catching his arm. The blow winded the Major, forcing him to let go of the spanner, but breaking free of Lynnford's hold, he slipped a foot behind his leg, tripping him over, and with the weight of his body pushed Lynnford backwards, his head just missing the glistening axle as both his head and shoulders fell through the opening. The Major fell on him, trying to push Lynnford's body fully out. The cold air struck Lynnford, his head dangling outside, the sails rotating behind him. He grabbed hold of the Major's forearms, trying to dislodge their grip. The Major was leaning over him, not saying anything, a silent fury filling his face. Still, his advantage of surprise was no match to Lynnford's strength, and bit by bit, Lynnford could feel the Major's hold weakening and, with his loss of strength, his desperation increasing. Lynnford kicked the Major's ankle. The sharp pain showed instantly in his face, but he held on, keeping Lynnford down with the weight of his body. The Major was pressing as hard as he could but clearly, he knew that all he was doing was holding Lynnford in place. Lynnford, pinned down as he was with his head and shoulders hanging outside, had no purchase with which to throw off the Major. It was a stalemate, for as long as the Major could keep Lynnford down. Stockton glanced around, looking for the spanner. It was lying where it had fallen on the planking next to Lynnford's foot, but he dare not reach down even though it was within his reach. Relaxing his hold on Lynnford would have his captive up at his throat before he could even touch the spanner with his fingers. Lynnford kicked it away, just to make sure. The tool slithered across the planking, the action seeming to make up the Major's mind. With a last surge of energy, he pushed Lynnford away and, turning, got to his feet. Lynnford tried to trip him with his foot but missed. The Major was already a

few steps ahead and racing back round the tower. Struggling
to his feet, Lynnford chased after him.

The Major had slipped into a low entrance, out of which
he must have come earlier, and was about to close the door
as Lynnford appeared. Just in time, Lynnford stuck his foot
into the doorway, jamming it open, and with his hands he
wrestled with the Major, who was still trying to pull the
door shut, his fingers gripped round the edge of the door.
Suddenly the Major let go. The door swung backwards with
the force of a catapult, knocking Lynnford over. Lying on
the timbered floor, he expected to hear the Major's footsteps
running down the stairs, only to see him reappear, his hands
back on the door, closing it in on him before Lynnford
could get back to his feet.

Now he was stuck. He had to break down the door, and
with the spanner he began hammering the wooden slats,
using all his strength. Anger and fury fuelled his muscles as
he counted the precious seconds that he was losing. Striking
the door in the middle, the thin wood splintered easily and
with another blow it split down to the bottom. Lynnford
continued striking at it. The surface of the door was now
damaged with holes and cracks, the freshly splintered
timber shining a very pale yellow. Lynnford struck his
elbow through the splintered panels, too damaged to offer
any further resistance. Stretching his arm through the
gaping hole, he unlocked the door and staggered through. A
staircase led straight down to a circular room. The Major was
nowhere to be seen. Lynnford ran down the steps, jumping
the last two or three. The room was full of coils of rope and
boxes. The dry sawdust and stale air caught the back of his

throat. Scuffed footprints in the dust revealed a trap door and through this, another staircase that wound down the middle of the mill from one floor to the next.

As he slipped through the trap door and started to descend, a rickety handrail guiding him, the Major's head popped out of a side room several floors below. Hearing the footsteps above him, he looked up and, spotting Lynnford, immediately withdrew into the room. Lynnford began to hurry down, taking the steps two at a time, momentarily losing sight of the room's threshold from time to time as he wound his way down the stairs. Seconds later, the Major reappeared, casting a glance up at Lynnford before darting down the stairs. Lynnford increased his pace. *Where is he going?* he wondered as he jumped down onto the next landing. *He can't hope to escape.*

He could see the Major now, almost at the bottom, one arm clutching a parcel to his chest. Crack! The wooden plank under Lynnford's foot snapped loudly as he landed. Crack! Crack! Crack! The sounds of breaking timber resounded all around him, up and down the staircase, and amongst the crash of splintering wood, Lynnford felt himself fall through the staircase, his arms uselessly flailing in the hope of catching hold of something to break his fall. A jagged piece of wood caught his hand, sending a searing pain up his arm.

The sounds of breaking wood still resounded in his ears as he hit the landing below, tumbling over. His shoulder thumped on the hard wood. Looking up on his back, a large hole in the staircase opened up above him, broken planks hanging from the edge of what remained of its frame;

others lay on the floor about him. Momentarily, the fall's pain and surprise were lost. There was something new. The strange sound of splashing liquid. He got to his feet, almost collapsing, his left foot throbbing with pain. Getting to his feet again, he hobbled to the edge of the landing. Standing close to the open entrance, at the bottom of the stairs, his back arched and a jerry can held in his two hands, the Major was shaking its contents out over the stairs. Paraffin!

Seeing Lynnford, the Major threw down the can and, to Lynnford's horror, pulled out a box of matches from his pocket. Dropping the lighted match at his feet, he turned and ran, an explosion of blue flame hiding his flight. Within a flash the flames were consuming the fuel, reaching out to engulf the liquid pool around the stairs, crackling on the dry wood and empty sacks of rye. The lower steps were lost in the flames, and the entire staircase was threatened. There was no way of putting it out, and no chance for Lynnford to break through the conflagration. He hobbled as quickly as he could over to the side of the landing furthest from the flames, and dropping to the floor, rolled over and holding onto the edge of the planking, let himself fall until he was hanging, suspended, some three feet or so from the floor below. The flames shot up the staircase, the heat almost scorching him. He released his grip, dropping down, trying to fall on his good foot. With luck he landed on some empty sacks, his feet sinking into the piles of soft sacking.

The flames were racing up the staircase like a lighted cord towards a keg of dynamite, rising ever higher. The heat was ever more intense, almost blinding him. The Major had disappeared. The grey afternoon light etched a rectangular hole in the wall of the mill, marking the door. The entrance was free of fire, the cold wind blowing in from outside, carrying the fire quickly up the stairs. Lynnford lifted his legs out of the sacks and stepped gingerly onto his feet. The pain from the twisted ankle was less intense now, allowing him to place his weight fully on the foot. He winced a little before hurrying towards the patch of grey light, the heat of the fire falling on his back as he stepped outside. Inside, the crash of timbers from the falling staircase filled his ears.

Lynnford did not bother looking back at the burning windmill, too preoccupied with the whereabouts of the Major, and he spotted him straight away, a hundred yards or so back down the path, running from the mill, one hand still clutching the parcel to his chest.

THIRTY-TWO
CHECKMATE

*H*e's heading back to the old barn and his car! Lynnford started to run as best he could, pushing out of his mind the sharp needles of pain springing up from his twisted ankle. Although clearly unconcerned as to whether Lynnford had perished in the fire, the Major was still not taking any chances and was continuing to run, and with dismay Lynnford soon realised he was losing ground on him. He could see the Major crossing the footbridge, and then, once across the water, turning back up towards the headland. Now the Major could see Lynnford but cared little, obviously thinking himself safely out of reach. The tall reeds, however, hid from him the small group of figures coming round the low-lying headland from the direction of the cottage – whom Lynnford, glancing across the water, now spotted. To his surprise, he recognised Victoria, a hand holding onto her beret as she ran, the collar of her gabardine up around her neck. Alongside her was Helen Stockton and just behind, Edwin Philips, the curator, clearly panting from the exertion, his thick coat slowing him down. The Major did not see them until they were fully round the bend. When he spotted them, he must have recognised his wife and Mr Philips as he stopped short in his tracks. Then, without further hesitation, he turned on his heels, heading back the way he had come.

Lynnford, who had continued as best he could along the path on the other side of the water, now saw his chance, and making another supreme effort to forget the pain, sprinted across the remaining ground to the bridge, hoping to cross it before the Major went past it on the other side. The Major was, however, too quick for him and reached the end of the bridge first, carrying straight on along the path without losing a moment. Lynnford was now only a few yards behind. Pounding off the bridge, he pushed himself even faster, fighting off the pain, and within a yard of him, gave a tremendous leap, diving forward with his arms outstretched, reaching around the Major's legs and bringing him down with a thump.

'Checkmate!' he gasped, for want of a better word.

The two men fell to the ground, the Major winded and pinned down by Lynnford's grip. This time there was no escape. Lynnford lay still and exhausted, hearing voices speaking excitedly as the chasing group caught up with them.

'Bravo, Lynnford! A tackle like that would earn you a place in the Lions Eleven.'

Lynnford recognised the voice of the curator.

Sitting up on the Major's legs, Lynnford took off the

belt from his coat and, bringing out the Major's arms from under his chest, wrapped it tightly around his wrists. 'Come on, Stockton, the game's up. Sit up!'

Lynnford lifted the Major up into a sitting position. The Major said nothing, a sullen expression of hostility on his face, angry not at his capture but at the loss of strength that seemed to have flooded away with his fall. His wife looked on, saying nothing. The parcel he had been carrying lay on the path in front of him. Lynnford bent forward and picked it up, handing it to the curator.

'Take a look, Mr Philips. I'm sure this is the real one.'

'Robert! Your hand, it's bleeding.'

'It's nothing, Victoria. I cut it on some splintered wood. It can wait.'

Lynnford shrugged off the pain in his hand. All he could feel was the throbbing ankle. Meanwhile, the curator had taken the parcel and was cutting away the string and feverishly unfolding the sheets of newspaper, letting them fall to the ground, until he came to a piece of silk. Lifting off the delicate tissue with his fingers, the others watching silently in a cluster around him, Leonard Stockton forgotten at their feet, the curator revealed a blue stone, large like a paperweight, shimmering as if moving, despite the grey light of the winter's afternoon that was almost at a close.

'It's magnificent!' Victoria cried out in a breathless whisper that seemed to echo the lonely flight of the heron earlier on.

'It's truly unique,' remarked Lynnford. 'What do you think, Mr Philips? Is it the real one?'

'No doubt about it. It's the Elephant's Sapphire all

right, but I'm still going to have a second opinion, at a suitable moment.'

The curator carefully replaced the silk scarf in which the Elephant's Sapphire had been wrapped.

'Leonard, how could you ever think of doing such a thing?' Mrs Stockton's voice was full of disgust.

'What's that?' Victoria cried out, her alarm drawing everyone's attention to the line of smoke spreading out across the reeds, a red glow scorching their tips.

'It's the windmill,' answered Lynnford. 'Stockton put a torch to it. It's all I could do to get out. It's going to be too late now to save it.'

'Pity,' remarked Mrs Stockton, adding, 'Good job they stopped storing flour in there long ago otherwise there would have been one almighty explosion. I doubt you would have got out alive, Mr Lynnford.'

'So, the fire should be safe enough,' concluded Lynnford. 'It'll burn itself out. There's nothing else there to catch fire.'

'Unless a wind springs up and blows the flames onto the reeds. Come on, we'd better get back as soon as possible,' urged Victoria.

'She's right,' agreed Mrs Stockton. 'We can call the fire brigade from Barton village. The sooner the better!'

'And what made you come out here, Victoria?' Lynnford asked. 'It was lucky you turned up when you did.'

'Jack.'

'Jack?'

'Yes, he had the sense to telephone Stephan at *The London Herald* this morning, just to let him know what was going on in case there was a problem.'

'Max?'

'Yes, Stephan Maxwell. He called me and I thought it best to get Mr Philips to drive me up here. You've got yourself mixed up with some very dangerous people, Robert! Once we arrived at Straw House Farm, Jack explained where you had gone and in Barton village, we came across a labourer who told us he'd seen your Morgan an hour or so earlier on the road just outside the village. Imagine how grateful we were when we spotted it parked here. Mrs Stockton was waiting there as you had instructed and pointed us to the path you had taken.'

'Well, I'm sure Nelson, her Great Dane, couldn't have done a better job in tracking me down. And very lucky for me indeed, I have to admit!'

Suddenly Lynnford had a thought. 'What about Matthews? Who's looking after him?'

'He's secure enough, Mr Lynnford,' replied Mrs Stockton. 'He's tied hand and foot, and back in the carriage.'

'Matthews?' asked the curator. 'Joseph Matthews, from the museum?'

'Yes, Mr Philips. I'll fill you in with all the details later.'

Lynnford prodded Stockton to his feet and, hobbling, with the Major in front, led the others back along the path to the cottage and the old barn, Victoria closing ranks at their rear. The walk back along the reedy water bank was slow and painful for Lynnford but, not too soon for him, they passed through the wicket gate at the back of the cottage.

'Victoria, you'd better take my car and drive straight to the village,' he directed. 'We'll wait for you to come back. Call the fire brigade and then Inspector Sheffield at Scotland Yard. Here's his number.'

'The police?' The curator gave a look of alarm.

'What do you expect?' replied Lynnford. 'We're going to need them if we want to sort this out. You had better get going, Victoria. I can't drive with this foot.'

'What do you want me to tell Inspector Sheffield?'

'To meet us at Park Mansions in London at about ten o'clock this evening. Oh, and tell him to send over a police car to pick up Joseph Matthews.'

The Morgan turned out of the yard and sped away, Victoria waving back at them.

'What's the problem? Can't we just get going? We've got two cars. We can all fit in,' the curator spoke impatiently, indicating Stockton's Rover motor car and his own.

'There's Matthews here, don't forget,' pointed out Lynnford. 'We should wait for the police to take him away.'

'What's he done anyway?'

'He's the man who stole your Napoleonic sword. There are also serious reasons for believing he killed your predecessor, or at least that he's an important witness to the curator's death.'

'Sir Christopher? I don't believe it.'

'I'm afraid it's true. He's wanted for questioning by the police in connection with the curator's possible murder.'

'And so, what was he doing here, in this awful place, anyway?'

'I guess he had hoped to steal the Elephant's Sapphire from the Major. One last chance to make his fortune before fleeing the country.'

'Well, Mr Lynnford, I've got what I wanted. You stay here and look after him until the police arrive. We'll get going.'

'Not so fast. I'd much prefer not to lose touch with any of you whilst you have the Sapphire in your possession,' objected Lynnford.

'I believe we somewhat outnumber you.'

Mrs Stockton intervened. 'Mr Philips, I think we should do what Mr Lynnford says, don't you? After all,' she added with a pointed look at her husband, 'he was clever enough to find both the Sapphire and the thief.'

THIRTY-THREE
AND PIGS WILL FLY!

'He's safe enough where he is, in the small sitting room, with Nelson and the police constable keeping an eye on him,' declared Mrs Stockton, with an air of reassurance.

She had rejoined the others in the drawing room in Straw House Farm after leaving the museum warder, still bound hand and foot, under the watchful eye of the Great Dane and the police constable, whom Victoria had brought back from Barton village. No police car had been available at the time. Suitably reinforced, and once a fire engine had turned up, they had decided to return to Straw House Farm, where they were still awaiting a police car to take away Joseph Matthews. A fire crew had gone over to the cottage and was attending to the burning windmill.

'And so what are you going to do with me?' The Major's voice was gruff and sullen. He was standing in front of the fireplace at the end of the room with the almost imposing air of being their host, except his hands were still tied and a resigned tone belied the bravado of his posture.

'You may as well sit down for a start, Leonard, and stop being so infuriatingly pompous. Nobody here is taking you seriously,' replied his wife.

'This is your decision, Mr Philips,' Lynnford addressed the curator. He was sitting in an armchair with his foot resting on a stool, the wound to his hand having been cleaned and bandaged by Victoria. 'But you'll need to make up your mind before we meet with Detective Chief Inspector Sheffield this evening.'

'I'm not sure that I follow, Mr Lynnford.'

'Either you hand over Major Stockton to the police or you don't. You have recovered the Elephant's Sapphire, but what are you going to do with the person who stole it?'

'And don't look at me,' interrupted Mrs Stockton. 'Leonard's no longer anything to do with me. He can rot in prison as far as I'm concerned.'

'Helen!'

'Considering the whole situation, I really would like to avoid involving the police,' replied the curator. 'A scandal would weaken the museum's reputation, and, if I understand correctly the sequence of events, it was my predecessor, Sir Christopher, who replaced the Sapphire with a replica that he had commissioned with the intention of handing over the original to a ring of international art thieves. Major Stockton simply took advantage of the situation and stole the Sapphire for himself.'

'Well, that's a rather generous view of the Major's

actions,' replied Lynnford. 'You know the art world, Mr Philips, and it's a small place. The Major has got himself into an enormous mess. But, whilst you might want to avoid a scandal, news of the theft has got out. From these sheets of newspaper, it looks like he got as far as Rome and Milan trying to sell the Elephant's Sapphire.'

Lynnford pulled out from his coat pocket the sheets of newspaper that the curator had let fall to the ground on the waterside path earlier in the afternoon when hastily unwrapping the parcel containing the Sapphire.

'It's last month's *La Stampa*!' observed Victoria, examining one of the sheets of newspaper.

'So, you see, Mr Philips, you need to find some way of re-establishing the public's belief that the Queen's Fine Art Museum does in fact possess the real Elephant's Sapphire.'

'Yes, of course, Mr Lynnford. What do you suggest? I'm at a loss.'

'The arrest of the thief would help.'

'Yes, but I don't like it.'

'But you can't let people think that they can steal from the museum with impunity.'

'That's something else. Mr Stockton is one of the museum's trustees.'

'More of a reason, don't you think, Mr Philips?' replied Lynnford.

'Maybe I have an idea.' The others looked at Victoria. 'The Prime Minister of Nepal,' she added simply.

'What about him?' asked the curator.

'Well, he'll be in London shortly, isn't that right, Mr Philips?'

'That's right. On Friday, in three days. And that's part of the problem, if not *the* problem.'

'No, it's the solution!'

'How's that, Victoria?' asked Lynnford.

'Well, a photograph in *The London Herald* of the Prime Minister of Nepal holding the Elephant's Sapphire, with the elephant beside him. The most important person in Nepal, after the king, wouldn't be seen in public with a fake, would he?'

'Certainly not! Yes, that might just do the trick,' replied the curator, hesitant relief edging his voice.

'And you'll let off Leonard?'

'Is that what you want, Mrs Stockton? Hasn't he done you the most harm?' observed Victoria.

'That's an understatement, Mrs Beaumont. He's ruined the two of us. He forged my signature on the mortgage deed. The house is lost. Leonard can look after himself, but what am I going to do? Where am I going to live?'

Lynnford tried to reassure her. 'You might still save Straw House Farm from the bank. You need to get the advice of a good lawyer, Mrs Stockton.'

'I'm happy to put your husband's adventure down to a simple error of judgement, but it'll be for the Board of Trustees to decide,' declared the curator. His self-assurance and pomposity now restored, he added, 'In the meantime, I'm sure you'll agree that it wouldn't be appropriate to release the Sapphire to you this Christmas, Mrs Stockton?'

'It won't be missed!' Mrs Stockton replied with bitterness. She continued, her emotion having suddenly evaporated and her voice now listless, 'They always said that in the wrong hands, the Elephant's Sapphire would only bring bad luck and misfortune. Well, it certainly has. Marrying Leonard, it has just brought me trouble. I couldn't bear to see it again.'

*

Later that day, in the evening, Lynnford, Victoria, Mr Philips and Detective Chief Inspector Sheffield were assembled in the drawing room of Lynnford's Knightsbridge apartment in Park Mansions. The Stocktons had remained at their home. The inspector was in a bullish mood.

'I fully understand your concerns, Mr Philips, but really the cat is out of the bag now, so to speak. The theft of the Elephant's Sapphire and its substitution with a fake is an open secret. Maybe not to the general public for the moment but I doubt that will be the situation for long.' The inspector cast a glance at Lynnford. 'And so, maintaining the museum's reputation is no longer a reason not to prosecute Major Stockton.'

'But the Sapphire belongs to his family,' objected Edwin Philips.

'Mrs Stockton's family, to be precise, and she certainly doesn't approve of what her husband did, far from it. Anyway, the Sapphire's held in trust by the museum, if I understand the situation correctly, so the Stocktons no longer own it.'

The inspector seemed to Lynnford to be replaying the very same conversation that Mr Philips had had with him when he had first explained the affair to him in The Golden

Fox, two weeks ago. The police officer continued, 'More importantly, he's been involved in criminal activity, and it beholds us to be transparent, particularly when it involves someone, like the Major, who has misused the public trust placed in him as a trustee of the museum.'

'But he didn't steal the Sapphire.'

'Well, yes he did, Mr Philips. He stole it from a thief, Sir Christopher, that's true, but he stole it nevertheless. Clearly, he had no intention of returning the Sapphire to the museum, did he? What do you think, Lynnford?'

'Well, it's your call, not mine, Chief Inspector. But it seems to be a matter for a court of law and jury now. Let them decide the Major's fate. And what about Joseph Matthews?'

'He's being questioned,' replied the inspector.

'Has he said anything?'

'He's changed his story a little.'

'Has he admitted killing Sir Christopher?'

Inspector Sheffield shook his head. 'No, although he does now admit to being there that evening and having had an argument with the curator.'

'And how does he explain the curator's fall?'

'He slipped as they were tussling with each other over the balustrade.'

'Will you accept that, Chief Inspector?'

The inspector shrugged his shoulders. 'We haven't finished questioning him yet. Let's see what more his solicitor will let us squeeze out of him. But maybe, as with Stockton, it'll be up to a court and jury to decide his fate.'

'Of course, Inspector, you can't do any more.'

'Good, then if there's nothing else, I'll be off.'

Showing the inspector to the door, Lynnford asked him quietly, 'And is there any news from Dundee? Did Chandra Bhat try to break into the councillor's home?'

Inspector Sheffield shook his head, 'No, he didn't turn up, and probably won't now, as soon as he hears that the museum has recovered the Elephant's Sapphire, if that's what he was hoping to steal.'

Lynnford smiled. 'So you saw through my ruse, Chief Inspector?'

'It wasn't too hard, knowing you as I do, Lynnford. But I warn you, Walter Duff will need some pacifying. I heard that his photographer and reporter were left kicking their heels outside the councillor's house, and that you might have had something to do with it!'

*

Late the following day, at the offices of *The London Herald* in Fountain Street, Lynnford breezed into the editor's assistant's small ante office.

'Is he in?' he asked.

Mabel Wainwright looked up from her typewriter, about to say something, but before she could the door to the editor's office opened with the abrupt apparition of Paul Kombinski, waving the day's edition of *The London Herald*, and smiling triumphantly. 'Now, that's a story, Lynnford!'

The break-up of the Alexandria Wharf Art Smugglers' Gang, as Lynnford had named it, and the recovery of the Westlake House paintings were spread across the front page.

'Pity not to have kept in the thefts from the Queen's Fine Art Museum,' regretted Lynnford.

'Irvine was dead against it.'

Indeed, Joseph Irvine, *The London Herald's* proprietor, had set his mind against it, arguing there was enough of a story without embarrassing the museum and its trustees. Lynnford had suspected that the proprietor was simply protecting his friend, Edwin Philips.

'Well, I don't think he's going to be able to hold out much longer. Not with this.' Lynnford held up the sheet of typed copy that he'd brought in personally for the editor's approval.

'What's this?' snapped the editor.

'The police have finally charged Joseph Matthews, a warder in the Queen's Fine Art Museum, with the manslaughter last August of its curator, Sir Christopher. Without a confession, they don't have enough evidence to charge him with murder.'

'So what was it, a brawl that got out of hand?' sniffed the editor.

'Something more than that, Paul. Deeply held hatred and a thirst for vengeance.'

'Sounds like murder to me.'

'They can only prosecute on the evidence they have. Anyway, it's part two of the Alexandria Wharf story. The death of the curator was tied up with his theft of exhibits from the museum and his links with the *S.S. Martaban*, the ship that was used to smuggle the stolen artworks out of London. And at the heart of the story, Joseph Matthews' children were corrupted and criminalised by Sir Christopher.

It's too big a story for Philips and Irvine to keep a lid on it now. What's out, will out!'

'Give it to me and come in!'

Kombinski pulled Lynnford into his office, closing the door behind them and pouring over the text as he strode over to his desk. He had finished reading it even before he'd sat down, and his satisfaction was plain to see.

'Excellent, Lynnford. Really good work. This will put Willy Tanner and his *Daily Chronicle* back in their place. Get it down to the print room immediately, and to hell with the proprietor! I'm the editor, after all.'

As he walked out of the editor's office and past the assistant's desk, Mabel Wainwright looked up and, noticing the smile on Lynnford's face, asked, 'A Christmas bonus, Mr Lynnford?'

Lynnford shook his head regretfully but without losing his smile, 'And pigs will fly, Miss Wainwright. And pigs will fly!'

*

Three days later, Maxwell was standing at the window, looking down at the passing traffic in Fountain Street, his hands in his pockets, idly waiting for the Saturday morning to draw to a close before going down for a drink in The Golden Fox.

'Ready for a drink, Lynnford?'

'In a minute. Look at this!'

'What is it?'

'A photograph of the Elephant's Sapphire. Look!'

Maxwell came away from the window and took the newspaper that Lynnford had been holding, reading out loud the short caption that accompanied the photograph, 'The Maharaja and Prime Minister of Nepal flew into London yesterday for urgent talks on the critical situation in his country with members of His Majesty's government, including the Prime Minister and the Foreign Secretary. At the end of a long day His Excellency still had time to visit the Queen's Fine Art Museum, where he proudly inspected one of his country's most famous treasures, the Elephant's Sapphire. His Excellency used the occasion to express his hope that, one day, conditions would allow for the historic jewel to be returned to Nepal.' Maxwell folded the paper and, indicating the photograph that had been taken to illustrate the scene, commented, 'And that's a nice picture, too.'

The photograph, reflecting faithfully Victoria's idea, showed the Prime Minister standing beside the bronze sculpture with his left hand resting protectively on the elephant's head, his fingers touching the precious blue sapphire.

'So, all's well that ends well?'

'Yes, Max. Whilst Mr Philips was obviously not too happy with us printing the story on Sir Christopher's plunder of the museum's vaults—'

'To put it mildly, I imagine.'

'We did help him recover the stolen Elephant's Sapphire and get it back into the museum in time for the Prime Minister's visit, and now he has the official seal on its authenticity. And that should go a long way in helping him to manage the task of restoring the museum's international reputation.'

'Well, I wish him luck with that. And what about the international criminal, Chandra Bhat? Wasn't he supposed to be another of your big fish?'

Lynnford shook his head with an air of disappointment. 'Too clever for us by far. He never turned up in Dundee. I guess on his way up to Scotland he must have had second thoughts, his instinct telling him something was amiss. My decoy, at least, did its trick! It got him away from Straw House Farm long enough so that we were free to tackle Major Stockton without fear of him interfering. That would have been too dangerous for us all, and, I dare say, a very different outcome.'

'And do we know where he is now? He's not going to be too pleased with you, is he, Lynnford?'

'I should be safe enough, Max. Inspector Sheffield told me today that he'd received an Interpol report informing him that Chandra Bhat had been arrested yesterday afternoon by the Italian police outside Venice, on his way to the free port of Trieste, or even Tito's Yugoslavia.'

'Perhaps then the Italians have done Bhat a favour. Trieste's a bit of a hotspot since Tito's split with Moscow, isn't that so?'

'Indeed. Anyway, let's hope he doesn't slip through their hands. The art world will be a better place without him.'

'Well, Lynnford, you can't win them all.'

'No, Max, like your races. Win some, lose some!'

'And what about Eddie Campbell? He should be happy with the end of the supply of illegal tobacco imports from the *S.S. Martaban*.'

'It seems his trade is back and he's doing well, for now at least. Fancy a game of chess before our drink, Max? Victoria bought me this…' Lynnford bent down and opened the cardboard box next to his chair, lifting out a wooden sculpture that he placed carefully on his desk, next to the typewriter. The two sculptured Korean chess players from Wheeler, Chambers & Son off St. Martin's Lane, dressed in dark greens and browns, continued to stare stoically at the pieces on the board between them, deep in thought. Lynnford looked up, a proud smile on his lips. 'What do you think of that then, Max? Beautiful, aren't they?'

'Come on, Lynnford, let's go for that drink!'